Nowhere to Run

N.J. Warner

Published in 2013 by FeedARead.com Publishing – Arts Council funded

Copyright © N.J. Warner 2013

A CIP catalogue record for this title is available from the British Library.

Acknowledgements

To my parents, my sisters Lisa and Kayleigh, and Maggie thank you for your unwavering support, encouragement and inspiration. I wouldn't be here without you.

To Rachel, my best friend, thank you for being my guiding light in more ways than one, for slogging through first, second and third drafts and being my no nonsense 'editor-in-chief'. Your overwhelming enthusiasm is much appreciated.

Thanks to the New family for their help with research and answering my never-ending questions.

Thanks to Nightwolf Kay for designing the front cover, it rocks!

For my parents, with love

To Kira,
Best Wishes,

Chapter One

Scared or nervous? Matthew Brennan could not decide which one he felt but he had to face them.

Bella's Coffeeshop was on Hanover Street, in the center of Billows Creek. It had been open since 7am, and the bustling breakfast rush was now over.

Two deputies and three mechanics sat in the coffeeshop, discussing the latest football results over their regular mid-morning snacks of blueberry muffins and toasted bagels.

Matthew entered through the glass paneled door. He carried a black suitcase and a crumbled bus ticket in his left hand. He felt more like a redneck than a lawyer, dressed in tight Levi jeans and a white T-shirt.

Placing the suitcase onto the floor, he rested his brown rimmed sunglasses on his head, pushing back his mousy blonde hair.

'Matt? Is that chu?' Rutha, the waitress, approached from behind the counter. She was in her mid-sixties, dressed in a brown floral print dress that stopped just below her thick calves. A brown head scarf, tied at the back of her head, tamed her wispy gray hair.

Matthew was conscious of faces turning to stare at him and the abrupt silence that followed. Even though he had expected their reaction, he froze, anticipating their next move.

'Lord, look at chu?' She kissed her teeth, making a sucking sound. 'All skin and bones.' Her face softened. 'It's good to see you, honey.'

'Thanks, Rutha,' he replied, somewhat embarrassed by the apparent change in atmosphere.

Rutha didn't seem to notice as she approached him. 'This town hasn't been the same without chu.'

'Yeah,' a female deputy whispered, 'the street's been kept in one piece for one thing.'

Matthew pretended not to hear.

Rutha looked up at him. 'Give the ole girl a kiss?' she said, chuckling.

He leaned down kissing her soft black cheeks. 'I see not ever' one shares your enthusiasm,' he whispered.

She turned deliberately on her heels to face the audience. 'Oh never mind them,' she said loudly, waving her hand. She turned back to face him. 'How are you doin'? You look good, healthier now.' She looked down at the suitcase next to his left leg. 'I see you've just arrived, you must be hungry?'

He smiled. 'Thanks Rutha, but I should be getting home. Anna doesn't know I'm back yet. I just came in to say hi.'

'Are you sure I can't get you somethin' to go?' She winked, smiling sweetly at him.

He chuckled. 'Thanks, but I must be going.' He picked up his suitcase.

'I suppose you haven't heard the terrible news?' Her smile faded.

'What news?'

She frowned. 'Bout Harry?'

He shook his head.

'He was shot the other night and his partner too, poor boys.' She shook her head sorrowfully. 'Harry's momma's a wreck, hit the family hard.'

'Shot?' His voice raised an octave. 'Is he-'

8

She cut him off. 'No, no. he's in intensive care. They say he'll be paralyzed.' She paused. 'But patrolman Collins, died at the scene; he's only lived here for six months.'

He stood open mouthed, remembering how vibrant and full of fun Harry was at his bachelor party last year. 'How is Becky holding up?'

She looked at the floor. 'Poor girl. She visits him every day. Young newly weds shouldn't have to...' she shook her head sorrowfully.

'I'll go and visit them tomorrow.' He stepped forward and rubbed her arm lovingly. 'I know Harry, he'll pull through. Don't you worry.'

She nodded in agreement.

'Have they caught who done it?'

'Omar was in here earlier he said they had a suspect. The whole town went crazy to find her. She fled the diner, that's where it happened, Omar and Willy hunted her down like a rabid dog.'

'It was a woman?'

'They should gas her,' the female deputy whispered. 'Traitor.'

Matthew didn't bother to turn around. He concentrated on Rutha's reply.

'Evil witch, so I'm told - got the devil in her.' She folded her arms matter-of-factually. 'They say she used to be from around these parts. Folks round here don't know what to do; they're terrified. Birchwood County has never had anythang like this happen, we're God fearing, not like those other folks. Well, you know being a lawyer an' all?'

He chuckled once. He and his partner, John Beaumont, were the only lawyers in a ten mile radius. Business was usually booming with civil complaints and land owning disputes, usually settled out of court. He had not had a murder case since he worked in Atlanta, after leaving law school fifteen years ago.

He paused. 'I bess get going.'

'All right honey, but don't be a stranger, you hear?' she replied, pointing a finger at him. 'Tell that wife of yours, I'll see her in church on Sunday.'

He nodded.

'He's gotta lot of nerve,' a mechanic from Pete's auto repair shop sneered as he walked from the men's room. The deputies and other mechanics mumbled in agreement.

Rutha walked toward the mechanic's table, picking up his empty plate. She gave him an evil eye, kissing her teeth again in disgust.

The mechanic looked up at her. 'Now don't tell me that you approve of this low-life comin' back here?' He fiddled with his baseball cap, which sat lop-sided on his Neanderthal head. He glared at Matthew. 'You should be locked up.'

'Don't listen to him Matt.' Rutha wiped the mechanic's table. 'Preston, you finished?'

He mumbled a reply.

'Get outta here,' Rutha said, sternly.

Preston made his way reluctantly across the coffeeshop. He nudged Matthew hard and headed toward the exit. He paused, placing his hand on the gold door handle, turning abruptly on his heels. 'Why are you so happy he's back?' he sneered, waiting for Matthew to bite.

Matthew gripped his suitcase; his heart rate increased.

Rutha placed her hands onto her rounded hips. 'Leave Preston.' She raised her eyebrows. 'Now.'

'Well I don't trust this damn fool,' Preston mumbled. 'He cost me over a grand in legal fees 'coz he didn't bother to show up, lowlife.' He left the coffeeshop mumbling under his breath and shaking his head.

'You go on home now Matt,' Rutha instructed.

Matthew stepped out onto the sidewalk, closed the wooden glass paneled door and breathed a sigh of relief.

He felt proud he didn't flatten Preston in a heartbeat and anyone else who intervened.

Matthew strolled across Hanover Street, trying not to whistle 'Eye of the tiger' by Survivor.

The heat penetrated the sunless sky. It consumed his body like a suffocating cocoon; he could not wait to be back in the safe clutches of air conditioning.

He studied the address his wife, Anna, had given him over the phone, and proceeded down Goodland's Avenue until he came to a two-story four-bed-roomed house, at the end of the quiet cul-de-sac.

He walked up the driveway, occupied by Anna's beige Volvo, along the path at the front of his house.

He had seen the photographs she had sent him, but he couldn't prepare himself for the bright yellow and white house until he had seen it in the flesh.

He stared at the pine trees that surrounded it and the tall brown spikes of grass that sprouted from the ground. He wondered what the wildflowers that occupied the tall wispy stalks were.

If he didn't know any better, he would have thought the front lawn was a nature reserve, not his front yard. It put the rest of the street to shame with their immaculately trimmed lawns.

He climbed the small bricked steps onto the front porch. On the left side of the porch sat a hand crafted two-seater swing. The slat-backed wood creaked as it rocked gently in the warm breeze.

Sure the lawn needs work, but it's home. He thought as he placed his key into the lock. His German shepherd, Rocky, barked from behind the door. He could hear Anna's voice from somewhere at the back of the house; it sounded as if she was on the phone.

He turned the key and stood in the doorway. He let the air conditioning caress his skin for a moment. It blew through his soaking hair and tickled his neck.

He heard footsteps approaching from the kitchen; he closed the front door and stood in the hall.

The hall was long and wide. It had the distinct smell of emulsion. The refurbished hardwood floor reflected the oatmeal colored walls.

'Matt!' Anna exclaimed. She ran toward him, her bare feet slapping on the floor. 'Why didn't you call me, I would have picked you up?' She wrapped her arms around his waist.

'I wanted it to be a surprise,' he shrugged. He dropped his suitcase onto the floor and wrapped his arms around her shoulders. He stroked her long wavy hair and inhaled the strawberry and vanilla fragrance of her shampoo.

Rocky continued to bark. He pounced onto Matthew; his huge feet were perched onto Matthew's shoulders.

'Missed you too, Rocky!' he exclaimed, gently pushing the hefty dog to the ground. 'I love the house, Anna.' He looked down at her. 'What's wrong?'

Her hazel eyes filled with tears. 'It's Sally.'

Chapter Two

'Arrested?' Matthew said, finally breaking the silence. He stared at the passing street.

Anna turned left at the next junction and they headed toward the county jail.

'What for? It doesn't make any sense.'

'I know. First degree murder... How can they think she murdered what's-his-name?' She shook her head, trying to remember. 'Collins, that's his name and shot Harry?'

The Volvo came to a stop in a parking bay.

'Sally has her faults but...She's never done anything illegal, I don't think. That's good though, right?' She shot Matthew a look, waiting for his confirmation.

'Yeah, don't worry, she'll be fine,' he smiled weakly. 'Has the Sheriff let your folks see her yet?'

She shook her head. Her voice was a whisper, 'First degree murder,' she repeated.

Images and scenarios plagued Matthew's mind. 'What was Sally doing here anyway?'

Anna shrugged.

* * *

The crime itself had been spread across newspapers and television broadcasts for days. It was the story that shook the county; the story that broke hearts - peace keepers slain in cold blood.

Every reporter, from local news stations to New York and Washington, were hungry for the latest information. They prowled around the small town of Billows Creek, moving into every available hotel, motel and bed and breakfast in the vicinity.

The reporters pounced on Matthew and Anna as they walked from the Volvo to the jail front steps.

'Are you the suspect's lawyer?' a female reporter asked.

'Is it true that Harry Richardson is currently in critical condition at Birchwood County memorial hospital?' another reporter interrupted.

'Do you think Mrs. Martinez is guilty?' a male voice said.

Matthew held up his hand. 'No comment, at this time. Thank you.'

The jail buzzed with excitement. Matthew could see the commotion through the inner door. If he did not know better, he would have thought it was the Fourth of July.

Matthew sat in the corridor next to his father-in-law, Arthur Owens, waiting for Sheriff Langford to let them in to see Sally.

Arthur and his wife, Linnie had rushed to the jail as soon as they had heard the report over the radio, calling Anna on the way.

Arthur caressed his black moustache with his thick rough fingers as he stared into space.

Linnie paced back and forth. Her fifty-nine-year-old body had been neglected over the years; it bulged from the cotton dress and wobbled when she walked. Matthew noticed her make-up was of its usual thickness and wondered how she walked in such tiny shoes. He tried to block out the click-click-click they made as she paced back and forth.

Anna stood by the window, biting her fingernail. 'Momma, why don't you sit down?' she pleaded.

Linnie didn't reply.

'You can go in now, Matt,' Deputy Porter said. He placed a biro behind his ear and sat at his desk.

Linnie stopped pacing. 'What about us?' Her cerise lipstick had become sticky in the heat; it made her lips smack together when she spoke.

Matthew noticed she swallowed hard, trying to hold back the tears that pricked her eyes.

'Visiting hours are over for tonight, Linnie. I'm sorry,' Deputy Porter said, softly.

Matthew stood. 'I'll go and see if she's OK.' He gripped Arthur's shoulder. 'Why don't you go home? There's nothing you can do tonight.' He looked at Anna. 'I'll come by in a minute.'

He entered the interrogation room and sat at a short wooden table. He heard movement from outside another door that led to the jail cells at the back of the station.

A key entered the lock and Deputy Patterson opened the door. He and Sally entered to the jingle of the shackles gripping Sally's wrists and ankles. Patterson closed the door behind him and stood at the far end of the room.

'Where are my kids? Have you seen them?' Anxiety flashed in Sally's ocean eyes.

Matthew pulled his eyebrows together, confused. 'Liz and Tom are here too?'

Sally nodded.

'I'm guessing the Sheriff's holding them in the conference room.' Matthew looked at Patterson. 'Can we take the cuffs off, please?'

Patterson sucked in his gut, rolling his eyes. Metal smashed against metal, echoing around the room as he removed the cuffs.

Without taking his eyes off Matthew, Patterson side stepped back to his position next to the door.

Matthew hardly recognized Sally in her orange jumpsuit. She crossed the room toward the nearest chair, rubbing her wrists. She had gained a few pounds since the last time he had seen her, and her small frame carried it well.

She sank onto the pine chair opposite Matthew. 'Do you think my Mom would…Can you take them to my Mom's? I don't want them to stay in this place. They must be so frightened.'

'Of course Linnie will take them. Now, tell me what happened?' he asked.

Sally sat with her palms facing the ceiling. 'I-I don't know…Joe had a gun…He shot those two policemen…There was so much blood,' her voice trembled. 'I was so tired, I had to pull over. We'd had a long drive from Atlanta, so we ate at the nearest diner.' She stared at him, a confused expression evident on her worn face. 'W-Why is this happening?' She interlocked her fingers and slammed her fists onto the table. 'Get me outta here, please!'

He reached forward, tapping her hands. He looked at Patterson. 'Ted, could you give us a minute?'

Ted Patterson bit at his tongue. 'Whatever,' he replied, belligerently. The keys rattled as the heavy door slammed shut.

Sally flinched at the sound. She coughed clearing her dehydrated throat and wiped her face with the sleeve of her jumpsuit.

Matthew frowned. He could see the pain in her eyes and felt awkward asking her to relive her ordeal. He could imagine it clearly - the Sheriff standing over her snarling obscenities and spitting in her face, the occasional slap just to get the point across.

He could almost taste the venom on the Sheriff's tongue as he threatened to take Sally's children away from her, if she didn't co-operate.

He noticed a purple bruise just below her left eye. 'How did you get that bruise? Did the police do that?'

She didn't reply, just sat frozen like an animal in headlights.

'What were you doing here that night?'

She avoided eye contact. 'It's the summer holidays. We were stopping off here, and going onto Florida to visit Miguel's parents. Obviously we weren't visiting mine,' she retracted. 'I'm sorry that was uncalled for.'

He sat back against the chair and let her continue without interruption.

'We ran into Joe at the diner. I haven't seen him in so long. He offered to buy the kids some ice-cream, but it was late – we were exhausted.' She swallowed hard. 'We left the diner and Joe followed us. He fell and couldn't walk to his car. He said he'd hurt his ankle, I was soaked and didn't want to stand around in the rain anymore,' she paused, brushing her hair away from her face. 'I couldn't just leave him there. He asked to sit in my car for a while until the rain let up. I didn't have the energy to argue.' She stared at him, her voice became coarse; her words were rushed. 'Then I woke up with a patrol car in front of me. The kids and I must have fallen asleep...I saw St... the police officer's body fall off the hood. There was so much blood.' She wiped her nose with her sleeve again.

He leaned forward and took her shaking hands. 'It's OK, everything's going to be OK. Now, who is this Joe?'

She sniffed. 'Joseph Mullen. Please get my children outta this place.'

He handed her his handkerchief. 'I will, I promise,' he sat back in his chair. 'Why do the police think *you* did this, Sal?'

17

She blew her nose. 'Joe hit me and put a knife to my throat…in front of Lizzie and Tom,' she gasped in-between sobs. 'I was so scared. I thought he was gonna kill me. He kidnapped us and took us to a motel. He locked us in the bathroom for hours.' She bit her lip. 'That's when the Police smashed through the front door and threw me to the ground. They took Lizzie and Tom and arrested me.' She put her hands over her ears. 'Lizzie screamed…I will never forget the look on Tom's face,' a tear fell from her chin and landed on the table.

'Listen, I'm going to help you, but I need to know everything. Now, did you give a statement?'

She looked at him. 'I didn't do this, Matt. The Sheriff thinks I did this, but I didn't. You have to believe me,' tears fell from her blood shot eyes. She rested her head in her hands, sobbing. 'He wouldn't listen!'

'OK Sal, I'll talk to him.' He picked up his cellular phone from the table.

'Who are you calling?'

'My associate John.'

'But I thought you were gonna help me?' Her voice was high-pitched and shaky.

'I'm going to get you out of here. I promise,' he comforted. He paused. He could not shake the uneasy feeling in his stomach. 'What is the evidence against you?' he said trying not to upset her further, but frustrated he was not getting a straight answer.

Wiping her face, she glanced over her shoulder checking the door was still closed. Turning back to the pine table she said, 'Isn't it obvious?' her voice became a whisper.

He frowned. 'Listen, I'm sure that's not the reason. I'll call John and talk to the Sheriff. Sit tight.' He stood to leave.

'If you're not gonna help me why did you bother comin' at all?' There was a hint of venom on her tongue.

He paused and contemplated taking her case. 'I'm not sure I'm the best lawyer for you right now.' He looked Sally in the eye.

'You think I'm guilty?' She leaned forward, desperation in her colorless eyes.

He took a deep breath and chewed his tongue, making a clicking noise in his throat. 'No I don't think you're guilty, it's just...' He frowned.

'Just what? Is it because I'm a Muslim?' She looked at him defiantly.

He put his hands on his hips. 'What-'

'I'm begging you Matt, please...think of Lizzie and Tom,' she cut him off. Worry lines appeared above her nose and across her forehead.

He was silent for a moment. 'Don't talk to anyone,' he sighed heavily. 'I'll come by tomorrow.' Before he made it to the door he said, 'And no it isn't because you're a Muslim.'

Chapter Three

Sheriff Omar Langford sat in his office. His capacious body leaned back against the leather cushioning. He held a cigar in his teeth. Matthew knew the Sheriff was oblivious to his presence in the corridor. He could see with each inhale, the Sheriff's nostrils were drowning in the pungent smell of victory.

Matthew knocked on the open door, hoping it would wake the Sheriff from his day-dream. 'Sheriff, may I have a minute or two please?'

'Well if it isn't Matthew Brennan…' Langford lit his victory cigar. 'Have a seat.' He pointed to the chair in front of his desk. The chair was lower than his over sized leather chair. He peered down at Matthew from his throne. 'What can I do for you?' He smirked, blowing thick gray smoke out of his mouth.

'I'd like to know what you have in terms of evidence against Sally Martinez.'

Langford rested his hands over his beer gut and crossed his fingers matter-of-factually. 'Are you here officially? I thought Judge Chamberlain disbarred you indefinitely?'

'He suspended me, that's not the same thing. Anyhow, you didn't answer my question.'

The Sheriff rolled his eyes. 'The revolver was covered in her prints and the lab confirmed she was covered in gun powder fragments. We also have witnesses.'

'Her fingerprints were on the murder weapon?' Matthew tried not to sound so surprised.

'She left out that detail, didn't she?' Langford leaned forward, tapping cigar ash into the ashtray. He rested his hands on the oak desk, 'I don't suppose she informed you the murder weapon, a .38 caliber revolver, was registered to a Miguel Martinez either?'

Matthew could feel his face drain of color.

'Yes, her husband.'

Why didn't she tell me? He thought angrily. He wondered where Miguel was at this moment. 'Can I have a copy of the police report?'

'It's being typed; you'll get your copy.' The Sheriff took the cigar from his mouth and held it in his thick fingers. 'So, you really are defending her – back in the saddle, eh?'

Matthew did not answer. He had not had confirmation from the judge whether he had permission to practice again and wasn't sure if taking the case would be a good idea. He decided not to correct the Sheriff and instead kept up the pretense. 'She said Joseph Mullen did the shootings. That was her statement to you when she was arrested.'

Langford gave a deep belly laugh. 'Yeah and Elvis is alive and well and living in Savannah.' He stood from his desk and crossed to the window, the cigar smoldering in-between his fingers. 'None of the witnesses saw a man with her at any point during her visit to the diner. This Joe Mullen is a figment of her imagination, I'm tellin' you.'

'Nevertheless did you investigate the possibility that this guy did in fact, do it? Did you interview her children?'

The Sheriff was silent for a moment. He rolled his tongue across his teeth. 'She did it, Mr. Brennan.' He turned back to his chair, leaning his arm on the backrest. 'Matthew, you've been out of the game a while, so I'm gonna give you some helpful advice – don't be fooled by

21

her story.' He placed his cigar into the ashtray to the left of the desk. He leaned toward Matthew with his lips curled. 'They changed their story so many times I had to have a refresher course every time I interviewed them,' he sneered. 'Guess you're gonna have to come to terms with the fact that your sister-in-law is a cop killer as well as a traitor to her own kind.'

Matthew leaned back against the cushioning of his chair. He crossed his legs, interlocking his fingers around his knee. 'Allegedly.'

The Sheriff stood wide-eyed. 'First she said the gun wasn't her husband's,' he chuckled, shaking his head in disbelief. 'Then she said the prints weren't even hers,' he shook his head again. 'Then she gave us a cock-and-bull-story that she had come down here to visit her folks. Now, we know that ain't true don't we?'

'She said she was visiting Miguel's parents in Florida.'

'Bullshit.'

Matthew stood. 'Do you have any objections to Linnie taking the children into her custody – Sally will sign the release forms?'

'Sure. Sure.'

Matthew crossed to the door. 'Thanks for your time, Sheriff.'

'Matthew, why don't we go for a walk?' The Sheriff picked up his cigar, making his way toward Matthew.

He led Matthew down a narrow corridor painted in a deep biscuit color. He nodded at passing officers and placed his arm across Matthew's shoulders. 'I didn't ask before - how's the family?'

'Fine,' Matthew replied, uneasy. 'Thanks.'

The Sheriff gripped the cigar in-between his index finger and his thumb. 'S'ppose you've heard Willy fixed his store? Only cost four thousand dollars. You started drivin' again?' The Sheriff smiled wickedly. 'What about ridin' that bike of yours?'

Matthew narrowed his eyes. 'Are you trying to get a rise outta me, Sheriff? It won't work.' he replied, firmly.

They stopped outside a room; the door was closed.

'Just making sure you realize what you're lettin' yourself in for. Listen, I know she's your sister-in-law and all, but if I were you I'd seriously consider dropping her case.'

'Why would that be, Sheriff?' Matthew turned to face him, shrugging his arm away.

The Sheriff moved closer. 'Now, Matthew,' his eyes widened. 'People in this town are distraught. Those two boys of mine were part of this community. Think about it. People take thangs to heart, you know?' He opened the door and gripped the silver handle. 'I can't be held responsible.'

'Are you threatening me?' he narrowed his eyes.

The sheriff smirked. 'Not at all.'

The children sat on the floor with a female officer. She was reading from a children's book.

'OK, Officer Ward. You can go back to work now. This here is Matthew Brennan, their uncle. Gonna take them home to Grandma's,' he said, ignoring Matthew's comment.

Matthew was shocked at how much the children had grown.

Elizabeth had her mother's tall shapely figure and her structured cheekbones. The mocha color of Elizabeth's skin resembled her Hispanic father, as did her huge brown eyes and thick eyelashes. Her satin-black hair was covered with a pink silk Hijab that draped down her back until it touched the waistband of the cream Jilbab.

The officer handed the eight-year-old the book.

'What about my Momma?' Thomas asked. He stood

23

from the floor, staring at the Sheriff expectantly. The five-year-old tugged at his denim pants that were two sizes too large for him.

Matthew could see Thomas was his father's son. He had his father's wilder beast stance, big stocky shoulders and a stare that could turn any man to stone.

He did that stare now at the Sheriff.

'Well, they're all yours,' the Sheriff replied.

Matthew noticed the Sheriff ignored the comment made about Sally going home.

'Don't forget to sign the release form,' he demanded and left the room.

* * *

Anna stood in the kitchen doorway at the Owens' home. She stared at Linnie with a worried expression.

Linnie leaned against the work top, looking out the kitchen window. Her white apron hung from her waist.

'Momma?' Anna's left hand ran along the worktop until she came to a stop next to her mother.

Linnie jumped. She took some glasses from the overhead cupboard.

'Are you all right?'

Linnie was slouched, almost frail looking. Her face was colorless and tired. Fine lines appeared around her eyes and across her forehead. 'Yes, darling.'

Anna took a jug of iced tea from the refrigerator and spooned sugar into the golden liquid. As she stirred, she said: 'Matt's on his way.' She placed the jug onto a tray. 'He said we should send over some personal items before the seventy-two hours are up. You know, toothbrush and underwear those kinda things.'

Linnie placed her hand across her stomach as if she were about to retch.

Anna looked at her mother's patented expression. She squeezed Linnie's arm. 'Don't worry Momma. John will sort out this misunderstanding, I'm sure. It has to be a misunderstanding, how can they think that of Sally?'

The front door closed.

Linnie jumped again. She could hear Matthew's voice in the hall. 'The children will need something to drink. I'll make them some Soda.'

Matthew entered cradling Thomas. 'Here take him.'

Linnie did as instructed. 'I'll put him in Anna's old room, he's exhausted.'

Anna carried the tea tray into the living room.

Elizabeth sat on the chocolate colored sofa, staring at the hardwood floor.

Anna took a long deep breath. 'Hello, Lizzie? Do people still call you Lizzie? Or is it Elizabeth now?' She approached, placing the tray onto the coffee table. She handed a glass of fizzing Soda to Elizabeth. 'My, how you've grown.' She perched herself on the arm of the sofa.

Elizabeth held the glass. 'Momma calls me Lizzie. Why can't she just come home?' she sobbed.

'Oh angel, your momma's gonna be home real soon.' Anna held her, caressing the silk Hijab over Elizabeth's head, with her finger.

Chapter Four

The sun set slowly over the town, washing the creek with an orange glow. The evening had become unbearably muggy; Billows Creek was deserted. Townsfolk had retreated to the comfort of their air-conditioned homes hours ago.

The Brennans were in bed. Matthew was engrossed in News Time on T.V. He scribbled notes and doodles onto his notepad.

Anna tried to read her adventure novel to no avail. 'How was Sal you didn't say much at supper?' She placed her bookmark against the pages.

'Scared.' He paused trying to find the right words.

'Should she be?'

He sighed, heavily. 'She asked me to defend her.'

'But you called John?'

Matthew bit his lip. 'No.'

'But you're gonna call John?'

'No.' He pointed the remote control at the T.V. raising the volume. '…The brutal murder of patrolman Collins and the attempted murder of his partner Harry Richardson, took place a mile from the fishing town of Billows Creek, southwest Georgia.' The reporter raised her arm and turned slightly to give the viewers a better look at the yellow police tape surrounding the parking lot.

Anna pressed the standby button on the remote control defiantly.

'I was watching that!'

She stared at him. 'Matt, you can't be serious about defendin' Sally?' She shook her head, frustrated by his apparent lack of interest in the conversation. 'C'mon Matt tell Sal you can't do. This. Right. Now?'

'She's your sister!'

'I know, but John can handle it. Tell Sal you can't defend her, I won't let you,' her voice grew louder.

'You won't let me?' He cut her off, throwing the covers back and walking to the window. He stood semi-naked, wearing blue striped boxer shorts. 'Stop treating me like a child!' His voice raised an octave. He spat into the drapes, hung in front of him. 'I can handle this – I'm a lawyer and dang-it I'm gonna do my job.'

'Doctor Adamson said you shouldn't-'

'I'll call Judge Chamberlain tomorrow and ask to be reinstated. My three months are almost up so I should be reinstated automatically.' He wasn't talking to Anna now. His mind raced through a to-do list. 'I'll file an affidavit of compliance with the order.' He shook his head frenetically. 'Thangs are gonna get ugly.'

'You. Selfish. Bastard!' She stormed from the bedroom, slamming the door.

* * *

Matthew slipped his feet into his chestnut moccasins. He perched on the edge of the bed, staring at the T.V., while playing with his wedding ring.

The news report had ended. A Jackie Chan movie flickered on the screen; Matthew had never heard of it. He sighed. *Why can't Anna understand why I have to do this?* He thought. He could not live the rest of his life pretending he was not a lawyer that the bills did not matter. He was cured now. He could cope. He just needed the chance to prove himself.

He pointed the remote control at the screen. The picture disappeared. He threw on his robe and crossed to the door.

Anna was in the living room. A glass of mineral water and the bible rested in her lap.

For a moment, he watched her sitting in the shadows from a small crack in the doorway, daring himself to enter the lair.

Her face was washed with red as she stared at the LED digits on the DVD player.

Taking a deep breath, he pushed the living room door with the tip of his finger. He cringed as the door creaked on its hinges, slicing the silence. 'Hey,' he whispered.

She turned her attention back to the digits. She shuffled on the sofa, covering her feet with the bottom of her nightgown.

He approached slowly, waiting for her to speak.

'You know,' she leaned forward, placing the glass on the coffee table in front of her. She made a fist with one hand, overlapping the other. 'When you came home, I thought thangs were gonna work out for us. I thought this new house would be a new start for us. Now, I'm not so sure.'

'Anna, listen to me-'

'No you listen!' She stood from the sofa and stepped forward, directing her emotions to the wall in front of her. 'Your head... your head was so full of hate – so full of bitterness.' She placed her hands onto the side of her face. 'You got this look in your eyes,' she paused. 'I-I never want to see that look again, Matt.' She covered her mouth with the back of her hand. 'I can't go through that again.' She brushed a tear angrily from her left cheek and looked at the ceiling as if talking to God. 'I beg you...' Her voice trailed off.

He bit his lip. 'I had no idea you felt this way.'

'Of course you didn't, you were so caught up in your own emotions you forgot I was involved too.' She sobbed. 'I kept trying to figure it all out. Why couldn't you open up to me? Was it my fault?' She reached for a tissue. 'Did you think I didn't care or that I wasn't hurtin' too?' She tried desperately to control each erratic breath.

He sat down. 'He was my son, and I couldn't save him. How would you feel?'

'He might not have been my son, but I couldn't save him either – no-one could have saved him. Matt, it wasn't your fault, it's no-one's fault. You did everything you could do. He's with God now.' She turned to face him.

'Spare me the bible bull,' he put his head in his hands. 'I have to do this.'

'No you don't!'

'Please trust me.'

'What if you can't handle the stress and start drinking again?' her voice raised an octave.

He looked up at her. 'I won't.'

'I've heard that before. The last time you said that we had to remove the Buick from the front of Willie's store at four in the morning.' She turned away from him again.

'Thank you. Thank you very much!' He stood, crossing the living room and slammed the front door behind him.

He sat on the swing staring angrily into space. He sucked in the air through gritted teeth.

Chapter Five

Matthew jumped as the persistent beep of his wrist watch alarm sounded. 7am. He wiped the sleep from his eyes before taking in his surroundings for the first time in daylight.

The living room was painted in a light peppermint green with a white European-style marble mantle around the fireplace.

He glanced at a photograph above the fireplace of his wedding day and wished he could go back in time when they were wild and passionate about each other.

Rocky entered the living room and made his way toward Matthew, wagging his tail once.

'Traitor,' Matthew said as he kicked off the blanket to stretch. He patted Rocky's head before picking up the telephone from the glass coffee table and dialing the Judge's number.

Judge Chamberlain, the superior court judge for the trial, answered on the first ring. 'Yes?' His tone was deep and thick with a Georgian accent.

'Good morning, your honor,' Matthew perched on the arm of the leather sofa. 'It's Matthew Brennan.'

'Mornin' Matthew, I take it this is not a social call?'

Matthew's smile faded. He cleared his throat. 'I'll get straight to it; I know you're a busy man. As you know I have been discharged from Summerdale rehab center, where I have completed my eight week program. My three month suspension is almost over and I-'

'And you were wondering if you could be reinstated?'

'Yes your honor.'

The judge was silent.

Matthew shuffled, making himself comfortable. *This is gonna be a long phone call*. He thought.

Governor Eleanor Francis appointed Chamberlain to the Superior Court bench six years ago. He had a decorative list of credentials to his name, courtesy of the University of Georgia and the University of Georgia School of Law. He took his role very seriously and was known for his no nonsense military approach.

'I was going to deny your request-'

'But your honor-'

The judge cut Matthew off. 'However, I feel you have complied with the order, and I shall reinstate you on one condition if you so much as smell a glass of liquor I will have you disbarred indefinitely.'

'Thank you your honor,' Matthew replied.

'Do I make myself clear?'

'Yes, sir.'

*   *   *

Matthew stood motionless, eyes closed, in the shower. The warm water soothed his sleep deprived body.

He dressed hastily, combing gel through his bedridden hair as he went downstairs.

He picked up the morning paper lying on the front porch and flipped it to the front page.

A picture of the officers, in their full regalia, stared back at him. *Last Christmas's charity event, no doubt to add more sympathy.* He thought. He read the headline aloud.

'Governor vows justice for peace officers.' He rolled his eyes.

He stood in the kitchen, placing the newspaper on the breakfast bar that ran snake-like down the center, with a cooking utensils ceiling unit hanging above it. 'I see the governor's up for re-election?'

Anna sat hunched over the breakfast bar, holding a glass of water. She was wearing a pink bathrobe. Her eyes were dark and distant, and her face was blotchy.

Rocky greeted Matthew.

'Hey boy,' he patted Rocky on the head. 'You wanna go outside?' He crossed the stone floor toward the back door, at the far end of the kitchen. Rocky barked excitedly, wagging his tail and bouncing around. 'OK, boy.' He unlocked the door.

Rocky flew up, past the dingy shed, to the end of the yard.

'Damn cat,' he sighed, shaking his head. He stepped backward, crossing to the nutmeg colored countertop that ran along the left side of the kitchen. He poured himself a mug of coffee. 'Where do we keep the sugar?'

'Don't you think you should lay off the caffeine?' she mumbled. She stared at him.

'It's my first cup since I've been back!'

She rolled her eyes. 'Top cupboard.' She spoke into her cereal bowl, 'Your lunch and snacks are in the fridge – make sure you eat six times a day to keep your blood sugar levels up.' She climbed off the stall, picked up her empty bowl and made her way to the sink. 'There are some muffins in the cupboard for your breakfast.' She placed her bowl into the sink and stared out the window at the backyard.

'Thanks.' He tried to control the antagonism in his voice. He hated being dictated to like a child.

'Are you going to visit Harry today?'

He sipped his coffee with vindictiveness, staring at the back of her head. 'Yeah, sure when I get a spare five minutes to scratch my ass.' Disappointed by her lack of retaliation, he crossed to the breakfast bar. 'Well, I bess get goin',' he said, finally. 'I want to be at the office by eight.'

'Don't forget your vitamins.' She threw a bottle of vitamins at him. It missed, crashing to the floor just behind his legs.

'Oh that's real grown up of you darling,' he snapped. He grabbed the plastic bottle from the floor: A Super nutrition's *Perfect Blend* with added evening primrose oil. He threw two tablets into his mouth, washing them down with the remnants of his coffee. 'Bye,' he picked up his motorcycle keys and stormed toward the front door.

* * *

John Beaumont entered Bella's Coffeeshop, whistling to himself. He carried his wallet to the counter, admiring the freshly baked flapjacks sitting on display. 'Gees Rutha, I can't wait any longer I'm wasting away!' he joked, pulling his famous toothy grin. He rolled up his sleeves, revealing perfect mahogany colored skin. He leaned against the counter.

'M-mornin' Mr. Beaumont.'

John turned in the direction of the young male voice. 'Oh, morning Roy, I didn't see you there.'

Roy was known around town as Roy the Retard. John hated that word and never used it.

'Have you enjoyed your breakfast?' John asked, louder than was necessary for Rutha to hear.

Roy chuckled. 'Yes Sir. I'm goin' to work now, Mr. Beaumont.'

'Good for you son.' He sighed, 'The service in this town gets worse and worse,' he joked.

Rutha placed her hands on her hips, looking up at him. 'Lord, I'm comin' you rascal!' She smiled, as she approached the counter. 'You know they'll be worth it, honey,' she shuffled a brown paper bag toward him.

He inhaled the sweet blueberry muffin aroma. 'Mmm, they're still warm.'

'Who's cellular phone is that?' Rutha narrowed her eyes; the beep-beep-buzz noise persisted despite her glare.

Fumbling in his pocket, John replied bashfully, 'Mine, sorry Rutha I forgot I had it on.' He stared at the caller I.D. on the screen. 'It's Anna Brennan, see you at lunch, Rutha. See you around Roy – don't work too hard.'

'Ok Mr. Beaumont,' Roy said.

'I guess you want the usual?' she called after him.

John smirked. 'You bet I want the usual. There's no way I'm missin' the Tuesday lunchtime special.' He chuckled once and inhaled the scent of the blueberry muffin in the bag. His stomach rumbled loudly. He placed his cellular phone to his ear.

'John, it's Anna.'

He smiled. 'What's up?'

'I'm worried about Matt. He has already phoned the judge; he's defending my sister!'

John had been Matthew's partner for seven years. They had met at Georgia state university.

After graduation, a corporate Law firm in Atlanta had accepted their applications and they had set out to change the world together.

But John hated the politics of being in a stuffy corporate firm. He wanted his cases to mean something to the people. The real people, people who were just like him.

They had always talked about opening up their own practice together and after three years in Atlanta, they came home.

'He's phoned the judge already?' John stopped mid-step in surprise.

Anna paused. 'John. I don't think he's ready for this. What should we do?'

John took a bite of his breakfast. He crossed the street to his restored Chevy Caprice and took out his keys. 'I'll talk to him, don't worry.'

'Thanks John.'

'Don't mention it. Is he settling in ok?'' he asked, changing the subject. He pulled out of the parking bay and headed toward Brennan and associates law office; his cellular phone did not move from his ear.

'He seems to be, I can't really tell at the moment, what with Sally's arrest.'

He nodded. 'Word is you've hired Linnie's famous gardener. Has he started the yard yet?'

She chuckled. 'You heard about him too, huh? No, he's dropping by later,' she paused. 'John, it goes without saying, but don't tell Matt I called.'

He could hear the anxiety in her voice. 'Ok Anna I won't. I'll be in touch and try not to worry.'

Chapter Six

Brennan and associates law office was on the corner of West Street, next door to Twinkles' toy shop.

The office was a historic two-storey building in a row of two-storey buildings, overlooking downtown Billows Creek. Downtown was where the small town's business was done.

The law office was quaint, compared to most. The downstairs doubled as the foyer and the secretary, Clara's, office.

On the second floor were two offices and a library.

Matthew parked his motorcycle in the reserved space below his office window. The aluminum frame reflected the brilliant sun like the eyes of a demon.

The V twin engine growled as Matthew rocked his hand back and forth on the throttle; adrenaline flowed through him.

He flicked the kill switch and the engine died. He took his helmet off, brushing his mousy blonde hair with his fingers.

A handful of reporters spotted him from across the street. They ran to him, armed with their tape recorders and microphones.

'Mr. Brennan, just a moment of your time?' a reporter from the New York Times asked. She pointed her small rectangular tape recorder in his direction. 'Is it true you are defending Mrs. Martinez?'

'Yes,' Matthew replied.

'Will she plead guilty?' a male reporter said.

'Do you anticipate the grand jury will indict the suspect?' another male reporter asked.

'Not with this lack of evidence,' he replied, swapping his helmet to his left hand. He took his keys from his right pocket.

A local female reporter thrusted her tape recorder toward Matthew's face. 'Is it true a Koran was found at the crime scene?'

Matthew raised his eyebrows in disbelief. 'No comment, but I'd like to know where you get your information.'

The female reporter smiled cockily. 'A very reliable source.'

'Are you still a regular patient at Summerdale rehabilitation center?'

Matthew raised his hands defensively. 'No comment at this time, thank you.' He walked to his office doors, flicking through the key fob, to find the right key. The reporters continued to spit questions at him. Matthew replied no comment several times before closing the doors.

He breathed a sigh of relief. *I should not have answered the first question.* He thought. He was not in the right frame of mind to be dealing with reporters. His head was filled with his own questions he needed to answer since hearing of Sally's arrest.

It had been eleven weeks since he had entered his office; the recollection of it escaped his memory. It was as though he had been reborn, without the memory of his previous life.

He picked up the mail at his feet and studied the foyer as if for the first time.

The walls, painted in a soft blue, made him feel refreshed. The smell of pine furniture polish enhanced the feeling. He smiled. Clara had cleaned up. It was one of her rituals before she left in the evenings. She felt a clean foyer was a welcoming invitation to potential clients as they entered through the doors the next morning.

She was more than just a secretary. The past four years she had worked for them, she had become more like a favorable aunt than an employee.

Her professionalism was acute, but when the work was completed, she offered a soft nurturing side; a character flaw they had grown to depend on.

Clara's antique mahogany desk was situated a few feet from the doors. It was organized to perfection, each pencil in its place, each file in its color coded order.

An array of freshly cut flowers stood in a vase at the end of the highly varnished surface. To the right of the vase, was a flat screen computer covered in a gray dust protector.

A black leather sofa sat against the wall, to the right of the windows; a waiting area for their clients.

He felt lured to the silver coffee machine next to the sofa but decided to continue past, climbing the dark blue carpeted stairs to his office.

He placed the mail in front of him on his newly polished L-shaped desk; it glistened in the sunlight from the window behind.

The clock tower above the courthouse chimed loudly at nine, snapping him into wake-up-mode. He buried his head into his daily planner, writing down a to-do list for the day ahead.

He finished scribbling and flicked through the mail. Several letters were for John, confirmations, appointments and a phone bill. *What's this?* He thought; he came across a blue envelope with the Birchwood County postmark on it.

It had a watermark halfway down, almost invisible through the pen inked address. It was the kind of stationery bought at an expensive stationery shop.

He ripped along the top with a brass letter opener and pulled matching colored paper from inside.

The words were typed in a clear bold font. It read: **She is guilty. Drop the case.**

He sighed, screwing up the piece of paper and slam-dunking it into the Trash Can to the left of his desk.

A loud commotion, coming from downstairs, suddenly disturbed the silence; he wondered what was going on and rushed to investigate.

Clara entered the foyer, carrying an oversized purse, an armful of books and what looked to Matthew like a cake tin. He hoped it was full of her famous pecan pie.

'Let me help you, Clara. Here have a seat.' He helped her to the leather sofa and placed the books on the seat beside her.

She took a handkerchief from her oversized purse and wiped her forehead elegantly. 'Oh thank you,' she exclaimed. 'I heard you were back in town, well look at you?' She studied him thoughtfully. Her bright pink lipstick creased on her plump lips as she smiled warmly. 'You're lookin' good, honey. I'm glad.' She rustled the cake tin. 'I've been baking all mornin' - just to say welcome home.' She pulled against the top of her dress, airing her pigeon-like chest. 'It's gonna be a scorcher, bess get the air conditioning set to *high*.' She shuffled in order to stand.

'Don't trouble yourself Ma'am, I'll do it.' He made his way to the far end of the room flicking the red switch on the air conditioning dial. The air conditioning system whistled and whirred into action like a jet engine.

She placed a slice of pecan pie onto a napkin and handed it to him. 'Well, we may as well taste a slice then we'll know what to look forward to after lunch,' she said, cheekily. She placed a delicate slice to her lips. 'Mmm.' She closed her eyes in delight as the pie dissolved sweetly in her mouth.

He rested the pie onto the corner of Clara's desk. He poured two cups of coffee from the machine and handed one to his secretary.

John entered holding the morning paper. 'Mornin', well look what the cat dragged in? It's good to see you Matt.' He bear-hugged Matthew, patting him on the back affectionately. 'How do you like the new house?' He waved the newspaper above his head. 'Damn gnats,' he grunted. 'I should have never given up smoking.'

Clara winked at Matthew. 'Well I guess you won't want a slice of pie then?'

'Miss Clara, being hounded by gnats gives me good reason to taste your delicious pie. Pecan pie makes the sun shine, the birds sing, and the cotton flourish.' John flashed his toothy grin and put his arm around her shoulders. 'And yours is the best in town.' He nudged her gently, giving her a wink.

She tapped his hand. 'All right enough panther piss,' she said, jokingly. 'I can't take anymore, here help yourself.' She handed John the cake tin.

John took it gladly, pulling off the lid and grabbing a huge piece. 'This place hasn't been the same without you, Matt,' he mumbled with a mouthful of pie. Crumbs tumbled down and rested in the creases of his shirt.

'Thanks,' Matthew replied. He took another mouthful of his coffee, swallowing quickly trying not to burn his tongue. 'I like the house, thanks for helping Anna with the move.'

John raised a hand, nodding; he took another bite of pie.

'I guess y'all have heard about Sally.' Matthew scratched at his face, looking at the floor he said, 'You're looking at her lawyer.'

He waited for the room to erupt with negative voices, shouting him down until he was on his knees; he was surprised by the silence.

John picked crumbs from his shirt and placed them to his lips. 'I trust you've thought about this?'

'Yes, I have,' Matthew replied, putting his hands into his pockets.

'You will need an affidavit drafted then,' she said, rolling her empty napkin and standing from the sofa. 'I'll send it over to the judge's clerk for you.' She crossed to her desk and sat down on the swivel chair in front of her computer. She took off the dust sheet, turned on the screen and began typing away.

'Thanks Clara.'

'You do know Helen Maxwell is the D.A?' John brushed the remaining crumbs off his shirt onto the floor.

Matthew watched Clara give John the evil eye from where she sat. John picked up the crumbs quickly and threw them into the Trash Can beside the front doors.

'When did that leech get elected?'

'While you were away…in the spiritual sense,' John replied. He crossed to the coffee machine and picked up the glass coffee jug. The coffee inside was still hot, steaming from the small triangle opening. He poured the liquid into a cup. 'It's a hell of a comeback. Maybe you should start on something less controversial. How about a nice little divorce case?' John said, softly.

Matthew sighed heavily. It was bad enough facing the day fighting with Anna; he didn't want to fight with John as well.

John raised his hand defensively. 'It was just a suggestion.'

Matthew picked at his slice of pie. 'I'll have to inform Sally of this. It didn't occur to me Helen was D.A. I thought Cleaver was…'

John placed his cup on the table. 'Let's go to the courthouse an' hand in your affidavit, then why don't we go over to the jail and have a chat with your sister-in-law?'

'You mean you're with me on this?'

'Sure, Buddy.'

Matthew gave a little nod. 'Thanks.'

Clara frowned. She stared at her computer screen. 'Matt, you'll wanna see this.' She nodded towards the screen.

The daily headlines flashed along the bottom of the webpage: Ned's bar and Diner reopens for business after heinous crime.

Matthew curled his fingers into fists. 'Forget going over to the jail.'

Chapter Seven

'Matt?' Helen Maxwell said, surprised. She stood staring at him as he burst into her office uninvited; John trailed behind. 'Is something wrong?' She brushed stray cat hairs from her navy pencil skirt, nervously.

His nostrils flared. He forgot the formalities. 'We have the right as defense counsel to view the crime scene and let our forensic team examine it. It's damn right dirty.'

He placed his hands on his hips angrily, glaring down at her.

The blue and white striped shirt hugged his chest and outlined the curves of his biceps.

'I have no control over Ned's diner,' she said, 'he was losing business and had to reopen,' her breathing was shallow. She tucked her straight black hair behind her ear. 'Look, I'm truly sorry for this mistake, I'll have my notes sent over to you.' She remained standing, still holding her pen in her left hand. 'Is there anything else?'

'Actually there is,' Matthew folded his arms matter-of-factually. 'The police report and case file, I haven't received my copy.' He held up his hand. 'Let me guess another mistake?' His sarcasm hung in the air.

Helen was silent. She looked down at her newly polished shoes.

Matthew noticed she swallowed hard. He knew she did not want him to head straight to the judge with his

43

complaints about ethics. It was important for her career she played nice with the opposition. The judge would surely put her 'career ladder' in a wood shredding power tool and hit mulch if word got to him.

'I'll have all the reports you need sent over a.s.a.p.' She busied herself and placed the telephone to her ear.

* * *

'Did you find anything, Glen?' Matthew said to a tall, slightly built man.

The defense forensic team had spent an hour trying to find untainted evidence, crouching in-between parked vehicles with their boxes of apparatus.

'No, I'm sorry Matt,' Glen replied, sheepishly. He stood, turning to face Matthew and John, who were leaning against the Chevy with their arms folded across their chests. 'The crime scene is completely contaminated.'

'Guess that's it then, we'll have to take the DA's reports as gospel,' John said, sighing.

'That's convenient,' Matthew intoned. He placed the last mouthful of his candy bar to his lips. He listened to the faint sound of traffic cruising along the I-75 and gazed up at the mass of fluffy clouds floating along the powder blue sky. As his gaze fell lower, he noticed a small security camera bolted to a metal stand just above the kitchen door. It faced out into the parking lot. 'Look,' he pointed to the security camera. 'Wanna see a movie?'

'Dang it. I forgot the popcorn,' John smiled.

Matthew crossed the parking lot. He made his way to the kitchen door at the back of the diner, screwing the candy bar wrapper in his fist. He lifted the lid of a Dumpster, standing to the left of the kitchen door, and threw the wrapper inside. The lid closed with a thud.

Matthew made his way toward the building's front entrance. John ran along side, huffing and puffing like an old sheep dog.

A sign advertising the bar hung in the entrance window, decorated with blue and pink strobe lights.

'Maybe you should wait here Buddy?' John said, opening the heavy glass door. 'I'll go inside and talk with Ned about the camera.'

'I'll be fine.' Matthew followed John into the foyer.

A pit-faced African-American boy greeted them. He was dressed smartly in a dark blue suit. Matthew thought he looked as if he had just graduated from high school.

'Welcome to Ned's diner,' the boy's voice was high pitched and shaky. 'Would you like a tour?'

Matthew narrowed his eyes. 'A tour?' he shook his head in disbelief.

John handed the boy his card. 'We'd like to speak to Ned.'

'Follow me.' The boy led them through the dining area to the bar. 'Wait here, Ned's in his office he'll be out soon.'

The diner was lit by twelve large dome shaped lamps hanging from the ceiling. There were several gold-framed lakeside fine art prints on the walls and references to fishing around the bar area.

John looked at Matthew. 'You OK, buddy?'

Matthew nodded. 'Yeah, just wondering where Sally sat that night.' He tried to focus on the bustling dining area ignoring the smell of liquor behind him. One question kept nagging him: why were the officers even here that night?

'Ned, how's the fishing - caught any big ones lately?' John said, to a tall bald headed man.

The man rested a fat hand on the bar. 'Caught some bass yesterday - fine specimens but I don't think you're

45

here to discuss fish?' Ned, stroked his gray moustache. 'Follow me.'

Matthew was pushed by a man trying to get to the front of the bar. The man raised his hand, a gesture of apology.

'I see business is doing well,' Matthew said, squeezing through a gap before treading on a woman's foot. 'Sorry, Ma'am.'

Ned lead them past the bar area, down a corridor and into a small room.

A steel desk stood directly opposite the entrance, with two security T.V screens on top. Four black and white images displayed on each screen, showing different angles from each security camera. The first screen showed the front of the diner, the other the back.

Next to the T.Vs was an IBM computer with a black leather desk chair in front of it. Ned took a seat, swiveling around to face them. He rested his arm against the fire exit door to the left of the desk. 'So what can I do for you?'

Matthew closed the entrance door behind him, creating more space in the tiny room. 'Ned, we are representing Mrs. Martinez.'

Ned nodded, before folding his arms across his beer gut. He leaned back against the chair, waiting for them to speak.

'We want to look at the security tapes on the night of the murder,' John said, taking out a note pad and pen from his inside pocket.

Ned's smile faded. 'Err see now here's the thing. I was sure I changed the disc that morning, pressed record and set the timer...' He scratched his cheek. 'But when the Sheriff came it was gone.'

'Gone?' John asked, surprised.

'Yeah, I tell ya my memory ain't what it used to be. My wife's always telling me that.' He chuckled. 'She's always saying "Ned you need to slow down - take a vacation -

you're not gettin' any younger"' having no hair proves that, I guess.'

John licked his lips. 'Could someone have removed it?'

Ned shrugged. He scratched his head thoughtfully.

'Who was working that night?'

'Sarah-Jane - she's serving at the bar. Shirley Baxter - it's her day off and me.'

Matthew leaned on one foot. 'Can we interview her?'

Ned stood. 'Sure.'

'Sarah- Jane?' Matthew said, handing his business card to a small but curvaceous woman wearing a blue and white striped Ned's diner uniform. 'We're investigating the Martinez case. We would like to ask you some questions?'

She took the card, glanced at it and continued to serve the awaiting customer at the bar. 'So ask,' she intoned. She wiped a wine glass and replaced it onto a rack above the register.

'We'd like to know what happened on the night of June 13th.' Matthew tried to catch her eye, but she remained with her back to him. He tried to stop his eyes from wandering along the collection of liquor bottles displayed behind the counter.

'Please, Miss Meadows?' John said, softly. 'Anything you can remember will help us.'

'*Remember?*' she chuckled once. 'Oh I remember it like it was yesterday Mr. Beaumont, was it?' She looked at him thoughtfully.

John nodded.

She smiled, and her posture softened. 'It was real busy that night; we were short staffed. No surprises there,' she said, sarcastically.

'Lady I've been standing here all day!' a deep male voice yelled.

'Two whiskeys on the rocks,' another male voice said.

'Shoot. Here take these to table twenty-five?' She placed two crystal glasses on the bar in front of Matthew.

He held the glasses. The golden liquid vibrated against the ice. He froze. His hands trembled.

As if reading Matthew's mind John said, 'I'll take them.' He took the glasses from Matthew's grip.

'They ate over there by the window,' she pointed to a booth on the far right near the doors.

'Did you notice anything unusual about the woman? Did she seem preoccupied or nervous?' Matthew asked, unable to look up from his notepad.

'Not that I recall. She seemed tired as if she had been traveling a while.' She placed her hand to the side of her mouth and whispered, 'She was wearing one of those –you-know- Muslim garments,' she shrugged, 'If you call that unusual.'

'What happened then?' Matthew raised his voice over the noise from the bar.

'They left round five, maybe ten after seven. I headed out the back to my locker, went to the restroom, and that's when I heard the shots.' She set six place settings around the table. 'Everyone was stunned. Someone shouted to call an ambulance, and I saw Ned grab the phone.'

'Excuse me, Ma'me?' An elderly man, who was sat a few feet from Sarah-Jane called. She smiled politely at him and crossed the runway to his table in the dining area.

Matthew and John shuffled along next to her. She nodded to the man, took his order, and crossed the diner toward the kitchen.

'Did you go outside - take a look?' Matthew raised his voice again as she drifted further away from him.

'No way!' she said over her shoulder.

John placed a stick of nicotine gum into his mouth. 'Do you know anything about the security disc?'

She avoided eye contact. 'Security disc? No, I don't know anything about it.'

'Ned says it went missing after the incident – any ideas where it might have gone?'

'Look, I'm real busy,' she replied. 'Excuse me.' She disappeared through the kitchen door. It swung violently back and forth.

'Thanks for your time,' Matthew mumbled. He turned to face John. 'Let's try Shirley, maybe she knows about the disc?'

Chapter Eight

The Chevy Caprice bounced to a halt at a stop sign, a mile from downtown Billows Creek.

Matthew had counted fourteen places where he could buy alcohol. He turned up the radio, trying to block the voice inside his head. He hoped his ears would drown in the relaxing sound of country music.

'What was the name of Shirley's street again?' John asked. He pulled away from the stop sign, taking a right onto Brighton Street.

Matthew unfolded a small piece of paper. He read from the address Ned had given them. 'Long Pine Road, it's just past the golf course.' He placed the paper into his pocket. 'It's just here,' he confirmed as John turned left into Long Pine Road. 'That's her house. Number 3425.'

The Chevy's brakes squealed as it came to a halt in front of Shirley Baxter's home.

'Nice neighborhood, for a single mother of two, huh?' John said, sarcastically.

They walked up the path toward her front porch.

The large rented ground floor apartment had recently had a coat of paint around the window frames; the red bricks surrounded the frames like neat borders.

The front lawn appeared newly laid with its immaculate green blades and perfectly weeded flowerbeds that led up the front path.

With the July heat murdering lawns and flowerbeds around the neighborhood, Matthew knew this picturesque yard would turn into patches of brown dust within a few weeks.

He figured this yard, like his own, had to have been in desperate need of refurbishment for the Baxter's to have bothered.

Standing on the front step, Matthew pressed against the doorbell with his finger.

Suddenly, the door flew open. A woman bouncing a baby on her hip stood in the doorway. 'Oh, I thought you were someone else,' she said, sheepishly. She was dressed in a white T-shirt tucked neatly into her denim shorts.

'I get that all the time,' John joked.

'Can I help you?'

Matthew handed the woman, who appeared to be in her early forties, his card. 'Mrs. Baxter? My name is Matthew Brennan,' He could see from the expression on her face she already knew whom he was, probably from the reports on television. 'This is my associate, John Beaumont. We were wondering if we could ask you a few questions?'

She did not seem to care what they wanted. She looked past them up the street, seemingly distracted by someone or something.

She focused her attention back to the men standing at her door. 'I know who you are. What questions?' she replied, bouncing her son on her hip.

'Well, we were wondering what exactly you saw on the night of June 13th?' Matthew flashed his winning smile, the one that never failed to get him what he wanted.

'They told me I didn't have to talk to you if I didn't want to.'

'Who?' Matthew asked as if he had not already guessed.

'Miss. Maxwell and Mr. Daly.'

Matthew's suspicions were correct. Helen was quick to ensure all her witnesses understood their rights as free citizens. No one was forced or coerced into doing anything, least of all share their experiences openly with the defense.

'But, seeing as you're here, you may come in. I have to feed the baby his lunch.' She gestured for them to enter her home, inconvenienced by their timing.

'Thank you, Mrs. Baxter,' Matthew said. He sat across the dining table next to John.

The dining room was at the front of the apartment over looking the front yard. Matthew could see John's Chevy from where he sat.

An expensive bouquet of flowers were arranged in a glass vase, in the center of the table.

Plant pots were along the window sill and a book case stood in the far corner of the room.

'It's Ms. Baxter - I'm divorced.' Placing the baby onto her lap, Ms. Baxter added, 'Can I get you anything - tea?'

Matthew shook his head. 'No, thank you. We just have some questions - we won't take up too much of your time.'

'You were working on the night of June 13th, is that correct?' John took out his note pad and biro from his pocket.

'Yes that's right.'

'Can you tell us what exactly you saw?' Matthew rested his elbow on the table.

'I wasn't supposed to be working that night, but someone has to keep a roof over our heads - my ex isn't exactly forth coming with his wages,' she flicked her long auburn hair away from her baby's grip. 'Anyway, the kitchen was so damn hot, I propped open the outer door. Actually, I was just trying to save my ears from the so called band Ned was auditioning for gigs on Saturday nights.' She mimicked her son's mouth movements as he ate. 'Just as I was about to go back inside and finish taking orders, I saw Sally Martinez fire her gun at the officers.'

'You actually saw her shoot the officers?' Matthew confirmed.

'That's right. I couldn't believe it,' she shook her head. 'I watched her jump in her car, a blue Ford bronco and drive off. She left them lying there in a pool of blood.'

This woman was good. Matthew sensed she had already had her rehearsal time with the D.A, passing with distinction. They would have to work hard to find some impeachable evidence against her.

'I was lucky enough, last year, to do a first aid course at the university, so I knew what I had to do. I kept Harry warm until the ambulance came. The other guy was…' she shook her head again. 'She deserves everything she gets if you ask me.'

Matthew was thankful he had not.

She took another scoop of brown mush and spooned it into her son's mouth. 'I'm just thankful that terrorist woman was caught, and no more people will get hurt.'

Matthew flinched at the word *terrorist* and was about to ask what she was implying when John spoke first.

'Did you see anyone else in the parkin' lot that night?' John scratched his cheek slowly studying her expression.

She finished feeding her son and wiped his face with a hand towel, 'Nope, just that Martinez woman.'

The baby cried in protest. He screamed louder.

'Do you know what happened to the security disc after the incident?' John yelled over the child.

'Sshh,' she soothed. 'Isn't it in the office? It should be with the others, Ned's very particular about his discs - they're useful in court.'

Matthew raised his eyebrows. 'Yes they are. OK, Ms. Baxter. I can see you're busy,' he rolled his eyes at John and they stood to leave. 'Oh, there is just one last question?'

She lifted her head and looked at Matthew.

'You said you propped open the outer doors, what did you use?'

'The same thing I always use, the corner of the closest Dumpster outside in the parking lot. Ned says it's a health and safety thing, but I say if we all die from heat exposure coz he can't pay for a new air conditioning system, who will run the diner?'

Matthew held out his hand. 'OK, thanks for your time.'

* * *

'Let's go to the station,' Matthew said. 'I'm curious to find out what kind of person Stephen Collins was.'

John turned to look at Matthew from the driver's seat. 'Are you thinking of putting the man himself on trial?'

Matthew shrugged. 'I don't know. We'll see what we find out.'

'It's odd that Ned would forget to put a disc in for the security cameras, isn't it?'

'Shirley seemed to think so, but who would remove it?' Matthew sat upright. 'Helen - that leech!'

John made a high-pitched noise in the back of his throat. 'Oh c'mon Buddy – you think Helen stole the disc, why?' He shook his head. 'For one thing, she would jeopardize her career – she's hungry for governor Francis' job.'

Matthew folded his arms. 'Yeah maybe you're right,' he sighed. 'Well, somebody stole it, and we have to find out who.'

John frowned. 'I wonder what she meant by Sally being a terrorist?'

'I have no idea. But she didn't seem to like the fact that Sally was Muslim and not Catholic anymore.' Matthew

54

shrugged. 'Maybe that's what she meant? I heard a cop call Sally a traitor in the coffeeshop the other day.'

John scoffed. 'A traitor? Some people,' he said, wearily.

Chapter Nine

They climbed the front steps of the police station and entered through the double glass doors.

Matthew approached the front desk. His shoes clicked against the stone floor. 'Morning Marty.' He stopped at the workstation and rested his hand onto the counter.

Marty Porter sat behind the workstation in front of a computer. He tapped away on the keyboard in front of him. 'Matt, can I help you?' He did not take his eyes away from the screen and continued to tap away regardless.

'We've got some inquiries and would like to conduct some interviews.'

Marty nodded. 'Do you have an appointment?' He hit the print button. The rhinoceros-sized machine, a few feet from the computer, revved into action, spitting paper out in seconds. 'All visitors must have an appointment.'

'Come on Marty, cut the crap. It'll only take a few minutes.' Matthew raised his eyebrows. 'Please? You owe me - junior year?'

Marty chuckled, 'Abe Lovett - you stopped him from kicking my ass,' he sighed, heavily. 'The Sheriff will have my ass for this.' He kicked away from the floor, and the office chair rolled away from the desk. It stopped at the phone area, to the right of the computer.

Marty picked up a visitor registration form attached to a clip board and placed it in front of Matthew. 'Sign here -

you too Johnny boy.' He opened a drawer and took out two visitor badges, handing them to Matthew and John. 'A few minutes, right?'

Matthew nodded. 'You're a good man, Marty.'

The men's locker room was on the second floor, at the end of a long narrow hall.

Matthew could hear voices somewhere at the back of the room. Three officers stood next to three open lockers.

The taller one wore a dark blue police uniform. He had removed his shoes and hat. He stared in the direction of the entrance. 'It seems we let any old scum in here these days.'

The other two officers turned to face the uninvited visitors.

The younger one had removed his jacket and had placed it on the bench behind him. He wore a white T-shirt tucked into his pants. He tightened his belt, staring at Matthew with a strange grin on his long face.

'We just want to know if Stephen Collins had any enemies,' Matthew replied, raising his hand. 'Or if he made any unusual arrests lately?'

The taller one stepped toward him. 'I ain't got nothing to say to you, counselor.' He folded his arms across his chest. 'What about you guys?' He did not bother to face his friends.

The other officers nodded in unison.

'I think you better leave.' He glared.

Matthew and John walked from the elevator, on the ground floor and made their way to the exit.

'No-one is gonna talk to us,' John said, with certainty.

'Guess we'll have to go to plan B.' Matthew placed his visitor badge on the counter.

'Hey,' a menacing voice echoed down the corridor.

Matthew turned to see Deputy Patterson charging toward them. His huge bulk bulldozed through office personnel at a heightening speed.

'You wanna ask questions, do you?' He was nose-to-nose with Matthew. 'Ask me.'

Spit landed on Matthew's cheek. He wiped it away with his right index finger aggressively. 'I think you better get out of my face, Ted.' He pushed out his chest forcing Patterson backward.

People suddenly appeared around opened office doors; a crowd formed along the corridor. Whispering and muttering channeled up and down like waves.

'Come on Matt, let's go. He's not worth it,' John intoned.

Patterson glared at John, his green eyes were wide. 'You got something to say?'

John turned away from Patterson, ready to leave.

'Negro chicken-shit.'

John spun three-hundred-and-sixty-degrees on his heels. He plunged his left fist into Patterson's gut.

A strange sound escaped from Patterson's lips as the force sucked the air from his lungs.

The presence of Sheriff Langford spooked the crowd; they diverged quickly. He walked preponderantly down the corridor, each heavy step was precise, as if he was moving to the beat of an invisible military drummer. 'What's going on here, Ted?' The Sheriff narrowed his eyes.

'Nothing, sir,' Patterson tried to control the shaking in his voice.

Matthew was sure Patterson was in pain by the way he stood hunched over, holding his stomach, his eyes watering like a steady stream.

'I think you better leave.' The Sheriff glared at Matthew, before turning back to Patterson.

Matthew and John made their way to the exit.

'I'm watching you Mr. Brennan – make one wrong move and I'll throw you in jail faster than you can blink!'

Matthew gave the Sheriff a little wave before closing the glass doors. 'He's not worth it, huh?' He raised his eyebrows at John as they walked toward the Chevy.

John shrugged. 'I didn't mean I couldn't hit him – just you couldn't. If you got arrested *again* your wife would kill me.'

* * *

They downed the whiskey as if it would be their last.

Thick cigarette smoke clouded the small room. The card game had finished hours ago; the rewards were already spent at the Seven Eleven.

Crushed beer cans littered the brown tiled floor. Cigarette butts overflowed in the ashtrays and empty chip packets lay scattered across the small wooden table.

'Let's go have some fun,' the taller one sneered.

The fat one grabbed the remaining liquor bottle from the table. 'Yeah,' he replied drunkenly. He took a swig and swallowed hard.

The youngest looked up to them in admiration. He wanted to be just like them; tough in every sense of the word. They were his heroes. He grabbed the beer bottle next to him and threw its contents down his throat. Yeah. It felt good to be one of them. Indestructible.

The taller one grabbed his car keys from the stained counter. He headed to the door. 'Bring the spray paint that guy gave us,' he ordered.

His disciples staggered after him, anticipating his next move.

Chapter Ten

Anna arrived home from spending the afternoon with her parents. She parked onto the driveway and walked along the path toward the front steps of the house.

'What…?'

Placing her hands over her mouth. She stared narrow-eyed at the words painted in red, spread across her front porch.

Traitor cop killers.

Horrified, she ran into the house.

Ten minutes later, she emerged from the front door, carrying a bucket and sponge. She scrubbed at the letters.

The remnants of paint turned the soapy water red, like fresh blood; the sponge became stained on one side.

She could feel their eyes on her, the neighbors watching from their upstairs windows.

She closed the front door. Exhausted, she made her way to the kitchen and poured the water down the sink.

'Shoot.' She dropped the sponge and bent down to pick it up. A splinter of glass caught her finger. She cursed and grabbed a dish cloth from the sideboard to cover the wound.

'How did that get there?' A wine glass lay smashed to the left of the sink. Thoughts and scenarios played in her head. 'Oh Matt, I told you not to take the case.'

Rocky growled.

'What is it boy?'

Tap. Tap. Tap.

A sharp cry escaped from her throat. She stood frozen, staring at three shadows outside her kitchen window.

The phone blasted the hallway.

She jumped, an impulse to run to freedom. She picked up the receiver. 'H-hello?' her voice trailed off.

'Knock, knock,' the male voice said. The tone was as deep and cold as it had been before.

She slammed down the receiver. It rang again. Hands shaking, she picked it up.

'Knock, Knock.'

'What do you want from me?'

A deep sinister laugh rippled across the line.

She slammed down the phone. It rang again.

Tap. Tap. Tap. Tap. Tap. Tap.

'Let us in, bitch,' an evil male voice said. His putrid breath fogged the front door window.

The two figures kicked the back door.

Laughter.

Too scared to breathe, she started to panic. Her eyes scanned the rooms. A carving knife sat on the breakfast bar. The steel blade reflected the moonlight coming from the window. She ran back into the kitchen and grabbed the knife. She took a firm grip on the handle, blood seeped from her finger through the dishcloth.

She watched the silhouette move around the front porch from the kitchen doorway.

Rocky charged down the hall.

'R-Rocky!' She could hear Rocky growling, scrapping claws against wood. 'Leave us ALONE!'

Suddenly the front door opened. She could hear whispering. Rocky yelped.

She backed away slowly, holding the knife in front of her, poised ready to thrust. Her arms shook with tension as

61

the silhouette entered the dark hall and walked slowly toward the kitchen. She swallowed hard. She could not breathe. Her heart beat inside her ear.

She wanted to scream, but no sound would come out. She backed into the wall with nowhere to run.

Chapter Eleven

The light from the kitchen washed over the silhouette.

'Stupid mutt,' Matthew chuckled, looking down at Rocky, who trotted along side. 'Gettin' your foot stuck in my pocket. Anna?' He cried, staring at his wife in horror.

Her face was frozen, eyes wide and blood shot.

'Anna!'

She collapsed to the floor; tears glistened on her cheeks. She dropped the knife beside her. The tips of her fingers tingled as the blood flowed, giving them life.

'Anna? What's goin' on?' he asked, bewildered. He walked toward her, kneeling beside her. 'You're bleeding?'

She gasped trying to breathe as she stared at her finger. She fell against his body, throwing her arms around him; she was safe in his arms.

* * *

'Why didn't you tell me about the phone calls?' Matthew stood naked in the shower. He turned the faucet, adjusting the temperature of the water flowing from the showerhead.

'I didn't want to worry you.' Anna sat hunched on the closed toilet seat lid. 'And now this,' she looked at her hands; red paint had seeped into her pores and around the crevices of her palms. Her finger pulsed under the band aid.

He stepped into the shower cubicle and pulled the curtain across, to stop the water escaping onto the floor. 'Did you call the police?'

'Why bother?' she said. 'Everyone in this town thinks the same thing. Sally's a cop killer and a traitor. Besides, I don't expect anyone saw anything.' She pulled her flower printed hoodie over her shoulders and tugged at the zipper.

'A traitor?' He pulled his eyebrows together, confused.

'They think she betrayed her people and the church.'

He appeared from behind the curtain. 'Because she became a Muslim?'

She nodded. 'Pastor Jones said Sally was brainwashed by the devil's book, and they should execute her to save her soul,' tears fell down her cheeks.

He raised an eyebrow. 'I knew that guy was a nut.' He poured lemon scented shower gel into his cupped hand and rubbed the cool liquid over his body. 'Do you think those punks who made the calls were the ones who sprayed the house?'

'I don't know.' She shook her head. 'What's happening Matt? The people in this town have gone crazy and the trial hasn't even started yet!'

He shook his head, raising his eyebrows. *The people of this town have always been crazy.* He thought. 'It'll die down, don't worry.' He wasn't sure who he was trying to convince - himself or Anna.

'No-one turned up for the cookout this afternoon,' she said. 'You should have seen the look on my parent's faces, I felt so sorry for them.' She shook her head. 'I don't understand – these people have known my parents for forty-something years and now they shun them as if they've got the plague.'

He slapped his forehead. 'I forgot about the cookout, I'm so sorry. I will phone Linnie and apologize; I'm such an idiot.'

'Don't worry,' she said. 'I'm sure Mom was glad you weren't there - you were working on Sally's case. Right?'

He felt a hint of uncertainty in her voice. He appeared from behind the curtain again, dripping from head-to-toe. 'You know I was,' he replied, innocently.

She handed Matthew a towel from the rack on the wall behind her. 'Yeah,' her tone changed. 'I'll get supper started.'

He was not sure how to react. He decided to ignore her uncertainty. She had had an upsetting day and was probably tired.

Once he was dressed, he perched on the bed and dialed the Owens' number.

Linnie answered on the second ring. 'Hello?'

'Hi Linnie.'

'Matt?' She jumped in before he could say another word. 'How's the case going? Is Sally OK? When can I see her again?'

'Linnie calm down,' he was beginning to think this case had made all the women in his life deranged. 'Actually that's why I called, I was wondering if it would be possible for you to collect some of Sally's clothes for the trial. I know you have a spare key to her house.'

He heard some commotion across the line. It sounded as if Linnie had cupped her hand over the mouthpiece.

'Arty!' Her voice still managed to deafen Matthew's ear. 'Arty, find Sally's spare key - you're going to Atlanta tomorrow after church!' More commotion, then she said, 'No problem Matt.'

He tried not to chuckle. Were he and Anna like that? 'Thanks. I was also wondering if I could talk to the kids.'

'They're in bed right now Matt - tomorrow would be best.'

Matthew nodded. 'Of course. Listen while I'm on the phone, I want to apologize for missing the cookout today.'

'You just concentrate on saving my little girl,' Linnie paused. 'Are they really gonna send her to the gas chamber?'

He wiped his face with his free hand. 'Not if I can help it. I'll see you tomorrow.'

Chapter Twelve

Matthew arrived home from his morning run. Rocky trotted through the front door, panting.

'Get a drink old boy,' he said, breathlessly. He wiped the sweat from his forehead with the back of his arm. He peeled the cotton shirt from his body and headed for the shower.

He lay on the driveway next to the Buell, cleaning the exhaust can. He noticed a red pick-up truck pull up in front of his driveway and stood to see whom the visitor was.

'You must be Matt? I'm Ritchie Tate.' He held out his thick hand.

Matthew returned the favor. 'Good to meet you Ritchie, I've heard a lot about you.'

Ritchie placed his hands into his pockets. 'Just dropping off some more cement for the yard.'

'Oh great – do you need any help?'

'No, no, you carry on doing what you're doing,' Ritchie turned toward his truck. 'I won't be long. Heard you had some trouble last night, is Anna OK?'

Matthew sprayed some cleaning spray onto a rag and lightly rubbed it over the tank. The gold flecks in the blue paint twinkled like stars in a midnight sky. 'Yeah, she's OK thanks.'

'Glad to hear that,' Ritchie replied before disappearing around the back of the house, carrying the cement bag.

Satisfied with his efforts, Matthew returned to the house.

He sat in the living room, with the television remote control in his hands, staring at the blank screen.

Anna had recorded all of his favorite T.V. programmes while he had been away. She had listed them in chronological order in a blue note book, which sat under the coffee table. They seemed pointless to him now. How fanatical he was about them? He would rush home from the office, grab a bottle of Jack Daniels and sit in front of the television, glued for hours. Immersed in an imaginary world to help him escape his reality.

He had had a strict regime every morning at the rehabilitation center. Now he was free to live a normal life, part of him did not know where to begin, and it scared him. Should he continue where he left off – watching sitcoms while the rest of the town was at church? Or should he find something else to do with his leisure time? But what could he do? The whole town was deserted on Sundays. The stores remained closed the entire day. It was like a ghost town.

He hated church. The smell of the furniture polish. The echo of voices. The coldness of the pews. He didn't understand the fascination of it all. He pondered that thought when Anna arrived home from the morning service. She made her way to the kitchen and poured herself a mug of coffee.

'Hi,' he called from the living room. He fumbled with his case files in an attempt to show he had been working while Anna was at church. 'Ritchie came to drop off some cement, you just missed him.'

He heard her footsteps run hastily upstairs.

'Anna?' He crossed the hall, making his way upstairs. He heard her vomiting in the bathroom. He knocked lightly on the door. 'Are you sick honey?'

The door opened and she appeared wiping her face with a wet washcloth. 'Yeah, I'll be OK - just a stomach bug going round.'

'Was church that bad?' he joked.

She flashed him a dirty look.

His smile fell. 'Maybe you shouldn't go to the memorial tomorrow if you're not feeling well?'

'No, I'll be fine I want to show my respect to patrolman Collins and Harry – you remember him?'

He rolled his eyes. Nag. Nag. Nag.

'I'm sure it's just a twenty-four hour bug.' She continued. Her voice was coarse. She walked gingerly toward the bedroom and lay on the bed, closing her eyes.

He sat beside her, stroking her forehead as if she were a child. 'Can I get you anything?' he whispered.

She shook her head weakly.

'Did Arthur go to Atlanta after the service?'

She cleared her dehydrated throat. 'He left about half an hour ago.' She gave a warm smile. 'The children gave Daddy a list of what they wanted him to bring back.'

He leaned down, kissing her forehead. 'Try and get some sleep. I'll head over to your parent's house and talk with the kids.' He turned back to face her. 'Will you be alright alone?'

She drifted off to sleep. He pointed at Rocky and gestured for him to stay in the room.

The children were playing in the Owens' back yard when Matthew arrived. Thomas played happily with a blue toy car. He included Matthew in the 'act'. Elizabeth sat sullenly staring into space, oblivious to the game.

'Lizzie, can I ask you what happened on the night you came down here?' Matthew asked, softly.

'What do you care? You didn't cared about us before our Momma was taken away.' She stormed passed Linnie, who had joined them in the yard. 'I just want to go home!'

69

'She's still a little shaky Matt, don't take it to heart. Here, give this to Anna. It will make her feel better.' Linnie handed Matthew an over-the-counter upset stomach remedy.

'Thanks,' Matthew frowned. Part of him had forgotten the children were caught up in this. He could see Thomas had not slept in weeks from the gray patches under his eyes. He swallowed hard, trying to clear the fist lodged in his throat. 'I like your car, Thomas. Can I see it?'

Thomas jumped to his feet, showing Matthew the three-inch toy.

'Wow, it's great,' Matthew swallowed hard, forcing back the tears that pricked his eyes.

Thomas pulled at the painted aluminum doors. 'They open – see?'

Matthew nodded. 'Wow.' He placed the car on the path and pushed it. It came to a stop at the grass verge. 'Your sister is upset with me, right now,' he said, solemnly.

Thomas picked up his car and sat down on the step next to Matthew. 'Will Daddy be here soon?'

Matthew wanted to know the answer to that question too. 'I don't know, Thomas. Where is your daddy?'

Thomas shrugged. 'At work. He's always at work.'

Matthew placed his arm across Thomas' shoulders to comfort him, feeling awkward, he removed it quickly. 'What happened the night you came down here, Thomas?' Matthew pushed.

Thomas shook his head.

'You can tell me.' Matthew tilted his head downward to catch Thomas' eye.

Thomas shook his head defiantly. He wrapped his arms across his chest, giving Matthew an evil glare.

'Ok,' Matthew sighed. 'You don't have to tell me if you don't want to.'

* * *

Matthew arrived home feeling frustrated by the lack of cooperation. He dumped his motorcycle helmet and gloves on the living room floor and headed upstairs to his wife.

She was sat upright holding a glass of water in her right hand. She rested it on her abdomen. She was still dressed in her best church clothes, a long black round neck dress.

He smiled, softly. 'Hey, how are you feeling?'

'Better,' she replied, shifting her legs so he could sit next to her.

'Your mother gave me this to give to you.' He handed her the bright pink bottle.

Her face twisted. 'No, I'll be fine. If I take that stuff I *will* vomit again.'

He laughed and stroked her leg. 'You know,' he said, 'I've been thinking that maybe you should go and see Sally when you're better?'

She did not reply. She studied the empty glass in her hand.

'Look, what Sally did to us at our wedding was unforgivable, she knows that. She made a mistake.'

Anna choked. 'A mistake? She missed our wedding because she sneaked off to cheat on her husband, in some hunting lodge, and forgot the time.'

He raised his hand. 'I know, but-'

She cut him off. 'She was supposed to be my maid of honor.'

'I know,' he rubbed her arm, lovingly. 'But despite everything she's your sister after all.'

'I know. Mom's already told me this. They have visited Sally every day since she was arrested.' She leaned toward the bedside table, placing her glass next to the night lamp, then lethargically fell back against the headboard again. 'I might go and see her tomorrow.'

'The kids are having a rough time, especially Elizabeth poor kid.'

'Yeah, I know. We kinda shut them all out after the wedding, didn't we?' Anna couldn't hide the regret in her voice. 'The argument was nothing to do with the kids.' Her face softened. 'I'll take them to the mall. That should cheer them up, what D'you think?'

Matthew nodded. 'Yeah.'

'Has Sally said any more about letting them go and see her?'

The phone rang.

Shaking his head, Matthew stood to answer it.

'Hi Matt, I'm still at Sally's house.'

'Art, how's it goin'?'

'I've just spoke to a woman, a Mrs. Moore, she said she's Sally's boss.' Arthur smacked his lips together. 'Nice woman, said she had heard about Sally and has offered to help.'

Matthew could hear what sounded like a door closing. The background noise changed. It sounded as if Arthur had come from inside the house and was now outside in the street.

'Anyway, she gave me her phone number, and I said you would call her.'

Matthew knew not to get too excited when it came to volunteer witnesses. More often than not, they hindered the case rather than helped. However, he was curious what Sally's boss had to say about his famous client. 'Thanks Art, I'll call her when you get back.'

Chapter Thirteen

Matthew had not slept most of the night. His mind was plagued with questions and worries he could not shut off.

Sally's story re-played in his mind until he was even more confused and suspicious, but he wasn't entirely sure it was Sally he had the problem with. He suspected, deep down, his feelings were brought on by the lack of confidence in his own ability.

He had arrived at his office at 6:15am and had began working on the case.

Clara had joined him three hours later. They had re-enacted several scenarios of what could have happened at the diner, but none of their enactments had fitted Sally's story; Matthew was discouraged with her version and doubted her innocence.

The mahogany Corsica conference room desk was hidden under documents, books and scrap paper.

A huge white board stood at the foot of the table. A diagram of Ned's bar, and diner and the state's witness's names were pinned to the board.

Matthew's head ached. He could not think anymore and needed to free himself. He headed to his office, taking a seat at his desk.

Checking the time on his watch, he pressed the phone receiver to his ear and dialed Sally's boss's phone number.

'Mrs. Moore?' He took a sip from his coffee; the remnants had become cold.

'Yes?' a sweet female voice answered.

Matthew introduced himself.

'I was telling Sally's father, I was shocked when I heard what had happened to the police officers on the news. How can they charge Sally with murder?'

He imagined her shaking her head in horror.

'I've known Sally for years - since she moved here from Birchwood County. I don't understand how they can think she did it?'

He wondered if she would feel the same way if she listened to the evidence and Sally's story. 'You told Mr. Owens you have been Sally's boss for a number of years. Have you ever had any problems with her?'

'No, no sir. She was always punctual and polite. I gave her a raise last month because of her hard work.'

Matthew nodded.

'Please, Mr. Brennan, if I can help in any way, please don't hesitate to call. I can't bear the thought of Sally...' her voice disappeared, and Matthew thought she had hung up for a moment.

'You have my number?' she confirmed.

'Yes thank you. I'll be in touch Mrs. Moore.' He hung up feeling blessed with a hint of hope suddenly. At least they had one possible character witness.

With a slight spring in his step, he crossed the hall to the conference room.

Clara was standing at the window with a bottle of water in her hand. She turned to greet him.

'OK what have we got?' he said as if some miracle had occurred while he had been on the phone. He stared at the white board with his hands on his hips.

Clara read from her neatly typed notes recapping the information they had so far. 'What about the waitress

Sarah-Jane? She was somewhat evasive when interviewed…' Clara flipped over the pages of her notepad.

'Yeah,' Matthew scribbled on his 'to do' list. 'We'll pay her another visit I think - find out what she knows.'

'And Shirley Baxter?'

He sighed, 'We're going to have to work hard to beat her testimony.'

John entered the conference room holding Helen's files in his right hand. He slouched on the chair opposite Matthew and lay the files and police report on the desk in front of him. 'Got the files you wanted. Any luck with Sally's boss?'

Matthew scratched his head. 'She's a sweet woman who obviously likes Sally a lot. She has even left Sally's employment position open until she returns.'

John raised his eyebrows.

'She may be useful.' Matthew looked over the reports, sipping a fresh cup of coffee. 'Three bullet casings were found a few feet from the bodies,' he intoned. 'The revolver was found two feet from the bodies in some hedgerow, and a key card for room number fifty-seven at the Northgate circle motel, the same room Sally had pre-booked, was found a few feet from the revolver.' He flipped over the pages and tossed the files onto the table. He gave a sigh before resting his hands onto his hips.

The phone disturbed Matthew's contemplation.

Clara stood, crossing to the conference room extension. 'Does Sally say how she got her finger prints on the gun?' She slipped her earring off her earlobe and picked up the receiver. 'Brennan and associates?'

'She says she doesn't know.' Matthew looked at Clara, anxiously.

'Probably another reporter,' John said. 'What is it?'

Matthew frowned, 'We've been getting calls.'

'Reporters?'

Matthew shook his head. 'No,' he said. 'Anna's pretty freaked, they only ring when she's home alone.'

'Probably just kids. There are some sick people out there, this case has shook 'em up a bit.'

Matthew nodded.

'I'm sure she's fine,' John comforted. He placed a stick of nicotine gum into his mouth.

'Matt, it's Helen Maxwell,' Clara whispered, covering the mouthpiece with her free hand.

Matthew looked at John, who shrugged and pulled a "don't look at me?" face. Matthew walked toward the phone and placed it to his ear.

'What does she want?' John asked as Clara took a seat beside him.

'She wouldn't say - just it was important she speak with Matthew right away.'

'More good news, I'm sure,' John replied, sarcastically.

Matthew felt his stomach drop when he heard Helen's voice. It was the same velvet voice he remembered, only with a hint of venom attached. He tried to sound confident, keeping his tone upbeat and lively, not the same tone he had had throughout the morning.

Helen's words past over him at first, until the reality of what she had told him sunk in. He stood motionless with the phone attached to his ear, long after she had hung up.

John picked up the files from the table and began to re-read the reports. 'Helen got a subpoena for Sally's cellular phone records.'

Clara fiddled with her earring, placing it back onto her earlobe. 'So?'

'She phoned her husband an hour before the murder at 18:20. The call lasted two minutes and fifty-five seconds.'

'So?'

John leaned forward. 'Do we know where Miguel was when she called him?'

76

Clara studied the report. 'There's another number here she called five minutes after the call to Miguel.'

John's eyes scrolled down the sheet of paper. 'There are several text messages to that number, also on the same day.'

Clara frowned. 'Maybe it was to her boss to say she was enjoying her vacation?'

Matthew slammed the receiver onto the handset. A glum expression on his pale and stunned face.

'Bad news?' John asked, staring at him.

Matthew sighed. He threw down his pen and slumped in his chair. He rested his chin onto his fist.

'Matt?' John stared, waiting for some kind of response.

'She was fucking him,' Matthew snorted.

'Who?'

'Patrolman Stephen Collins of the Birchwood County police department.'

Matthew placed his head in his hands.

John ran his finger along the table. He stood, crossing to the white board. 'Well that makes things interesting. Guess that explains the other number on the phone records.' He licked his lips. 'OK, let's concentrate on impeaching Shirley's testimony.' He sighed, staring at the whiteboard with intense concentration. '*Ms.* Baxter claims she came out the back entrance…' He pointed to the back entrance of Ned's diner on the diagram, with his ball point pen. 'Here…Sally's car was parked here at the back of the parking lot and the patrol car was parked at a slight angle…Here,' he placed a hand to his chin, staring with narrowed-eyes at the diagram. '…a few feet in front of the Bronco.'

'Did you hear what I just said?' Matthew raised his right hand, palm toward the ceiling. 'The D.A has a tape recording dated two days before Stephen's murder. He threatened to tell Miguel of their affair! To top that off she also threatened to kill him in an email because he dumped her!'

'Do you honestly think Sally did this?' John asked, frankly.

'Hello?' Matthew tapped his head angrily. 'Am I the only one hearing this? The evidence speaks for itself! They have means, motive and opportunity!'

'Honey,' Clara said, calmly, 'maybe you should calm down?'

'Calm down? Calm down!' Matthew's voice raised an octave. He waved his arms in the air erratically, pushing law books off the table.

'All right that's enough!' John yelled.

The room was silent.

John inhaled slowly, trying to find the right words. 'This is not you talkin' Buddy. This is not the brilliant lawyer talkin'. You're going through withdrawal or something OK, and I know it is tough for you.' He sighed heavily. 'She's your sister-in-law, Matt. Are just gonna give up? Give up trying? Give up searchin' for the truth?'

Matthew leaned back in his chair and ran his fingers through his hair. Taking a breath to calm himself, he stared at the white board.

Clara tidied the law books and papers that littered the floor. She found a candy bar under a sheet of paper and handed it promptly to Matthew.

Matthew looked at her sheepishly. 'Thanks.' He leaned forward, placing his hand on hers; a token of apology. She tapped his hand lightly before using the table to help her to her feet.

Matthew chewed the candy bar. He threw the wrapper in the Trash Can across from his right leg. 'Shirley claims she *saw* Sally fire the weapon?' He studied the white board, before turning back to the Trash Can. He sat in silence for a moment.

John nodded. He turned to face the white board. 'What are you getting at?'

Matthew picked up the Trash Can and placed it onto the table. 'Trash,' he took another bite of the candy bar. 'Her vision was blocked by the Dumpsters.'

John gave a wry smile. 'That's my boy.'

* * *

Anna jumped as the heavy gray doors closed behind her. Although the room was long and wide, she could not help but feel claustrophobic.

Thirty-five chairs stood facing a large glass screen. Behind the screen was another row of chairs and another door; it led out into the jail area.

The smell of shoe leather and body odor lingered in the room.

The guard showed her to a plastic chair in the center of the row. 'Have a seat,' he intoned, before turning to face the next visitor entering the room.

She tried not to jump every time she heard the bang of metallic doors closing; the rumble echoed throughout the jail.

With a loud buzz, a line of glum faced female prisoners followed a female guard through the jail doors.

She waited patiently for Sally to come waltzing through the door, her envious thick hair flowing down her shoulders and her ocean eyes sparkling like huge jewels.

She stood instantly at the sight of Sally pigeon-stepping toward the glass partition. The golden hair Anna had envied as a child was matted and lifeless. It was pulled back and tied with a band that strangled each strand of frizzy hair. The ocean eyes were shipwrecked and cloudy.

Sally placed the phone to her ear. 'Hi, Anna,' her voice trembled. 'How do you like my new place?' she joked, trying to lighten the atmosphere.

'I can't hear you?' Anna faced the crowded room, her eyes pleaded for the volume to diminish. Sally repeated her joke. 'That's not funny. How can you joke at a time like this?'

An awkward silence.

Anna sighed, placing her hand to the glass.

Sally reached forward and returned the gesture. 'Are the children OK?' she said, finally.

'They need their mother,' Anna snorted. She rolled her eyes, feeling guilty by her evil comment. 'Look, I didn't mean that.'

'It's OK - you're right.' Sally looked passed Anna at the floor. 'There is something I need to say - should have said a long time ago.'

'Please don't,' Anna interrupted.

'It needs to be said Anna.' Sally leaned toward the glass. 'I need to apologize. I'm sorry I ruined your wedding day. I never meant to hurt you.' She slammed her fist on the wooden counter. She paused. 'It kills me knowing I missed your special day, and I was the one who spoilt it for you. Forgive me,' her voice trailed off.

Anna took a long breath. 'You let me down Sally for some guy you just met. You were my maid of honor.'

Sally raised her hand. 'I know. I let everybody down, but he wasn't just some guy...I loved him.'

'What about Miguel – he's your husband?' Anna shook her head. 'I don't understand how you could destroy your family like that.'

Sally wiped tears from her cheek. 'I'm a new person now, I've found my purpose. The Koran has shown me the way.'

There was silence between them.

Anna's head pounded with every echo around the jail. 'Is there anything you need? The children and I are going to the mall we could get you something?' She noticed Sally's body language softened.

'No. Thank you,' she sniffed. 'Are Lizzie and Tom getting on OK with Bobby?'

Anna bit at her lip. She swallowed hard. 'No, Matt's son died last year. He had Leukemia.'

Sally's bottom lip trembled.

'I'm sorry I thought Dad told you.'

Sally shook her head. 'Matt must have been a wreck?'

Anna nodded. She gripped her fingers, swallowing hard.

'I'm sorry Anna. Bobby was an angel.'

Anna tried to stop herself from sobbing. 'So are your children Sal. They miss you so much.'

Sally sniffed. 'I didn't do this Anna. You have to believe me. You have to...'

Chapter Fourteen

Lunchtime. Matthew could not eat. He could not do anything until he had heard the tape for himself.

The hall was packed with various personnel, visitors and what looked to Matthew, like a group of school children on a field trip courthouse tour.

He could not remember the last time he had seen the courthouse looking so busy. He pondered on that thought as he crossed the marble floor toward the elevators.

Helen's office was an uncomfortable elevator ride two floors up. He shared the elevator with what seemed like the entire courthouse.

Finally the doors opened and a tidal wave of people stepped out, taking him along with them.

He felt crosshairs on the back of his neck as he waited for the secretary to finish her phone call.

'Can I help you?' the secretary asked, finally. Matthew could tell from her turned up nose she was not impressed to see him. Her eyes narrowed somewhat from behind her small rimmed glasses. 'Do you have an appointment?'

'Yes I have an appointment. Please inform Helen I have arrived.'

'Matt? Come through.' Helen said, from the doorway to her office.

Matthew smirked at the secretary and walked passed her desk toward Helen's office.

'Sally,' said a deep husky voice, 'you know who this is if you don't stop calling me I'll ruin you... I'll tell your fucking husband everything...You won't get a penny in the divorce hearing. I've got someone else...It's over. Do you understand? It's over. Leave me alone...Or I'll ruin you, I swear.'

Helen pressed the stop button on the tape machine.

Matthew was bewildered.

'We recovered this from Sally's answering machine. Here is a copy of the emails we recovered from Stephen Collins' computer hard drive from your client.'

Matthew took the sheets of paper. He tried to focus his eyes on the printout. There were enough obscenities to impress Ozzy Osborne.

He had read enough to understand where the D.A was coming from, with this kind of rage it was easy to see Sally just snapped.

He crossed to the chair opposite Helen's desk, to the right of the window. He wondered why Sally didn't delete the message in case Miguel heard it when he came home from work. He sat down again, crossing his legs. 'Let's talk business. You're charging my client with murder one and assault on a peace officer?' He tried to overlook everything he had just read and found himself saying: 'She's a housewife and mother of two - member of the PTA and she has no criminal record.'

'She fled the crime scene and went on the run for two days before the Sheriff caught her.' Helen paced slowly back and forth behind where he was sitting. As if rehearsing her opening statement, she said 'the facts speak for themselves. The defendant's finger prints were on the murder weapon, it is registered to her husband and she was at the diner waiting for her victims.

'We have witnesses who saw her at the scene and she booked the motel room three days before the murder.

'She changed her damn story three times. First she said this guy did it, then she said she didn't know who shot the peace officers.' She shook her head. 'When the Sheriff confronted her about the murder weapon being registered to her husband she claimed it mysteriously vanished three days before the murder!' She turned toward him, remembering he was the only one in the room. 'Come on Matt the woman is lying - we have means, opportunity and *now* motive.'

'Let's just say, for arguments sake, Sally committed these crimes. What can you offer?' He placed his foot onto the ground, scratching at the stubble on his chin.

'She killed a peace officer.' She looked at the floor.

He could see her mind working overtime, trying to please everyone. He felt exhausted just watching her.

'Tell me what you think I should offer?'

His gaze wandered up the wall behind Helen's desk. There hung a photograph, in a gold rimmed frame, of a young boy holding a fishing rod. 'I remember when that photograph was taken,' he said, changing the subject. 'Bobby looked so good that day.'

'Yeah, it was his sixth birthday. We spent the entire day fishing. He begged you to climb the tree with him.' She smiled, turning to face the photograph.

'You know Sally's kid, Elizabeth? She is the same age as Bobby.'

She turned on her heels abruptly. 'Leave Bobby out of this!' She rested her hands onto the desk in front of her, leaning forward slightly. 'Bobby has nothing to do with this – you're confusing the issue!'

'Oh I'm confusing the issue?' He raised his hand and pointed his index finger accusingly. 'You're the one who is willing to send a mother of two children to the gas chamber, because you're so far up the governor's ass you've lost all direction!'

Her eyes narrowed and her face flamed with rage. 'How dare you? Let's not talk about who has lost all direction here, Matt! I'm not the one who had to spend twelve weeks on a rehabilitation program.'

He stood from his chair. He tried to hold onto his anger, but it escaped with tremendous force. 'You're a cheap and nasty whore, Helen Maxwell and let me tell you something else, kissing the mayor's ass isn't going to change what you are!' He made his way to the door and stood in the doorway. 'Maybe you should try coming up for air once in a while - might help the oxygen flow to your brain!'

'Get the fuck out of my office!'

Chapter Fifteen

Matthew knew what he had said was uncalled for and hated himself for thinking it in the first place. Why did Helen make him so angry? What was it about her that made his blood boil? Whatever it was, he knew he had to apologize. It seemed all he was doing was apologizing lately to the women in his life.

John greeted him at the bottom of the courthouse steps. He had called John suggesting they confront Sally about her affair with Stephen. The conversation had been sharp.

'OK what is it?' John took a stick of nicotine gum from the inside of his pant pocket and placed the pink stick into his mouth.

Matthew stood with his hands inside his pockets, sucking in warm air.

'Guess the chat with Helen didn't go well?'

Matthew shook his head, making a face 'like don't go there'. His stomach growled angrily. He had forgotten he had skipped lunch. He did not have time to eat, maybe later.

John slapped Matthew's back, a gesture of encouragement, and they made their way to the jail.

'I was lonely,' Sally leaned back against the chair, staring at Matthew with intensity. 'Miguel goes away for days with the trucking company. Stephen had pulled me over for speeding in May last year, and that's how we met. He was so…rough. Those eyes.'

Matthew looked at John and raised his eyebrows incredulously.

She licked her lips. 'He made me feel alive again. We would meet each other three nights a week at my house. The children would stay at Miguel's parents. Everyone thought I was working at the store.'

'Did Miguel know about your affair?' Matthew leaned back, resting against the chair.

'No. No. If Miguel ever found out…' She shook her head.

'Then why did you leave a recording of Stephen threatening to tell Miguel on your answering machine?' Matthew fanned himself with his notebook.

Her mouth fell. 'I-I didn't.' She looked bewildered. 'Stephen didn't leave any messages.'

Matthew sighed heavily.

'When exactly did Stephen call it off?' John asked, resting his index finger onto his cheek.

'He dumped me months ago,' she replied, unconvincingly. 'Just before he moved down here.'

Matthew and John looked at each other; an expression of disbelief.

She placed her hands up. 'All right. I admit…' She took a long breath. 'He dumped me two weeks before his…death.'

Matthew noticed she could not bring herself to say "murder".

'Why lie to us?' John said, matter-of-factually.

'Well, I know where y'all are going with this. You think I killed Stephen because he dumped me, but that ain't so.'

Matthew slammed his arm down. 'No Sal, that's what the prosecution think. You had motive, means and opportunity. Your prints are all over the murder weapon, and you were in town on the exact day your ex-lover is murdered.' He leaned forward and looked her straight in the eye. 'Sal, you're on trial for your life here. You're going to be put to death if we can't get your story straight.'

She was silent.

'Tell us the truth, what were you doing here that day?' Matthew remembered what Sally had said the night he had come to visit her at the jail. 'I'm guessing you weren't visiting Miguel's parents at their summer home.'

She held up a surrendering hand. 'Fine. The truth is I came down to see Stephen. Just to talk. I wanted to apologize, to try and work things out. I couldn't leave the children with Miguel's parents because they had gone away with church.' She placed her hands on the table in front of her and began picking at the cuticle on her thumb.

'We were gonna make a little vacation of it,' her voice became a whisper.

There was silence in the room.

Matthew fiddled with his biro thoughtfully. Suddenly he sat upright. 'Wait a minute,' he said, confusion in the tone of his voice. 'You knew Stephen from Atlanta right?'

She nodded.

'What was he doing here in Birchwood County?'

She tilted her head downward. 'He used to work for the Atlanta PD, but he came to see me about six or seven months ago and told me he had to be transferred. He said something about cut backs at the station. A job was going here for a patrolman, and he took it.' She moved from her cuticle to a piece of skin at the corner of her thumbnail; she picked at it unconsciously.

'Why didn't you tell us this before?' Matthew shook his head.

'I-I couldn't I was scared. I …I'm sorry.'

Matthew could tell by the way she bit her lower lip, she was trying her best not to cry. He sighed. 'Is there anything you need: dental floss? Magazines?'

She shook her head. 'Daddy is bringing my things during visiting hours.' She gave a nervous laugh. 'I feel naked without my Hijab.' She touched her uncovered head.

Matthew raised his chin and headed for the exit. He was done talking.

*   *   *

'We should check out the real reason Stephen left Atlanta,' Matthew said as he stopped at the curb outside the jail's front steps.

'That's if her story is true? Do you believe all that beef about Stephen transferring because of cut backs?' John replied, frankly. 'The tape's authentic and so are the emails. With the pre-nuptial agreement Miguel and Sally signed, if either of them cheated during the marriage, the guilty party would get nothing if they divorced. She would have lost everything.'

They made their way down the jail parking lot, weaving around parked vehicles, toward the Caprice.

Matthew shrugged. 'At this stage what choice do we have? We have to believe what she tells us.'

'She's a liar, and I don't trust her.' John sighed. 'A classic crime of passion. She murdered her ex lover in cold blood.' He stood in front of the Caprice and slapped the back of his neck. He could feel his skin being eaten alive by gnats hovering above his head.

'Allegedly.' Matthew placed his hands into his pockets, pulling out his motorcycle keys. 'Anyway, I thought you were the one who was trying to convince me she was innocent?'

John shrugged. 'Things don't add up, that's all. She's lied once what's to stop her lying again?'

Matthew rolled his eyes and was silent for a moment. 'Plan B. We'll concentrate on Stephen. I want to know everything about him – his hobbies, habits, bank accounts – whatever.'

'No-one is gonna talk to us. What about a plea bargain?' John could not understand why they didn't just do a deal with Helen and close the case. He didn't like surprises or being lied to, and he was getting both barrels from this piece of work.

'My last meeting with Helen…' Matthew sighed heavily. He ran his fingers through his hair.

'Speak to Helen again - she'll change her mind.' John studied his face. 'What is it Matt, you look as if you said something you regret?'

Matthew shrugged. 'See you tomorrow.'

John gave a wave and climbed into his car. He was thankful he did not have to work opposite *his* ex. He could not help but smile; after their divorce, she had moved three hundred miles away to Alabama, taking her high-maintenance attitude with her. 'There is a God, and he loves me.'

Chapter Sixteen

Monday. 12pm.

Black limousines beat up Toyotas and marked police vehicles invaded West Street. They parked strategically around the hotel parking lot, on the surrounding grass verge, ready for Stephen Collins' memorial service at St. James' church.

Glum faces exited the vehicles and gathered like a black cloud. Stephen's father, Billy-Ray Collins, greeted them, shaking hands and making idle conversations.

Stephen's body had been buried three days ago in his native home of Atlanta. His family wanted to be close to him and decided his final resting place should be next to his grandparents.

An army of reporters gathered outside the church trying to catch statements from the early arrivals.

Sheriff Langford gave a statement before asking the reporters to clear the churchyard entrance and move to the sidewalk.

At 2pm, West Street was declared closed to all traffic. The Sheriff placed barricades along the street to allow the cavalry to escort the mourners downtown, where Stephen Collins' name would be added to the officer memorial plaque.

Governor Francis' grandfather had hand carved the plaque, and it had remained at the heart of the town since the late 1980's.

Two names on the plaque dated back to the civil war.

The Birchwood County flag flew above downtown. Today it was raised to half-staff as Governor Francis took to the podium, ready to address officers and their families. Many of whom had traveled from all over South Georgia.

* * *

'What if members of the Collins family come back here?' Matthew asked.

Matthew and John arrived outside Stephen Collins' apartment down a quiet country gravel road, just off West Street.

'They won't,' John replied, smirking. 'They're all downtown and Rutha's cooking up a free memorial buffet lunch, courtesy of the governor herself.'

The apartment was one of twenty in an off-set apartment block overlooking the forest surrounding Billows Creek.

John led the way up the stone steps, along the balcony toward Stephen's front door. He began to feel around the door frame for a key.

'Oh yeah, a cop is just going to leave his door key outside his apartment for us to find!' Matthew said sarcastically.

'Sshh. Just help me look OK?' John whispered, trying not to attract attention.

'Fine,' Matthew sighed. 'I can't believe we're doing this.' He lifted a plant pot next to the front door. A present from a caring neighbor Matthew assumed. 'This is ridiculous,' he protested, putting the pot back. He cupped his hands trying to look through the window.

An off-white curtain hung from the window and camouflaged most of the living room, making it difficult to see anything of value.

'You said it yourself – Stephen was clean. He paid his bills on time, he didn't gamble, and he didn't have any unusual bank accounts. What do you expect to find in his apartment?'

'A-ha,' John exclaimed not listening to his partner. He found a long piece of string attached to the inside of a mail box, bolted to the side of the apartment building. He pulled it out to reveal a gold key attached to the end of it. 'Ridiculous ha?'

Matthew shrugged. 'You win.'

As the door opened, a strong, musky smell blasted from the apartment.

John entered first, leaving Matthew to close the front door behind him.

In the living room, an old brown leather sofa stood near the wall. Several cardboard boxes and a roll of bubble wrap lay across it.

A high-tech stereo system was to the right of it with surround sound sub-woofer speakers in each corner of the small room. A wide screen digital T.V hung from fixings in the center of the wall.

'The Collins family must be coming later to collect his things.' John said. 'I bet the neighbors loved this guy. Wow, would you look at this stereo he's got here!' he exclaimed and pushed the *on* button. The screen lit up with electric colored demonstrations and function displays.

Metallica blasted from the speakers, vibrating off the walls and surrounding the entire apartment with their high pitched chords. John pressed the *off* button hastily, his cheeks flushed. 'Sorry,' he huffed, trying to catch his breath.

Matthew rolled his eyes and crossed to a dingy kitchen at the rear of the hall.

An over used Emerson microwave oven rested on a small worktop near a sink area and a notice board was nailed to the wall above an Avanti compact refrigerator.

Bills and odd bits of paper stuck to the notice board with small brass pins.   Matthew lifted a yellow Post-it. 'Reminder notes,' he intoned. 'More reminder notes.' He read from a scrap bit of paper. 'Leave laundry outside for Mrs. Pullman to collect on Thursday.'   He assumed Mrs. Pullman was the same kind-hearted neighbor who had bought the plant outside the front door.

A reminder for Mrs. Pullman's payment was also pinned to the notice board along with the 'babes in bikinis' annual calendar. He lifted the calendar from the pin.

He stood suspended in animation, day-dreaming of January's long smooth thighs wrapped around him tightly; her long dark hair drowning him in paradise.

John entered the kitchen holding an envelope in his left hand. 'Hey look at this?' He spied the calendar. 'Babes in bikinis I've not seen this issue.' He took the calendar from Matthew. 'Is December in this one?'

John flicked through the months until he reached December. His mouth widened.

'Nice huh?' Matthew said, swallowing hard. 'What did you want to show me?'

John blinked several times and cleared his throat. He handed Matthew a blue envelope. 'Open it,' John instructed. 'I think you'll find it very interesting.'

Matthew opened the envelope, pulling a letter from inside. It read: **Run, run as fast as you can...**

'Weird huh? What do you think it means?' John asked, picking up the calendar for one more look.

'Sounds like someone was threatening him. Where did you find this?' Matthew re-read the words on the blue paper.

'It was in the Trash Can at the side of the sofa,' John replied, staring at December with goggle eyes.

'The post mark is dated two days before his murder. There might be some more, help me look will you?' Matthew opened the cupboard under the sink and pulled out the Trash Can.

John rolled his eyes. 'Fine,' he huffed, placing the calendar onto the counter. 'I'll check the bedroom.'

Matthew used his pen to poke through the leftover Chinese food, cigarette packets and Soda cans; the putrid smell slapped his nostrils with every movement. He could taste the vomit in the back of his throat.

Halfway down the Trash Can he found several blue envelopes, dotted and stained with leftover food. 'There's more in here too,' he raised his voice hoping John could hear.

'Matt, look at this?' John called from somewhere at the front of the apartment.

He made his way in the direction of John's voice.

John stood over several sheets of paper he had arranged on the bed. 'There's an old gas bill for an apartment in Et Lanna and several other utility bills registered to Stephen for the same apartment.' He read from a phone bill. 'It says here he moved out six months ago. Looks as if Sally was telling the truth.' He shuffled the sheets together.

'Yeah. Maybe Harry knows why Stephen moved away so quickly.' Matthew checked his watch. 'It's 5:30pm, visiting hours have just started.'

Chapter Seventeen

Birchwood County memorial hospital was 0.2 miles from Stephen Collins' apartment.

The Birchwood County Renovation Authority renovated the hospital in the late nineties after damage sustained during the Great Flood of '94.

Before making their way to the first floor, Matthew and John stopped in the gift shop; buying chocolate candies and 'get well soon' cards.

As they walked through the corridors, Matthew noticed a sign for the children's ward on the second floor.

John gripped his shoulder. 'Harry's room is down the corridor, room 4563.'

Matthew nodded.

'What's going on here, then?' John said, aloud.

Matthew shrugged. He figured the crowds outside room 4563 were family and friends waiting for their turn to see Harry.

They entered through the double doors, heading toward the crowd evasively.

Several deputies and patrolman loitered in small groups around family members, who sat in the seating area along the corridor wall. They were still dressed in their finest uniforms from the memorial earlier that afternoon.

Deputy Patterson stood leaning against the wall chewing on a toothpick.

'That son of a bitch,' Patterson snapped. 'He's got no right.' He lurched toward Matthew, pushing passed Sheriff Langford, who had just exited Harry's room.

Patterson glared at Matthew. 'You ain't welcome here.' He and Matthew were nose-to-nose. 'You lawyers make me sick. You think you're such a hot shot. Well, hot shot, let's see how hot you are against me?' He shoved Matthew, his green eyes wide and threatening.

'Look Ted. This ain't the time or the place,' Matthew replied. He stepped back with his palms up in front of his chest. 'Think about it.' He raised his eyebrows to the crowd, who stared silently in their direction.

Sheriff Langford placed his hands onto his hips. 'Ted it ain't worth it,' he whispered.

Without turning, Patterson signaled to the Sheriff he was calm, with a little wave. He snorted loudly, glaring at Matthew, like a predator fixed on its prey. He gave a wry smile before he bulldozed through the double doors, in the direction of the elevator.

The Sheriff placed his thumbs into the loopholes of his pants. He followed Patterson slowly.

Matthew knocked at Harry's door politely before he and John entered. Harry's wife, mother and father, stood around Harry's bed. He was awake and making coherent conversations.

Matthew smiled. 'Mr. And Mrs. Richardson, Becky,' he held out his hand. 'Good to see you Harry.'

'Why can't you people leave my boy alone? Hasn't he been through enough?' Daisy Richardson pushed Matthew's hand away angrily.

'Why don't we go and get some coffee?' George Richardson held his wife, kissing her forehead. 'Let Harry talk to Matthew and John a while.'

They left the room.

'Hey big boy? How are you feeling?' Matthew hitched up his pants and took a seat next to Harry's bedside.

'Got you some candy.' John placed the gifts in Harry's lap.

'Thanks, these are my favorites - how did you know?' Harry unwrapped the candies and placed one into his mouth.

'Harry, can we ask you some questions?' Matthew asked, softly.

Harry nodded, popping another candy into his mouth.

'Can you remember anything about the night at the diner?'

Harry pondered the question a while, making the most of what was left of the candy in his mouth. 'Well, I started the day as I always do. Stephen picked me up at home,' he smiled. 'He always picks me up - Stephen has to pass my house to get to the station. That's the benefits of living closer to work, I suppose.'

Matthew smiled back, listening intently.

'We chatted with some other officers, before heading to the locker room. That's when Stephen received a text message on his cell from *the bitch*.' Harry cocked his head. 'That's what he called her – I never did know her name.'

Matthew looked to the floor. He had a pretty good idea what *The Bitch's* real name was.

'Anyhow, I said to him, I said "is that woman still bothering you? Man, you should call somebody." And he told me she was on her way down to see him – from Atlanta!' He shook his head. 'I told him he needed to call a lawyer, but he wouldn't listen – told me he was just gonna tell her husband.' He chuckled in disbelief.

Matthew returned the wide-eyed 'he must have been crazy' look.

Harry tried to sit up but was unable to move.

Matthew propped a pillow behind his head. 'What happened then?'

'After we collected our supper from Bella's we got a call about an abandoned vehicle in the parking lot of Ned's. We've been having a lot of those lately - kids.' Harry rolled his eyes. 'We had some bad weather that night too, thought we might get a hurricane. The fields looked like something outta a Stephen King novel!'

Matthew smiled.

'Stephen flipped a "heads", so I had to get wet,' Harry groaned. 'He's the luckiest person I've ever met, hell.'

Matthew noticed Harry hadn't used the past tense when talking about Stephen. He hoped one of Harry's family members had told him of Stephen's death.

'I checked the perimeter. I didn't expect to see people in the front seat – nearly had a heart attack!' Harry chuckled again. 'Tourists, I told her to move on - no place for kids to sleep.'

'Did you notice anyone else in the lot?' John asked, folding his arms across his chest.

'Naw,' Harry winced. 'Just the woman and her husband.'

'Do you want some water?' Matthew leaned toward the table and picked up a cup at the side of a cooler.

Harry sipped slowly, making slurping noises.

'The woman was with her husband?' John arched his eyebrows.

Harry tried to shrug. 'I guess so, he was a lot older than her though. You can't tell these days.'

Matthew scratched his cheek. 'What did he look like – was he Hispanic?'

'Naw, black about fifty.'

'And where was he exactly?' Matthew sat forward.

'In the passenger seat.'

Matthew licked his lips, before turning to face John. John raised his eyebrows, and Matthew knew John was thinking the same thing. Joseph Mullen.

'What else do you remember?' Matthew said, turning back to face Harry.

Harry rummaged through the candy bag and said, 'The next thing I remember is the sound of the gun shot and the pain in my lower back.' He swallowed hard, remembering the severity of his wounds.

'Did you see who shot you?' John asked, taking a step forward.

Harry shook his head. 'Naw. The bullet came from behind. Everything went black. When I woke up, Shirley was leaning over me. I can't remember anything else.'

'Thanks Harry,' Matthew said.

'The Sheriff told me they got the bitch, who did this?'

Matthew nodded sheepishly. He did not want to tell Harry they were defending 'the bitch'. Changing the subject, he asked, 'Did Stephen ever tell you why he left Atlanta?'

Harry shook his head. 'He didn't like to talk about it. I got the impression someone died, like his sister or cousin, I can't really say who.' He scratched at the stubble on his face. 'Wait now,' he gave a nervous laugh. 'Why are you askting me all these questions?' He stared at the two of them and shook his head, disappointment evident across his face. 'Y'all didn't come here to see me, did you?'

Matthew frowned. 'Harry…'

'You're defendin' her, ain't you?' Harry interrupted Matthew's explanation. 'Get outta here, I ain't got nothing more to say.'

Chapter Eighteen

Last night had not gone to plan. Matthew felt bad about deceiving Harry and knew there was no way of making it up to him.

He sat in his office with the phone receiver resting on his shoulder. He had put off calling Helen. If he were honest with himself, he did not think he had the guts, but he needed to apologize for Sally's sake as well as his own.

If he could get Helen on board for a plea bargain, maybe he could save Sally's life. He could not allow two children to grow up without their mother.

'Helen?' Matthew breathed a sigh of relief when he realized he had Helen's machine. 'Are you there?' He hoped she wouldn't suddenly pick up the phone. He cleared his throat nervously. 'Helen,' he placed his head in his hands. 'I'm sorry. I-I didn't mean what I said. Please forgive me?' He hung up quickly. 'Chicken-shit!' he said, aloud.

He flipped open his memo pad and stared at the remaining list of tasks. Phone calls, statements he needed to read over and various documents that needed to be sent to the judge's clerk.

He still needed to find evidence that would impeach the prosecution's witnesses, but one question kept nagging him.

He closed his memo pad, put it to one side, and punched in the Atlanta police department's phone number.

The desk clerk answered on the first ring. 'Hello, you're through to the police department. My name is Ginger, may I help you?'

Matthew explained he was a lawyer investigating a case and needed information about an ex-employee. 'I believe he was a Deputy within your department six months ago, Stephen Collins?'

'Oh,' the desk clerk said. 'I'm sorry Mr. Brennan I don't recognize the name, but I'm new here. Listen, why don't you call back at around 1pm my boss will be available then - he should be able to help?'

Matthew nodded to John who had just entered the office. 'Thanks,' he said to the desk clerk, and he hung up the phone. 'What's up?' he said, staring at John's glum expression.

John's frown deepened. 'Think you'll want to read this,' he placed a newspaper in front of Matthew on the desk.

Matthew flipped over the folded paper to the front page and read the headline. 'Islamist's lawyer brainwashed!' He looked up at John. 'They can't be serious?'

'Yep. They're claiming while you were away, supposedly at rehab, you were actually involved in a Muslim cult.'

Matthew laughed deeply. 'Who makes this stuff up? It's priceless!'

John frowned deeply and raised his eyebrows.

'Oh, come on, people don't actually believe this, do they?'

John shrugged. 'It says they have a reliable source. Townsfolk seem convinced, what are we gonna do? There's some kind of hate…organization on the rampage now, there'll be riots in the streets. It's all over the internet.'

Matthew placed the newspaper into the Trash Can beside his left leg. 'A *reliable* source, that's what that reporter said to me.' He leaned back in his chair. 'We have to put a stop to this. Who could it be stirring up all this shit?'

John took a seat opposite Matthew. He lifted his legs up, placing his feet on Matthew's desk. 'How long have you got?' he joked.

*   *   *

Anna sat on the edge of a medical bed in the examination room. She found it difficult to breathe.

As if hearing her thoughts, Doctor Holmes said, 'It's a shock, huh?' He threw the paper towel into a Trash Can. He was wearing a blue overcoat showing a crisp white shirt and a silver tie with multicolored shapes scattered along it. His silver rimmed glasses rested perfectly against his roman nose.

'Yeah. I thought I had food poisoning or something. I mean…a baby? Now?' She stared at the floor. *How am I gonna tell Matt?* She thought.

'You mean with the trial and everythang at the moment, it's not the right timing?'

She nodded.

He took a yellow candy from a glass jar on the shelf above the washbasin. He approached the medical bed and gave her the wrapped sweet. 'Hey, c'mon. You know my door is always open if you need to talk?' He nudged her slightly. With a soft tone he said, 'You're gonna be just fine.'

She smiled at him. 'Yeah. I'm gonna be a mom.' Tears formed in her hazel eyes. She hugged her stomach maternally.

The doctor replied, 'It's a good day, huh?'

103

'Yeah, the best. Thanks, Doctor.' She climbed down from the bed and picked up her purse from the floor.

'You take care now, Anna. Come see me in a few weeks, OK? But call me anytime, if you need to.' He showed his 'I mean business face' by pulling down his glasses to the end of his nose and staring over the rims at her.

'Sure, I will.'

* * *

At just after 1pm, Matthew tried for the second time, to contact the Sheriff of the Atlanta PD. He was put on hold.

'Sheriff Drano,' a gruff voice answered.

Matthew pictured the Chicago Bears NFL player, William Perry, wearing a police uniform two sizes too small for his three-hundred-and-eight-two pound frame, squatting on a desk chair as if it was a child's.

Matthew introduced himself.

'Brennan...' Drano cleared his throat. 'Yeah Ginger said you called. You wanna know something about an ex-employee?'

'Yes. I was wonderin' if you could tell me any information about Stephen Collins. He transferred six months ago, and I want to know what the reason was.' He pictured the ball player scratching his head.

'Stephen Collins, did you say? Does this have anything to do with his death?'

'I'm afraid so.' Matthew did not want to reveal any further details, what with the *ball player* being a law abiding Sheriff and all. But he figured what the hell – maybe this Drano did not like Stephen and would be happy to help? 'I'm defending Mrs. Martinez and any information you can share about why Stephen Collins was transferred, would be much appreciated.' *Go for the flattery approach.*

104

He thought. 'I realize you must be extremely busy. I could call back when it is more convenient if you like?'

'No…lunchtime is usually pretty quiet.'

Matthew could hear some papers shuffling in the background and what sounded like a filing cabinet closing.

'All I know is, as soon as the hearing was over Stephen up and left.'

'The hearing?' Matthew searched around his desk for a piece of paper and a working biro.

'Yeah. Stephen and his partner were in the pursuit of a drug dealer over on 9th.'

Matthew tossed the first biro into the Trash Can at the side of his desk; it chimed against the aluminum bottom. He hunted in his drawer for another.

'Stephen chased him on foot down an alley, behind a dental hygienist practice,' Drano paused. 'Anyhow, the perp fired, Stephen returned fire, just as a bystander was leaving the dental practice. She was killed instantly.'

Matthew dropped the second empty biro onto the desk. 'Poor guy - he must have been distraught?'

'Sure. Sure. It devastated him. Even after it was concluded her death was accidental.'

Matthew leaned back in his chair. He rubbed the stubble on his chin as he listened intently to the Sheriff.

'Of course that's only my opinion on the whole thing.' Drano sniffed. 'Others say Stephen left because of the death threats.'

'Death threats?' Matthew sat up as if being struck by a lightening bolt.

'Yeah, from the Comancheros's gang member, Jay Keller A.K.A Killer J.'

Matthew pictured the classic John Wayne western and wondered if that was where the street gang got their name.

'Stephen arrested him two months prior to the

105

accidental shooting. Got him for rape, murder, and dealing - you name it.'

Remembering the letters John found in Stephen's apartment Matthew said, 'Were any of these threats mailed to Stephen's address?'

'No, no letters. They trashed his car and threw a rock through his window – we got the little bastard. Thirteen-years-old. Someone had paid him to do it, he went home crying to Momma.' The Sheriff laughed at his recollection. 'Wish they'd all do that.' Clearing his throat, he said, 'That's all I can tell you.'

'There is just a couple more questions,' Matthew took the only working biro he had from his jacket pocket and scribbled in his notepad. Fishing he asked, 'What was the name of the bystander that was killed?'

'Monette, Monette something, hold on a second…' Drano's voice disappeared.

Matthew could hear papers shuffling again and what sounded like a filing cabinet closing. It thudded and clanged.

There was more movement across the line before Drano said, 'Monette Williams, that was her name. Her husband identified her body at the morgue. Poor guy.'

Matthew narrowed his eyes, fishing again. 'Do you have his address?'

More shuffling, 'Bernie Williams, 3317 Cypress Street, Eastville.'

Matthew scribbled frantically. 'Why do you think the hearing was the reason Stephen asked to be transferred? I mean, being on a gang member's hit list is pretty scary, huh?'

'I don't think Stephen took the death threats as seriously as everyone thought.'

'Why?'

'He joked about it, but I guess it could have been a front?'

'This accidental shooting…any connection with the gang?' Matthew scratched his cheek.

'No.'

Matthew bit at his lip. 'Thanks for your time, Sheriff Drano. You've been extremely helpful.'

'No problem.'

Around dusk, Matthew left his office. He noticed three local reporters loitering on the sidewalk. They looked as if they had been hoping to catch him before he left; they sprang on him with eager anticipation.

'Mr. Brennan, do you have any comments about the memorial held yesterday afternoon in honor of the fallen officers?' One reporter asked as he thrust his microphone into Matthew's face.

He stepped back onto the sidewalk so everyone could see him. 'The family of patrolman Collins has my deepest sympathy. My thoughts are with Officer Richardson, I sincerely hope he makes a speedy recovery.' He placed his office keys into his jacket pocket, fastening the zip.

'When will the arraignment be held?'

'The arraignment will be Thursday morning at 9am,' Matthew replied.

A male reporter stepped forward with his notebook and pen at the ready. 'Do you have any comments about the reports of you and your client being involved in a Muslim cult?'

Matthew smirked. 'Yes. The reports are utterly ridiculous.' He pushed through the reporters making his way to his motorcycle. He placed his briefcase on the Buell's passenger seat, covering his briefcase with a cargo net to secure it in place.

'Has Mrs. Martinez confessed?'

'Of course not.' Matthew replied, angrily. He mounted the Buell, fastening the helmet strap around his chin. 'Thank you for your time.' His voice was muffled under the helmet.

The welcomed cool breeze blew around Matthew's body as he headed home via South Hall Road. He could not help but feel freedom as he cruised down the wide sweeping road, passing pecan trees on either side. The adrenaline exploded through him like a volcano.

The orange sky ahead reflected off the silky road; he accelerated toward it.

* * *

'That's the 21st commercial for Springfield liquor store in the last forty-five minutes,' Matthew moaned.

The Brennans lay in bed, leaning against the headboard. Anna had her nose in her adventure novel. The lace shoulder strap on her nightdress fell down one side as her hair draped, meeting her chest. 'Maybe you should turn off the T.V. Why don't you read your motorcycle magazine?'

He found it hard to read. The desire to drink and the desire to work on Sally's case plagued his mind. It became a battle inside him, and he wasn't entirely sure which side he wanted to win.

'I'm going to get some water,' he sighed and threw the covers back.

Rocky followed Matthew downstairs to the kitchen. Rocky watched Matthew pace up and down, before collapsing in his doggy bed.

Matthew's head ached. *Who else could have a grudge against Stephen or Harry? What about this gang?* He thought wearily.

'What about Miguel?' he said, aloud. 'What if he did know about the affair and did the deed himself then framed Sally for it?' He stopped pacing. 'Where is he now?'

He remembered six years ago. A gang of kids picked a fight with Miguel's younger brother, Juan. Miguel hunted them down like a rabid dogs. Two of them never walked again.

If Miguel did know about the affair, it was a safe bet he made sure Stephen did not walk again either.

'Maybe Miguel hired this Joe Mullen to kill Stephen? If I could find out what happened to the diner's security disc, maybe I would have some answers?'

The Springfield liquor store theme tune ran around his head. He tried to block out its hypnotic jingle.

Chapter Nineteen

Matthew sighed heavily and rubbed his eyes. He stared at the witness and evidence lists he had received from the courthouse clerk. There were as usual, pages of it.

Seventy names and addresses filled the watermarked pages. The assortment always seemed to Matthew to be deliberate in their quantity. Some he was sure, had nothing what-so-ever to do with the case. He knew it was customary for the D.A. to put as many names as possible on the list, just to give the defense extra legwork, but he felt like everyone was out to get him.

'Shirley Baxter? Did we find out any info on her?' he asked, knowing the answer before John even opened his mouth. Shirley was the next item on their schedule, along with several others.

'Not yet,' John replied. He did not lift his head from the sheet of paper he was reading. 'I've got another client coming in at…' He checked his watch. 'Five minutes ago. I'll join you when I'm done.' He stood from the conference room desk and grabbed his blue pinstriped jacket from the back of his chair. He crossed the room, in the direction of his office, across the hall.

Matthew frowned. He glanced at the next name on the list. Nelson Boone. The notorious forensic expert had put away hundreds, if not thousands of suspects on his testimony alone. Juries trusted him. He had the persona of a favorite uncle. It was sickening watching him smile and nod at the courtroom, like a holiday elf in Santa's grotto; the candy he handed out was for the prosecution only.

He rolled his eyes. Boone would be a problem. Matthew hoped he had some magic up his sleeve that would help the jury to understand the technicalities of revolver discharge.

Her name was Judy Fong. She was a professor for the Atlanta state university. She had written hundreds of books about firearms and had been a forensic scientist for over twenty years.

He wanted to introduce, in particular, Judy's book on ballistics. In chapter nine of that book, Judy explains revolvers can deposit residues to other persons at close proximity, even if they had not fired the weapon.

He had left several messages. He had not received a reply. He feared Judy was on vacation.

Deputy Patterson's name was next, along with Sheriff Langford's. They would, no doubt, testify to what they witnessed at the crime scene. Matthew was sure Sheriff Langford would tell the tale of Sally's arrest.

Cathy Woodall was a finger print analyst with a yard of letters after her name. Matthew had not come across her before, so he was not familiar with her presence in the courtroom.

However, he was certain she would testify that Sally's fingerprints were indeed on the murder weapon.

He skipped Mr. Collins name. It was obvious he would testify to the identification of his son at the morgue and identify his son's voice on the answering machine tape.

The next two names Matthew noticed were from Atlanta. Mr. Newson's address was the same street as Sally. A Mr. Kirkland lived several blocks west.

Clara entered the conference room. She was carrying a tray with two mugs of steaming coffee. 'There you are,' she said, placing the mug in front of him.

'Thanks,' he said, leaning back in his chair.

'I see the D.A will need some more Xerox paper?' She glanced at the pages, scattered across the desk.

A loud bang at the window made Clara jump.

Thick red paint smeared down the window pane, drying instantly in the sticky morning heat.

Matthew leapt from his seat, his heart beat racing in his ear. He crouched on his knees peering over the window ledge. He hoped no more missiles were thrown through the window.

He could see the pale turquoise color of the sky and the top of the courthouse clock tower across the street. He shifted to the left until he could see the sidewalk below.

Suddenly he saw them standing next to two pick up trucks under the canopy of a Nuttall Oak tree. They were in deep conversation and pointing at the blood-like stain on the glass. He could just make out the words printed on the first man's T-shirt: Stop Islamization.

'What's going on?' John asked, his eyes wide with panic as he stared at the window.

'They're wearing white masks.' Matthew swallowed hard.

'How many of them are out there?' Clara shivered.

'Ten maybe more.'

John crossed to the phone. 'I'll call the Sheriff.'

'Don't bother, they're going now,' Matthew said, his eyes fixed on the street below. He watched the pick ups disappear around the corner. 'It was a warning.'

John nodded. 'I've got a bad feeling about all this.' He comforted Clara.

Matthew placed his hand over his mouth thoughtfully. 'Clara?'

She stared at him with a worried expression on her face.

'Find out where Miguel Martinez was on the night of the shootings - get a copy of his schedule from his boss.' He looked at John defiantly. 'They're not going to stop me.'

'You think Miguel might have known about affair?' John ran his fingers through his hair as he stared at the painted window pane.

'Just thinking aloud. But I want to cover all angles.' Matthew followed John's gaze. 'I'll call a window cleaner.'

'It's OK, I'll do it,' Clara said. She folded her arms across her chest, took a deep breath and headed slowly down to her desk.

They followed her.

'I'm going over to the jail - start preparing Sally for the arraignment tomorrow. Why don't you take Clara home?' Matthew spun on his heels. 'Oh, you have a client coming in?' he tut-tutted.

'Not anymore, they cancelled. Fifth one this week.' John looked at Clara. 'I'll drive you home, OK?'

Matthew looked at Clara. 'Call me if you find out anything.'

*   *   *

The outer door slammed shut, echoing around the small interview room. Matthew arranged his briefcase on the wooden table, shuffling papers and scraps, just passing the time.

She entered for the first time wearing a dark blue Hijab covering her head; it clashed horribly with the orange jumpsuit. She had a sullen expression and looked to the floor.

The female guard took off the cuffs and exited the room, waiting outside for the lawyer and client to finish.

'Your arraignment is tomorrow at nine,' Matthew said, sternly. He did not make eye contact with Sally as she sat down opposite him.

'Matt, before we start there is something I need to say,' she placed her hands in front of her on the desk. Staring at her cracked cuticles she said, 'I want to apologize for lying to you the other day.'

He tilted his head and stared at her blankly.

'I'm just finding it hard to cope in here, I guess I panicked. Allah was testing me. I know you can help me. I want to get out of here. No more lies.'

He closed his briefcase and placed it on the floor. 'No there won't be, or I'm out.'

'I know.' She sat up in her chair. 'During Salah last night Allah showed me who could have stolen the gun.'

A loud bang. The locking system's high pitched buzz followed. She did not flinch at the sound. She appeared not to notice as she continued, 'Three weeks before Stephen's death I hired a handyman, just to do some odd jobs around the house. The thing is I think he stole Miguel's gun because I'm sure it went missing right around the time I hired him.' She leaned forward. She had a strange grin on her face.

He did not say a word. He was not sure how to respond, so he let her continue.

'I told you about him, Joseph Mullen. He is the only one who could have taken it.'

'Wait a minute? You're telling me the guy you told me about…this Joseph Mullen was your handyman?'

She nodded. 'Yes.'

'And you hired him three weeks before the murder?'

'Yes.'

He raised his eyebrows in disbelief. 'Why would he want to kill a cop two hundred miles away?'

Her jaw fell. Clearly she had not thought about that.

'Let me get this straight,' he ran his tongue across his teeth, making a sucking noise. 'Your defense *is* a guy you hired as a handyman came down to Birchwood County, ate at the same restaurant as you, on the *same* day and murdered your ex-lover with *your* handgun,' he slammed his fist onto the desk. 'He kidnapped you and locked you and your children in the bathroom of a motel room that you booked in advance. But you don't know why. Is that what you want me to tell the court?' He could feel the mist sinking over his eyes. 'Cut the crap, Sal. Jesus.' He stood, knocking the chair backward. He came to an apparent halt next to the window. Focusing on the window pane, he stood sucking in the air through his teeth, trying to calm himself.

* * *

Matthew had no idea where the anger had come from. He had apologized to Sally, but he knew his outburst had upset her by the way she avoided eye contact as if his eyes would scald her if she looked.

He wondered if she were playing mind games just to get a reaction. Maybe she did murder her ex-lover out of revenge, and she was just trying to make him lose his focus? It worried Matthew that he could not answer that question.

On the way out of the jail, his cellular phone vibrated in his back pocket. He flipped it open and placed it to his ear. 'Clara?'

'Matt, I've been in touch with the trucking company Miguel works for. He was in Florida at the time of the shooting. He is currently on his way back from Savannah.'

He frowned. 'Thanks, Clara. I'll see you in the morning.'

115

He slipped his cellular phone back into his pocket and mounted the Buell. He couldn't shake the feeling that he was being watched.

The streets were eerily quiet. There were no reporters ready to pounce on him. No locals on their way home from the grocery store. No sound of traffic. Nothing but the sound of his heartbeat echoing in his ear.

He took a left down Hanover Street, riding past Betty's hair salon, toward his house on Goodland's Avenue. He found himself searching for people as he rode by, wondering where townsfolk were.

*　　*　　*

'The only good Muslim is a dead Muslim!' Pastor Jones's husky voice echoed around Saint George's Catholic church. 'They threaten us and our constitution!' the hate exploded from his mouth.

The church-goers cheered and clapped in agreement as they witnessed the theatrics before them.

He raised a fat hand in the air. 'We must protect ourselves from anyone who chooses Islam, this woman betrayed her people and her own family,' his fist punched the air. 'She must be executed to save her soul!' He gestured for the altar boy to pass the collection plate round. 'We must kill the traitor!' he yelled.

'Kill the traitor!' their chants echoed around the church.

'Kill the traitor!'

'Kill the traitor!'

Chapter Twenty

'State versus Sally Martinez, case number 23453, step forward please,' the bailiff said.

The bailiff removed her handcuffs, and she followed Matthew to his honor's bench. A few coughs echoed around the courtroom as Judge Chamberlain read over the indictment silently. He peered over his glasses, looking in Sally's eyes. 'Are you Sally Martinez?' he asked.

'Yes,' she replied, nervously. She stared up at the judge.

'Is Mr. Brennan your attorney?'

'Yes.'

The judge held up a green file. 'I am holding a copy of the indictment here returned against you by the grand jury. Have you been served with a copy of it?' He rested it onto a pile of other green folders.

'Yes.'

'Do you understand the charges against you?' he asked.

She looked at Matthew, who smiled at her reassuringly.

'Well, Mrs. Martinez? Do you understand the charges against you?' the judge repeated.

'Kill the traitor!' A male voice yelled, interrupting the judge. He sprang from the back of the room, charging toward Sally and Matthew. Two bailiffs ran after him, trying to take a firm grip on the skinny runt of a man. 'Kill the t-traitor!' his voice disappeared as the bailiffs ushered him out of the court room.

'Order!' Chamberlain slammed his gavel down twice. 'Order!' The courtroom was silent.

Matthew raised his eyebrows at Clara, who sat in the front row. He scratched his ear and turned back to Sally who stood with her arms crossed over her chest, swaying back and forth.

'Mrs. Martinez?' Chamberlain sighed heavily, taking off his glasses and rubbing his nose. 'Do you understand the charges against you?'

She looked at the floor. 'Yes, your honor,' she replied, finally.

Chamberlain nodded once and replaced his glasses. 'Trial date is set for 25th September at nine AM. Any pre-trial motions to be filed before 30th August.'

'At this time, your honor my client is requesting bail,' Matthew asked.

Helen stood abruptly. 'Your honor we consider this defendant a flight risk and ask bail be denied.'

The judge frowned. 'As the defendant does not reside in the county, I am inclined to agree counselor. Bail is denied.'

'But your honor, my client has family in this county. There would be no reason for her not to attend,' Matthew pleaded. He could see the judge was unfazed by the simple dismissive shake of his head. This was a capital murder case, and Matthew knew the judge's rules.

'Bail is denied.' Judge Chamberlain slammed his gavel down.

'But...' Sally shook her head in disbelief. 'No... Please!' She watched the judge leave the courtroom.

Matthew reached forward. 'Sal, it's going to be OK,' his voice was smooth and even. He gripped her shaking hands. 'I promise.'

* * *

'John, I've been thinking about Harry and I think it would be wise to get him to sign an affidavit confirming he saw someone else at the diner that night.' Matthew shielded his eyes from the sun's glare. They were making their way across the courthouse parking lot.

'Have a hunch, do we?' John replied, taking his keys out of his pocket.

'Just want to cover all angles.' Matthew unclipped his helmet from the padlock attached to his motorcycle. Placing his helmet onto the floor, he pushed a small silver key into the disc lock on his back wheel. With a twist, the lock unclipped, releasing the motorcycle.

'Visiting hours don't start until two. I'll get an affidavit drafted, and then go over to the hospital,' John replied. He shook his head. 'I don't know,' he sighed. 'Sally looked devastated by the bail verdict, feel kinda sorry for her.'

'Yeah I know.' Matthew placed the disc lock under his seat. Lifting his helmet up from the floor he said, 'I'll go talk to the children again. They must have seen something?' He mounted the machine.

'Did she agree to let them see her?'

Matthew nodded.

'Well good luck buddy,' John called from inside his car.

* * *

'Hi Lizzie!' Matthew tried to keep his tone upbeat.

Elizabeth turned to see Matthew towering above her holding two peanut butter and jelly sandwiches on blue plastic plates.

'Here, I made it myself.' He frowned.

119

She turned back to her brother playing on the Owens' back lawn. Thomas approached excitedly and took a colored plate. 'Thanks,' he said, taking a bite of the sandwich. His face was full of delight as he chewed the crunchy filling.

She rolled her eyes.

Matthew sat down beside her on the step below, next to her foot. 'Not hungry, huh?' he sighed. 'I know how you feel.'

She did not bother to look at him. She fixed her attention on a blade of grass.

'Listen Lizzie, I know things are tough for you right now and I am going to do everything I can to help your mom.' He ran his fingers through his hair. 'How would you like to go and see her this afternoon?'

Thomas sprang from the ground, jumping in the air and waving his hands above his head. 'I'll go tell grandma,' he beamed, running to the house.

'You mean it?' she asked, staring wide-eyed at Matthew.

He could not believe the family resemblance. He remembered when Sally had had the same child-like vulnerability. 'Sure I mean it. Your grandparents are taking you.' He was not sure how she would react.

Her bottom lip trembled. 'Thank you,' she whispered.

The lunchtime heat became unbearable. Matthew's shirt was covered in wet patches, and he could feel himself starting to sway on the step, his eyes becoming blurry. 'Why don't we go inside to the kitchen? It's cooler in there?' he suggested, picking up the plate next to her foot.

They sat opposite each other at a granite breakfast bar. Matthew said, softly, 'Can I ask you some questions? You don't have to answer if you don't want to.'

She nodded.

Matthew watched her studying the contours of his face. He smiled nervously, unsure how to word the question.

120

'Do you remember the night you ate at the diner?' he asked, picking at the hard skin on his right thumb.

Elizabeth sat up. 'Why?' A confused expression on her face. The same expression Sally had shown on the night Matthew first saw her at the jail.

'Lizzie, you're a big girl now, and I know you're smart, so I'm going to be honest with you OK?' Matthew placed his hands on the counter interlocking his fingers in a business-like manner. 'Your Mom's in a lot of trouble. I'm going to help her, but I need you to help me?'

She mimicked his posture.

'Now do you remember a man speaking to your mom that night?'

Elizabeth was silent for a moment. 'There was a big storm,' she said, finally. 'The lady on the radio said that we might get a hurricane. Mom was worried, I could tell.' She slapped her pink pencil lips together. 'I wasn't afraid.'

He smiled.

'Mom said I was a good girl because I spotted the sign for the diner first.' She started to wiggle a loose upper incisor with her tongue.

'So you found the diner for your mom? Good job.' he praised. 'Did you have something nice to eat?'

Nodding, she said, 'Yes, but I wanted some ice-cream, Joe said we could have some but mom said no.'

'Joe? Who's Joe?'

Shrugging, Elizabeth said, 'Joe. He cleaned my dad's garage and cleaned my bike, but he didn't clean my room.' She put her finger in her mouth. 'But I don't like Joe anymore. He's mean.'

He cocked his head. 'Why is Joe mean?'

'Mom said he tried to hurt her with a knife and wouldn't let us out of the bathroom.' She jumped off her chair.

'Where are you going?' he asked, placing his hand into his lap.

'Watch cartoons.'

He nodded.

Turning back to face him, she asked, 'You will help my Momma, won't you?'

'I promise,' he replied.

* * *

John was waiting for the bell to indicate visiting hours had started. He wandered aimlessly in the corridors when at two minutes past two, the chime sounded.

He was the first visitor into Harry's room.

'Hi Harry,' John said, smiling. He handed Harry a bag of grapes and took a seat next to Harry's bedside.

'So more questions?' Harry said a hint of aggression in his voice.

Sensing hostility, John said, 'C'mon Harry. We've been friends a long time.'

'Yeah, a long time so why are you two defending the woman who did this to me?'

'She's Matthew's sister-in-law, man. What would you have him do?'

Harry shook his head. He tried to reach a copy of *Billows Creek* Gazette resting on the table. With no luck, he retreated back against the comfort of the pillows. 'They're saying he hasn't seen her in over a year - she didn't even go to his wedding?'

'That's families for you. Look, Matt feels bad, but he's stuck between a rock and a hard place.' John took out the affidavit from his jacket pocket.

'What's that?' Harry pointed at the document; an achievement he had recently mastered.

'It's an affidavit,' John sighed, 'Harry listen, about before…we're both sorry we didn't come to visit sooner.'

Harry nodded. 'And you want me to sign this?'

'Yeah. It's just to confirm you saw someone else at the diner that night.'

'You mean someone else who could have done this to me and killed my partner?'

John licked his lips, looking to the floor he replied, 'It's possible.'

'Look I'll sign your affidavit,' Harry said, 'but I hope you have a casket picked out 'coz when this goes down,' he winced, closing his eyes until the pain lessened. 'I'm telling you this woman is guilty.'

Chapter Twenty-One

'All signed and dated,' John said, into his cellular phone.

It was 3pm, and the weather had taken a dramatic turn for the worst, as far as Matthew was concerned, rising to ninety-two degrees.

Since arriving home from the Owens's, he had tried numerous attempts to cool himself. He was comfortable now, wearing nothing but a pair of boxers.

The Whirlpool air conditioning unit thudded and drummed loudly from its place in the kitchen window.

He walked from the kitchen, the phone against his ear and a cold Soda in his left hand, to the living room. 'Good job. I spoke to Lizzie she confirms her mother's story.'

'Bingo,' John replied. 'So all we have to do is find this Joe Mullen and discover his motive, right?'

Matthew sighed, 'I don't know.' He flopped on the sofa, moving the cushions to one side.

'What D'you mean you don't know?'

'It was something Lizzie said. She said Sally *told* her Joe Mullen tried to hurt Sally.' Matthew took a sip of Soda. He balanced the can on his abdomen. The sudden coldness on his skin made the tiny hairs stand on end.

'So?'

'So, if Lizzie were there she would have seen Joe threaten Sally with the knife? Why did she need to be *told*?' He lay his head back against the sofa rubbing the

124

bridge of his nose, wearily. 'Anyway, we'll go through the whites pages tomorrow and see if we can find this guy. He must know something?'

John sighed. 'Who knows buddy?' he sighed heavily making the line crackle. 'Do you ever get the feeling you're being screwed?'

Matthew nodded and rubbed his eyes. 'All the time lately.'

* * *

The Brennan home had become an industrial freezer. Anna had complained when she had arrived home that it was warmer in Antarctica.

At the risk of starting a feud over the fact it was over ninety degrees outside, and too hot to function as a warm blooded mammal, Matthew had turned the dial down a couple of degrees.

They sat in silence now, eating their cold supper at the breakfast bar.

'So how was your day?' Anna asked, pouring ranch dressing onto her salad.

He shrugged. 'Ok I guess.' He stabbed his fork into a tomato.

'Ritchie came today. He thinks it's a good idea to make the flower bed wider to cut away some of the lawn. He's going to do some plans for me to look at.' She put down her fork. It chimed against her glass of lemonade. She sighed, heavily. 'What is it Matt? You haven't listened to a word I've said?'

He looked up from his plate. 'Oh, sorry. What did you say?'

She shook her head. 'What is it?'

He frowned. 'I think your sister is guilty.'

125

'What?' She leaned forward, stretching out her hand to make peace. 'Why do you think that?'

He shook his head. 'I can't get a straight answer out of her. Just when I think I've got the truth, someone springs up another version, and I'm right back where I started.' He took his wife's hand and gripped it gently. 'I just don't know how I can help her if she won't tell me the complete story.'

'What does John think?'

'The same as I do, I think?'

She took back her hand and placed it in her lap. 'I know Sally didn't do this Matt and deep down I know you feel the same way. Whatever her reason is for being evasive I'm sure it has nothing to do with Stephen Collins' murder.'

'I think it might, Anna,' he took a slow breath, trying to work out how to word his next sentence. 'They had an affair – he had dumped her before he was murdered.'

She bit her lip. 'Has she said how long she was with him?'

Not seeing the relevance he said, 'About a year, so she said. Why?'

'The guy Sally sneaked off to see during our wedding - his name was Stephen.'

Chapter Twenty-Two

At 8am, Matthew arrived at his office. He had not bothered to comb his hair when removing his helmet, instead let nature do its worst.

This morning his body felt drained of all its energy as if a giant mosquito had sucked the life out of him in the middle of the night. He did not know if it were the weather or fear that kept him tossing and turning all night.

It was too much effort to move. He slouched in his office chair, leaned back against the leather cushioning and closed his eyes. *Just a quick nap.*

Clara arrived loudly carrying the mail.

The sudden noise made him jump. 'What?'

She looked stunned. 'Good morning to you too!'

'Sorry, morning Clara, what time is it?' he yawned, stretching his arms above his head.

'It's ten to ten.' She stared at him narrowing her eyes. 'Are you all right, Matt?'

'Sure,' he replied, dismissively. 'I didn't sleep well last night.'

She cocked her head. 'I expected to see you working on Sally's case, not sleeping; I thought you had arrived early to find Joseph Mullen?'

He sat up in his chair and flicked through the mail aggressively. 'Yes well I'll start in a minute!' he snapped. 'That will be all, Clara.'

The audacity. Trying to tell me what I should be doing in my office? How dare she? Who does she think she is? He thought.

He paced angrily back and forth. If he had been a bull at a bull fight, he would be seeing red right about now.

Taking a long deep breath, he sat down at his desk. He grabbed the first letter from the pile. Another blue envelope.

He sliced along the top with one quick even stroke of his letter opener. It read: **She is guilty. Drop the case or your wife dies.**

He screwed the letter, throwing it into the Trash Can. He tried to control his breathing as he went to the book shelf. Lifting phone directories from the shelf, he noticed a glass bottle. 'When did I hide that there?' He stared at the bold white letters on the black label as if being reunited with an old friend. He reached for it, holding its square body in one hand. 'Made in Tennessee,' he said, before rotating the bottle. He read from the label, 'Whiskey made as our fathers made it.' He smiled to himself and unscrewed the lid.

Chapter Twenty-Three

Matthew stood in the restroom adjacent to his office. He poured the golden liquid in the sink, watching it disappear down the plughole. *I shouldn't have been so hard on her.* He thought. He stared at himself in the rectangular mirror above the washbasin. His face had changed and he knew it, since his return to work. Dark circles shadowed under his eyes. *Is that a gray hair?* He thought. He examined each strand with precision and pulled the culprit from his head.

Carrying the phone directories in his right hand, he headed downstairs.

Clara and John were standing near the entrance window. They were whispering, leaning toward each other, careful not to raise their voices. However, Matthew could hear Clara's reply, 'He looks awful, and he's been sleeping in his office again. The last time I saw Matt sleeping at his desk he was dismissed on the grounds of incompetence.' She shook her head. 'He should never have come back to work – he's not ready to handle this.'

Matthew placed the books onto Clara's desk.

The sudden noise made her jump. 'Matthew would you like some coffee?' She crossed to the coffee machine hastily and began to pour a cup of coffee for him.

'I don't think there are enough books here, Matt?' John joked, with a slight nod in the direction of the desk.

Matthew took the first book from the pile. 'Bess get started.' He took Clara's arm gently. 'I want to apologize about earlier. I shouldn't have snapped at you.'

She nodded, a sign of forgiveness and handed Matthew his coffee.

* * *

'Try this one,' John said. He read out the phone number.

Matthew punched in the digits onto the phone pad.

They had spent the entire morning searching through the directories, and the whole exercise was becoming tiresome. If Matthew did not speak to another Joseph Mullen, it would be too soon. 'Well, I've had it,' he sighed, replacing the handset onto its base. 'That was his sister. Joseph Mullen is ninety-years-old and has lived in a home for the last fifteen years.' He rubbed the bridge of his nose.

'This is ridiculous,' John placed the phone directory onto the desk with a thud. 'Hasn't it crossed your mind that she just made up this Joseph Mullen?' He stared at Matthew with questioning eyes. 'She could have grabbed the name from the white pages herself?'

Matthew flicked through the white pages aggressively. 'No, it isn't possible,' he protested. 'We're missing something.' In the corner of his eye, Matthew could see John turn to Clara and mouth something unintelligible. *Maybe John's right? Maybe Sally did make all of this up?* He sighed, closing the hefty book. 'I'm hungry; I'm going to get something to eat.'

'I'll come with you,' John replied, following him out into the street.

* * *

130

Anna leaned against the side of the house and admired her yard. Ritchie had extended the borders and was now digging up the cracked path.

She had pulled out the weeds and began to rake over the rich dark soil. 'Ritchie, how 'bout some lemonade?' She wiped her sweat-laced brow.

'Sure.' He straightened his back. He placed the shovel and pickaxe on the lawn and walked exhaustedly toward the back door.

'Here,' she handed him a glass of chilled lemonade.

He drank it hastily. 'That was lovely, Anna. You make wonderful lemonade,' he said, catching his breath. Puddles of sweat seeped through his sleeveless shirt.

'Why, thank you,' she smiled. 'Would you just look at my yard?' They both admired their efforts.

She walked toward a ceramic pot she had planted daisies in earlier that day. She crouched, pushing the pot to the left of the patio.

'Oh!' She could feel her face drain of color. The yard twirled around her. She straightened up again, holding her head and closing her eyes.

'Are you OK?'

'Yes, just a little faint that's all.'

He rushed toward her. 'Come, sit down.' He led her into the air conditioned kitchen. 'Here,' he poured her another glass of lemonade and handed her a handkerchief from his pocket.

'Thank you.' She noticed the embroidered design on the corner of the handkerchief. 'Oh that's beautiful.'

'Yes, my wife made it for me.'

'She has quite a talent.' She sipped the lemonade. 'Do you have any children, Ritchie?' She wiped her forehead with the handkerchief.

He sat at the breakfast bar, opposite her. 'Sadly no, I wish now we had. My wife was everything to me.'

131

She noticed his face sadden. 'I'm so sorry. How long ago did she die?'

'Seems like yesterday…'

'Oh…' She sat with her mouth open. 'I'm terribly sorry I had no idea.'

He leaned against the wooden breakfast bar. 'My work keeps me going. Do you and your husband have any children?'

She swallowed hard. 'Actually I'm expecting, but I haven't told anyone yet.'

'I won't tell anyone. Congratulations.'

'Thanks. With the trial and everything it's not the right time,' she explained.

He nodded. 'I see.' He stood from the breakfast bar. 'Well, I bess get on home. Put these sore muscles under the shower.'

She smiled.

'I'll see you tomorrow.'

*   *   *

'Sheriff Drano? It's Matthew Brennan.' He sat tapping his biro against his notepad.

He had had enough of the wild goose chase and had decided twenty minutes ago, he would search for another angle for Sally's case. If he could add reasonable doubt by giving another scenario of events, then maybe she would be freed.

'Ah, the lawyer. How can I help?'

Matthew smiled, looking down at the list of questions scribbled on his notepad. 'I was wondering if you could share some more information about the Comancheros and if you would be willing to testify?'

Drano picked the remnants of food from his teeth with a toothpick. 'Sure. No problem.'

132

Chapter Twenty-Four

'Here you are, Mom.' Anna placed a glass of lemonade onto the living room coffee table and perched herself on the brown leather sofa.

Linnie stood in front of the television, ironing Arthur's shirts. 'Thanks.'

The children giggled at the cartoons; Linnie smiled at them, pressing the iron against the clothing on the ironing board.

'Ritchie has done an excellent job of the yard.' Anna sipped slowly from her glass, hoping the cool liquid wouldn't make her sick *again.*

Linnie nodded. 'I told you he would do an excellent job. He's an angel.'

A rattle on the screen door interrupted their conversation. Linnie placed the iron onto the stand. 'Well who could that be – better not be another reporter.'

Anna stood and followed Linnie as moral support, in case things became ugly.

'M-Miguel?' Linnie stood in the doorway, her hand resting on the doorframe.

'I wanna see my kids!' He demanded. His muscle bound body filled the doorway. His eyes burned with rage. His features were made even more prominent by the acne scars across his chin.

Linnie gripped the front door with her right hand. She looked helplessly at Anna, pulling the door closer toward her. 'What are you doin' here?' she said to Miguel.

'I came to get my kids. Now let me see 'em.' His tone was deep and menacing.

'Now, Miguel. Step away from the door…We'll call the Sheriff?' Anna said, trying to breathe normally.

He did not blink. He stared straight at them. 'Now why would you do that? I just want my kids, they're my kids, not yours…Tommy?' he yelled. 'Tommy boy, come 'ere!'

Thomas ran to the hall. 'Daddy?' he said, smiling.

Linnie stopped Thomas from reaching the door. She held him securely in her arms. 'Miguel, you can't see them right now,' she protested.

Miguel opened the screen door and grabbed Thomas' arm. 'I've been on the road for sixteen hours, now I want to see my kids - Linnie give him to me!'

'No. I'll call the Sheriff, I swear!' she threatened.

Anna rushed toward the kitchen, grabbing her cellular phone from her purse. She dialed frantically, not taking her eyes away form the commotion at the front door.

Miguel and Linnie struggled over Thomas. Their grip on Thomas' arms became unbearable. He screamed with agony.

'Stop it! Stop it!' Elizabeth screamed. 'Let my brother go!'

Miguel released his grip. Linnie pulled Thomas toward her. With one sweeping motion, she slammed the front door.

'They hung up!' Anna held her cellular phone away from her ear. 'They actually hung up!'

Linnie held Thomas in her arms. She rocked him gently back and forth. 'Do you think he's gone?'

Anna ran to the window and peered above the curtain, out into the street. 'I can't see anyone.' She sighed heavily, 'I can't believe the Sheriff would hang up on me.'

'I hate you!' Elizabeth stormed upstairs.

A moment later, Elizabeth slammed a bedroom door.

Linnie bit her lip. 'Maybe I should have just let him take them?' She wiped tears from her cheek. 'What's that noise?'

'Look, it's Miguel!' She watched Miguel kick the wooden front gate at the end of the front yard until it flew off its hinges.

Linnie peered over the curtain and followed Anna's gaze. 'Looks like he's callin' someone on his cell phone.' She squeezed Anna's arm. 'You don't think he's callin' his brother and his friends do you?'

Anna held her stomach. 'Lock the doors quickly!' she bit her fingernail. 'Where does Daddy keep his baseball bat?'

Chapter Twenty-Five

Matthew and Anna sat in front of the T.V with a cold supper on their laps. Matthew changed the channel for the news update.

'We were so scared - I thought he was going to kill us.' She brushed her hair away from her eyes. 'The Sheriff hung up on me!'

He swallowed hard. 'He hung up?'

She nodded.

He pulled his eyebrows together. 'That's unbelievable! I'll file a complaint.'

She turned toward the T.V. 'My, lord?' she cried. Pictures of Linnie and Arthur's home flashed across the screen.

Matthew's heart sank. A sick feeling washed over him.

The young female reporter smiled enthusiastically. '...This is the house Sally Martinez grew up in. Her Mother and Father, Linnie and Arthur Owens, still reside here.

'You spoke to Sally Martinez earlier today, can you tell me, in your own words, what she confessed to you?' The camera panned to the left.

'Miguel!' Anna stared wide-eyed at the screen. 'So that's who he was calling this afternoon?' She placed her supper on the coffee table and stared wide-eyed at the screen. 'What do we do?' she asked, running her fingers through her hair.

'Call your mother – see if they're all right,' he replied. He did not take his eyes off the screen.

'...She confessed to me she hated that cop.' Miguel said. 'She told me she wanted him to pay for destroying our family. She's not sorry for her actions, only God can forgive her now.'

Matthew wanted to throw up. *Why did she talk to him? Surely she knew Miguel would blab to the nearest reporter he could find?* He thought.

This confession would undoubtedly slam dunk the state's case against her, and even if it were not true, it would remain fresh in the jury's mind.

Matthew knew he would have to file a motion to request the jury be sequestered. He didn't want any more of Miguel's antics to poison the jury's view of Sally even further.

Anna returned from the hall. She rubbed her eyes wearily. 'Daddy said they're coping, but there are reporters camping outside their house.' She sighed. 'Why would Miguel do this?'

He gestured for her to sit beside him on the sofa. 'I don't know. I guess he's hurtin'.'

* * *

'Am I speaking to John Beaumont?' a soft female voice asked.

John lay across his sofa with a copy of *Billows Creek* Gazette in his hand. It was folded neatly in half, revealing a cross word puzzle.

He rested the handset on his shoulder and tilted his head to speak into the mouthpiece. 'Why, yes? And who's this?'

'I don't know if you remember me. My name is Sarah-Jane, I work at Ned's diner?'

He shone his pearly whites at his recollection of the leggy blonde. 'I remember you Ma'me, how can I help you?'

'Well, I had time to think the other day - you know after you left the diner. I remember Sally Martinez talking to an African American man just before the shootings.'

He sat up, straightening his back. 'Really? Do you remember anything about him? Did he have any distinguishing features, how tall was he?' He fumbled around the cushions, trying to retrieve his pencil from the depths of the sofa.

'He was about fifty, between five-foot-eight and five-foot-nine. He wore a bandana around his neck.'

Having pulled out leftover crumbs of his pastry supper: a couple of coins and finally his pencil, John scribbled on the corner of his newspaper. 'Thank you for calling. You've been a great help.'

'You're welcome.'

Chapter Twenty-Six

'Matt, phone?' Anna called from the garage.

Matthew stood next to a bucket of soapy water, a wet sponge in his hand. The Buell stood on its side stand reflecting the afternoon rays in its gas tank. He dipped the sponge into the bucket and began to coat the machine in suds. 'Who is it?' He did not want to talk to anymore reporters.

'It's John.'

He took the phone with wet hands. 'John.'

'Matt, got some news for you.'

Matthew's shoulders slumped. 'Not more bad news?' He threw the sponge into the bucket.

John told Matthew about Sarah-Jane's phone call.

Matthew scratched his cheek. 'You think it's Joseph Mullen?'

'Could be.'

Matthew placed a wet hand onto his hips. 'They can't all be lying? We'll have to find this guy – interview her some more.'

'Sure I can handle that.'

Matthew laughed. 'It's a tough job?'

'But somebody's gotta do it,' they replied in unison.

'Heard the news - how are the Owens's handling all the hoopla?' John asked, changing the subject.

'I think they're doing their best to cope with it. Anna's dropping by later to check on them.'

John raised his eyebrows. 'He has really thrown a spanner in the works hasn't he?'

'Gotta hand it to Miguel, he knows when to show his ugly head.'

'Have you thought about filing for a change of venue?'

'I'll file a motion, but Chamberlain will deny it. I'll ask that the jury be sequestered.' Matthew scratched his head. 'We have to change the public's view of Sally.'

'That's going to be tough, everyone is rooting for the state on this one,' John huffed. 'Including Harry.'

Matthew frowned. 'Do you think Sally confessed to Miguel?'

'Naw, he's just pissed his old lady two-timed him and who can blame him? Anyhow, I heard he got a nice sum of cash for telling his story.'

'Yeah, you're probably right, but I need to ask her anyway.' Matthew ran the cotton cloth over the Buell. It sparkled in the last rays of sunlight disappearing behind the forest. 'I'm almost done here - I'll head over to the jail.'

'Hell,' John chuckled. 'It's been a while since I've heard a bedtime story – I'll come with you!'

*   *   *

'Is it true? Did you confess?' Matthew stood glaring, watching closely for some sign Sally was lying, a twitch in her body language or the dilation of her pupils.

Sally stood against the back wall. She rubbed her face in desperation. 'What, you think I would tell that son of a bitch anything? You think I would tell him where my children are so he can stir up all this shit?'

Matthew had never heard her curse before. He could see the stress and anxiety was starting to get to her.

He noticed her body language was different. Her back was arched, and her shoulders were slumped; when she spoke she hissed and spat like a cornered cat.

'Y'all think that I would put them in danger like that?' She looked up to the ceiling. 'Allah please...' She shook her head. 'I didn't do anythin' wrong. I didn't shoot them officers, I swear it on my children's lives!'

John raised his hand, a shrug of his shoulder like how many times had he heard that before.

As if Matthew had somehow heard John's thoughts, he turned away from Sally, staring out the window.

The buildings had become gray shadows that seemed to sway in the muggy heat. The locals had left the streets for the night; front porches glowed with torches.

Tall whispering shadows staggered from the Tavern Bar. They maneuvered slowly to the end of West Street, toward the motel on South Hall Road.

'Do you think I'm guilty?' she asked. 'Tell me now and I'll get another lawyer.'

Matthew rested his head against the coldness of the window. The sweat dripped from his forehead down the back of his neck. 'No, we don't think you're guilty,' he mumbled.

She wiped her tears angrily. 'Now are you gonna help me, or not?'

Matthew turned to look at her. She sat hunched against the far wall, her hands resting in her lap. She did not make eye contact, just stared at the floor.

'Yes, we're going to help you. Of course,' Matthew replied, sincerely. He walked over to her and leaned down, looking her straight in the eye. 'All I'm asking is for you to tell me the truth.'

'I *am*. Please just get me out of here?'

Matthew turned to face John. 'Can you give us a minute?'

John nodded and left the room.

The room was silent.

Matthew studied her expression.

She smiled at him. 'I want to thank you for sticking by me,' she paused. 'Do you ever wish you'd picked me?' She studied his reaction. 'We could have been good together.'

He didn't know what to say. For the first time in her presence, he felt uncomfortable and tried to remember why he asked John to leave. He moved away, sitting at the table.

Sally moved close, straddling a chair. She leaned forward. 'I always thought you were a real man. Not like the men I'm used to. You would have never done me like Miguel. I admit,' she said, shrugging. 'I was jealous of Anna when she told me she was marrying you. Maybe that's why I missed it?'

He crossed his legs casually. 'No,' he replied, coolly. 'You missed our wedding because you were screwing Stephen Collins.'

She cocked her head, frowning. 'Yeah, do you know why I fell for him?'

He shook his head. 'Why?'

'Because he reminded me of you.' She frowned. 'You're the one I really wanted. I bet you know all the right spots, huh?' She licked her lips.

He leaned forward, narrowing his eyes. 'Did you murder him?'

She didn't move away. 'You know the answer to that.'

He could feel her warm breath on his cheeks.

She licked her lips again. 'What I want to know is, have you ever wished you'd picked me?'

He swallowed hard. 'I love my wife.'

'I know, but sometimes you need something sweeter. All men do and guess what I do too, and there's nothing wrong with that. We're consenting adults.'

He could feel his face blush. He leaned back against the chair. 'There is when you're married to someone else and you've signed a pre-nuptial agreement.' He scratched his head uncomfortably and crossed to the window.

'I know what I've done, and I deserve my punishment whatever Allah sees fit.' She pulled at her ponytail and allowed her long, wavy locks to trail down her shoulders.

He thought about running his fingers through her hair, down her soft cheeks, across the contours of her jaw line. He shook his head, clearing the images from his mind. *What the hell is wrong with me?* He thought.

He wondered if she had somehow seen what he was thinking. He cleared his throat. 'Are you involved with a Muslim cult?' He raised his hands defensively, 'I know it's a stupid question.'

She raised her eyebrows. 'A cult?'

'It's a rumor going round.'

She cocked her head to one side. 'A rumor? What else has Miguel said about me?' She didn't wait for an answer. She stood from the chair and began biting her fingernails.

He wanted to walk toward her and comfort her but thought better of it. Instead he placed his hands into his pockets again and said, 'I had to ask.'

Her eyes filled with tears. She stared at him.

'Can I ask you something?'

He nodded. 'Sure.'

'Do you believe in the constitution?'

He pulled his eyebrows together. 'Of course it's the supreme law of our government, don't you?'

'Of course I do.' She stared at the table and then at the floor.

He scratched his head. He didn't understand the relevance of her question. 'Is there anything else you can tell me about Joseph Mullen?' he said, changing the subject. 'An address maybe?'

143

She tied her hair back into a ponytail. 'No, I've told you all I know.' She knelt and wiped the floor with her sleeve. 'I have to pray.'

He nodded. 'OK get some sleep.' He was surprised how fast he made it to the door. 'I'll see you tomorrow,' he said, over his shoulder.

Chapter Twenty-Seven

Matthew paced the dark blue carpeted foyer, rubbing the sweat from his chin wearily. He didn't look at John who was reading the *Birchwood County Times* while drinking some water.

At 9am, the heat had already reached eighty degrees; Matthew cursed the air conditioning unit for taking too long to work. He fiddled with the dial as he said, 'Did Sarah-Jane tell you anymore?'

'No, nothing that would be of any help to us.' John stretched his arms above his head, straightening his back against the black leather sofa. 'Did Sally enlighten you anymore while I was outta the room last night?'

Matthew sat beside him. He could feel his face blush as he remembered her proposal. Or at least that's what he thought it was. He had gone over their conversation in his mind first, thinking she was coming on to him and second, thinking she was trying to make him lose his focus. What he couldn't figure out was why. The part that scared him most was that he liked it. He hated to admit it, but she was attractive. 'She's not involved with any Muslim cult, and she doesn't know Joseph Mullen's address.' He shrugged when John raised his eyebrows.

John took a long sip from his cup. 'Does she know who has been stirring up the whole cult/traitor theory?'

'She thinks it's Miguel.'

John licked his lips. 'Possible. But surely he would have stated that in his *overplayed* interview with the reporters?'

Matthew had not thought about that. If Miguel were the one doing it, he would shout about it during every interview. He yawned. 'Who could it be? It has to be someone who knows Sally converted to Islam.'

'Beats me.'

Matthew sighed. 'How are we going to find this Joe Mullen?'

'I don't know.'

Clara entered, looking tired and pale. 'Morning,' she intoned. 'You two look like you didn't sleep either last night.'

Matthew poured some coffee into a Styrofoam cup. He chuckled once. 'It's like trying to find the invisible man.'

Clara perched herself on the edge of the chair and turned to face her computer. 'Are you still struggling to find Joseph Mullen?'

'Yep.' Matthew leaned over her, the computer screen illuminated in his eyes.

She tapped at the keys. 'I'll find him.'

A list of names appeared on the screen.

'We've already spoken to these people,' Matthew said, discouragingly.

She tapped again. 'It's searching,' she said, resting her chin on her fist. 'Here we are,' she moved the monitor so Matthew could see the list of possible candidates more clearly. 'There's a Joseph P. Mullen, with an "e" living in Cartersville, Joseph Mullen JR. in Newton and a Joseph Mullen...there's no address but a phone number in Mayhaw County. Would you like me to give him a call?'

John stood next to Clara and stared at the screen. 'How did you...?'

'It was easy.'

Matthew raised his eyebrows, confused.

146

'There are two ways you can spell Mullen - with an "e" or with an "a". You obviously tried with an "a" and came up short, so I tried "e".' With a cocky smile she said, 'That's what you pay me for.'

John shook his head, smiling in disbelief.

Matthew squeezed her shoulder lovingly. 'What would we do without you? You deserve a raise,' he beamed.

'I know,' she replied, smiling.

* * *

Matthew tapped a pen on the corner of his wooden L-shaped desk. He had called two of the Joseph Mullens on the list Clara had printed from the search engine. Another dead end.

He tried the last number on the list. He felt the hairs on the back of his neck rise. Everything rested on this conversation; it was the last lead they had. 'Hello, can I speak to Joseph Mullen please?'

'Who's this?' a young female voice with a strong Georgian accent said.

'My name is Matthew Brennan. I am an attorney in Birchwood County.'

'A-ha and what you want with my cousin?'

Matthew stopped tapping his pen. 'I was wondering if I could speak to Joseph?'

'What he do?'

'Oh no he's not in any trouble. Actually I was hoping he could help me solve a case I am working on. Do you know where Joseph is?'

'A-ha. But I don't think he'll be any help to you.'

He could hear voices in the background.

'Listen I can't talk now.'

'Please don't hang up, Miss Mullen. It is vital I speak to your cousin. Any information you have about your cousin's whereabouts will be a great help.' He could hear the girl breathing over the line. 'Please?'

'Fine. You like eggs Mr. Brennan?'

He tilted his head, a confused look on his face. 'Yes.'

'Good, we own a farm just off Adam's called The Grove. Come by later and I'll tell you everything you need to know.'

'Is that in Mayhaw County?'

'A-ha. 1825 the Grove.'

He scribbled the address onto his notepad.

*　　*　　*

Matthew and John traveled west along Hopeland Street, toward Beachhead Road, in the direction of Mayhaw County.

'Would you look at that?' John cried.

Row upon row of pecan trees lined the two-lane blacktop road. Farmers chugged back and forth in their tractors, with their Combines in tow, collecting cotton from the fields.

'I love summer, don't you?' John said. 'Ever' one running here and there collectin' corn and cotton. Eatin' ripe peach cobbler and homemade pecan pie,' he grinned.

Yes. Matthew thought. *Summer is grand, except for the kamikaze gnats that fly at you left and right.* He slapped his neck.

After four miles, John turned right into Adam's Street. They traveled along the dirt road, leaving a trail of dust behind them, bouncing over pot-holes until they reached a small dirt track to the left of an old oak tree.

'This must be it?' John said, in a kind of question kind of answer tone.

Matthew looked at the address he had ripped from his notepad. '1825 The Grove,' he replied, reading from the note.

John turned cautiously into the small one-lane dirt track, being careful of any oncoming traffic. 'Start praying that any oncoming vehicles aren't of an enormous size, OK?'

Matthew chuckled.

Trees and bushes lined the track, blocking out the baking sun. Three squirrels sheltered in the shade and John's slow approach startled them.

'It's clearing; I can see a house up ahead.' Matthew said as he leaned out the window.

The Mullen's owned a run-down farmhouse toward the end of Adam's Street in-between Billows Creek and Newton. The Grove had been in their family for three generations and Edith Mullen's father now owned the farmhouse.

John pulled up in front of the farmhouse slowly, making sure he didn't hit any wandering chickens. They waddled along the dirt road in front of the Caprice; clucking loudly at the inconvenience of having to move from their eating spot under the shade.

Matthew and John stepped out of the car and looked around the yard. A rusted station wagon sat in an overgrowth of grass and weeds at the side of the track. Next to the car were some old children's bicycles and a broken chicken coop.

John stepped on the porch. He approached the front door cautiously. Matthew followed.

The wooden boards creaked and vibrated with every movement begging them to get off. John knocked at the screen door eagerly.

Matthew cleared his throat. He gave John a look of desperation. They both looked down. 'I hope these boards hold?' Matthew rested a supporting hand on the doorframe, just in case.

'I got it Grandma,' a female voice behind the door yelled.

Footsteps approached the front door and with a loud creak, the door opened. A tall skinny girl stood in the doorway. Matthew figured she was around twenty-years-old. Her short bobbed afro had seen its weekly visit to Betty's hairdresser's and was relaxed to perfection.

'Mr. Brennan, I presume?' she said, smiling. 'You're on time.'

'Miss Mullen?' he replied, softly. 'This is my associate, John Beaumont.'

'Edith, call me Edith.' The girl did not smile, just nodded.

An elderly voice mumbled in the background. Edith turned around then yelled, 'It's OK Grandma, just those lawyers wantin' to buy some eggs, I'll show them out.'

Edith turned toward face them. 'Follow me. I just made tea, you want some?'

They welcomed the young girl's offer and followed her out into the yard at the side of the house, thankful to be on safe ground.

An oak tree towered over the patio. A wooden rectangular table and four chairs sat under the tree's shade. A red and white coloured square cloth lay neatly over the table with a silver tray placed on top. A tall jug of lemonade waited patiently to be poured out.

They took a seat and Edith poured the tea into awaiting glasses.

'I'll be right back,' she said and disappeared into the house through the side entrance.

Matthew looked around the elegant looking yard. 'The yard doesn't look as if it's part of the same house, does it?'

'Naw,' John took a sip from the glass in front of him. 'Just the way I like it.' he said, catching his breath. He placed his empty glass back onto the table.

The side door opened and Edith appeared, pushing an elderly woman in a wheelchair. Matthew guessed the woman was her grandmother.

She was in her early seventies, wearing long baggy pants and a pink over blouse. The neckline had a lace design around the edges. A huge pink summer hat tamed her wiry silver hair.

Pearl earrings hung from her earlobes; they caught the side of her neck as she moved.

Edith placed the occupied wheelchair under the oak tree. She handed a glass of tea to the woman before taking a seat opposite Matthew and John.

'I'll get right to it Edith,' Matthew said. 'We're here to ask you some questions about your cousin, Joseph Mullen?'

'OK?' Edith poured more lemonade into John's empty glass.

'Thank you,' John replied. 'Does your cousin reside in the Et Lanna area?'

'Used to.'

Matthew made eyes at John before turning back to Edith. 'We really need to speak to him, have you got a contact number for him?'

Edith shook her head defiantly.

'Please, a woman's life depends on what Joseph knows.'

'It don't matter what Joe knows.' The voice came from across the lawn where the elderly woman sat under the tree.

They turned to acknowledge her.

She raised her summer hat elegantly. Rays of sunlight danced in her deep brown eyes.

Despite her appearance, she had a youthful and vibrant tone to her voice. 'He dead. He was killed in May of this year. Drive by shooting.' The woman leaned forward.

151

'Where were you *lawyers* when he bleeding on the streets? I didn't see y'all come to buy no eggs then?'

Chapter Twenty-Eight

'He's dead!' Matthew's voice echoed around the interview room. 'Joseph Mullen died during a gangland shooting four months ago, six blocks from your house, convenient huh?'

'No! I hired him.' She slammed her fist onto the table.

'You hired him?' John asked, confused.

'Yes as a handyman, I told you!'

'Well, I hope the pastor who buried Joseph Mullen knows there's an empty coffin in his churchyard on Mondays, Wednesday and Fridays. I'll tell him Joseph Mullen is in the habit of working as a handyman on those days!' Matthew's voice bellowed. 'I'll tell the pastor to keep an eye out for his corpse, roaming around your neighborhood!'

'That's enough!' John's voice echoed around the room.

There was silence for a moment. Matthew stood sucking in the air by the window. He clenched his fingers into fists.

'Tell us exactly when you hired him?' John asked, calmly.

'Eight weeks before this happened. He was working for me three days a week until Stephen and I broke up. Then out-of-the-blue Joe called me and told me he couldn't work for me anymore.'

'Why?' John asked.

She shrugged. 'I don't know. He just told me he couldn't work for me anymore.'

John looked at Matthew and gestured for them to leave the room, with a tilt of his head.

Leaning against the corridor wall John whispered, 'I think you should cut a deal.'

Matthew placed his hands into his pockets wearily.

John shrugged. 'Hey, it wouldn't be the first time we've defended a guilty client.' He straightened his back.

Matthew told John about the conversation he had had with Sheriff Drano at the Atlanta police department. 'Now, this *Killer J* dude has connections. What if this Joseph Mullen was hired by this gang leader to kill Stephen?' He suddenly felt as if he was clutching at straws. His *other version* of events sounded better in his head.

John shook his head. 'Stephen was planning to tell Sally's husband about their affair for Chrissake. She would have lost everything.' He placed a comforting hand onto Matthew's shoulder. 'Cut a deal.'

* * *

'Helen, the governor will see you now,' said a female clerk.

She stood and buttoned her blue jacket. She held her briefcase in her right hand, making her way swiftly to the governor's office.

Governor Francis smiled warmly. 'Helen, have a seat,' she said, with a thick Georgian accent.

Governor Francis was unattractive with beady eyes, thick glasses and a splotchy complexion.

She was born into a devoutly religious family and carried the Bible everywhere. She was never married and never wanted to date. Gossip circled years ago, she was in love once with a cable repair man. He ran off with a younger more attractive woman, leaving her bitter, resentful and power-crazed.

Helen placed her briefcase on the floor and took a seat opposite the governor's oak desk.

'You know why you're here,' the governor leaned forward, 'How is the case going?'

Helen smiled. 'I'll get a conviction.'

The governor lifted the latest copy of the *Birchwood County Times* from her desk. 'I see you've already done what we spoke about.'

'Yes.'

The governor frowned and interlocked her fingers, resting them on the desk. 'I thank we need to raise the bar on this matter to be absolutely certain of the outcome. We must thank about my voters who will one day if you continue as discussed, be yours.' She cocked her head.

Helen could not help but compare the Governor to a leap-of-faith healer. She sat up. 'But Governor I've already stated that I will get a conviction.' She could not disguise how offended she was in voice. After all, she had done exactly what was asked of her, why did she need to do more?

A knock at the door disturbed Helen's contemplation.

'Come in,' Governor Francis said. 'Why are you here?'

Helen turned to see Deputy Patterson standing in the doorway.

'I-I mean,' the governor cleared her throat. 'Helen, why don't we continue this conversation at another time?' She smiled wickedly. 'Ted, have a seat.'

*　*　*

'Thanks for meeting me.' Sarah-Jane squeezed herself along the booth, opposite John.

She was wearing a tight fitted black dress and white canvas shoes. A row of cream beads surrounded the nape of her neck.

'You said you had some information?' John took a handful of peanuts casually, from a small basket on the table in front of him.

'I remembered something about the man I told you about on the phone the other day.'

He placed the peanuts into his mouth. 'OK?'

'I saw him about a week before the shooting. He got into a black Jeep and headed in the direction of the freeway.' She shivered. 'He gave me the creeps.'

He could not help but noticed how soft her skin looked in the Tavern bar's dim lighting. 'Would you recognize him again if you saw him?'

She nodded. 'I think so.'

He raised his eyebrows. 'Would you be willing to testify?'

Her smile faded. Her eyes became glassy. 'No I can't testify. The only reason I'm telling you this is because I want to help you.' She unraveled her legs, grabbing her purse. 'You're a nice guy. Please don't make me testify?' She stood, charging toward the exit sign.

He followed her into the parking lot. He grabbed her arm pulling her close to him. Sobbing, she sank into his chest.

'Is someone threatening you?' he asked after a long silence.

Biting her lower lip, she looked deeply into his brown eyes. 'Please I just wanna go home.'

He kissed her forehead. 'I'll drive you. Is there someone at home, I don't think you're in any state to be alone tonight.'

She nodded, wiping the tears from her cheeks. 'Yes, my roommate Amanda.'

He pulled out of the parking bay and headed toward her house two miles away.

'I'm sorry,' she said, sheepishly. 'I'm just a little jumpy lately.' She blew her nose. 'I was followed the other night by a red pickup; I couldn't see who was driving.'

He shot her a look. 'Why would someone be following you?'

She folded her arms, shivering. 'I've been getting calls too.'

He reached behind, pulling his jacket from the backseat, and draped it over her shoulders. 'What do you know Sarah-Jane? Talk to me. I can protect you.'

She sighed heavily. 'There's my house. Thanks for the ride.' She handed him his jacket. 'Night.'

Before he could say anymore, Sarah-Jane hurried from the car toward her front door.

Chapter Twenty-Nine

Matthew took his seat in the courtroom. He placed his briefcase in front of him, took out two red files, and placed them to one side.

The courtroom was crowded. He had never seen such enthusiasm for voir dire and wondered what the trial would be like.

Reporters lined the gallery; their heads were down with looks of narrowed concentration on their faces.

It seemed the entire Birchwood County police department had taken up the first half of the courtroom. They whispered and nudged, with occasional glares in Matthew and Sally's direction.

He opened his trial notebook and flipped the index tab marked *Jury*. He took out his biro and studied his notes. He wanted as many young single women as possible, hard-working mothers, gun owners and anyone who appeared to be unbiased against switching religions, which in itself was going to be difficult.

During a capital case in Georgia, the court impanels forty-two jurors for the state, and the defense to strike jurors.

Because the state announced its intention to seek the death penalty, each side was entitled to fifteen peremptory challenges.

'Sally Martinez is charged with first degree murder and assault on a police officer. The indictment was returned by the grand jury for the state of Georgia.' Judge Chamberlain had begun the voir dire process by asking the usual string of critical questions to the mass of prospective jurors. They had already answered several questions pertaining to their qualifications to serve as jury members.

The last eighty people sat in the gallery in uncomfortable silence, only daring to speak when spoken to.

The judge gave the order for the clerk to continue. She read off twelve names, and the courtroom became animated with movement. They filed down the runway, through the partition and into the jury box.

'Does anyone on the panel know the defendant?' Three hands shot up. They were excused subsequently from the courtroom. 'Does anyone know the victim?' No hands rose. 'Has anyone been the victim of a crime?' Five hands shot up. 'Does anyone have a policeman as a relative?' Two hands rose slowly as if they were confessing to having the plague.

Both lawyers made notes and studied the potential jury member's body language like picking the best athlete for their team.

Matthew narrowed his eyes. *Would number nine be sympathetic? What about number four's body language - did he just clench his fist? Why is number seven smiling?* He thought.

It was a grueling process and after three hours, Matthew found himself doodling in his notepad.

At quarter to one, both attorneys had run out of challenges and a panel of twelve jurors and six alternates remained.

The alternate jurors had gone through the same procedure and examination as the chosen panel. When selecting alternate jurors, both sides were allowed additional peremptory challenges.

Matthew was disappointed with the outcome of the chosen panel. He was faced with eight males, the majority of which were married, and only four females, two of which were single.

* * *

Matthew and John drank cups of water from the cooler in Matthew's office. 'I got another letter,' he said, showing John the blue typed paper. He wiped the sweat from his forehead with the back of his sleeve.

'Is it from the same writing set?'

Matthew frowned. 'Yeah, it's the same.'

'Probably just some nut.'

Matthew screwed the paper into a tight ball and threw it into the Trash Can. 'Ok, we don't have much time. The trial is in less than two weeks, and we only have two witnesses.' He sat at his desk. He was careful not to sit too far back until the manufactured air had had a chance to dry his sweat-laced shirt.

He rested his chin onto his knuckles and tilted his head toward the mountain of memory sticks next to his computer monitor. 'Let's concentrate on the other state witnesses.' He scratched his face. 'Clara found out the witnesses from Atlanta have been given rooms at the Quality Inn, obviously the D.A intends to call them.'

'Have you spoken to Sally about them?' John placed a stick of nicotine gum in his mouth.

'She's clueless. My guess, these witnesses,' Matthew ran down the list to the witness's names. 'Mr. Newson and Mr. Kirkland must know something about the affair; maybe they saw Sally and Stephen together? Anyway, find out what they know. I'll concentrate on the trial.'

'Did you request a change of venue?'

'Denied.' Matthew took a candy bar from the drawer on his right.

'Are you gonna request that the jury be sequestered?'

Matthew nodded and looked down at a copy of the *Birchwood County Times* sitting in front of him. 'Yeah he has to grant it,' he said in a question- answer tone. 'I can't believe this?' He stared at the headline. Anti-Islamist organization takes to the streets.

John shook his head. 'Everyone's talking about it. Apparently they're gathering downtown for a protest march tomorrow.'

Matthew rolled his eyes. 'What are they protesting?'

'Islamization of America.' John nodded at the newspaper. 'They think if Sally's released then Muslim extremists will take over the town. Mosques will go up everywhere, and Islamic schools will be built here in town.'

Matthew shook his head. 'What a load of media-fueled horse shit.'

'I know it and you know it, but I tell ya, folks around here…' John sighed. 'I'm sure the University students will have something to say about all this.'

'What do you mean?'

'I can't see them letting the AIO have all the publicity – they'll march against them.' John sighed again. 'It'll be carnage.' He shook his head. 'I'll go talk to the witnesses.' He gulped the remnants of his water and headed for the stairs.

Matthew tapped his biro on the newspaper. 'I'll call the judge.'

* * *

'What about this one, aunt Anna?' Elizabeth pointed at a shelf of stuffed toys in Randy's toy store.

161

The toy animals were displayed in color coded order. Pink elephants sat on the top shelf, yellow horses on the next row and a collection of assorted colored teddy bears on the bottom.

Elizabeth had picked up a blue bear wearing a white T-shirt. It had the word 'daddy' embroidered in the center.

'Oh, Lizzie he's so cute. Uncle Matt will love him. Good job.' Anna beamed. She held the three inch toy. 'Let's pay for him. How about we go get some ice-cream?'

'Yay!' The children yelled in unison.

They walked along South Hall Road. The street was filled with shoppers who suddenly stopped in their tracks; their vulture-like eyes fixed on the children.

'Why do people keep staring at us, Aunt Anna?' Elizabeth held Anna's hand tightly.

Anna comforted Elizabeth stroking the pink embroidered Hijab covering her head. 'Take no notice, sweetheart.' She exaggerated her smile at passersby. They glared, shaking their heads and whispering to each other.

A shiver ran up Anna's spine.

'What's wrong, Aunt Anna?' Elizabeth said, looking behind them.

Anna stopped, looking over her shoulder. 'Oh, it's nothing. I thought I saw someone following us.' She patted Elizabeth's hand. Smiling she said, 'It's nothing. Let's go back to Grandma's OK.'

'But what about the ice-cream?' Thomas pouted.

Anna smiled. 'We'll have some at home, OK?'

They turned into Goodland's Avenue, heading toward the Brennan home. Anna brushed her hair away from her eyes. She could not escape the feeling someone was watching her. She folded her arms across her stomach. 'Stay close Thomas. Don't run off.'

Chapter Thirty

'Did you find out anything?' Matthew asked. He replaced a dictionary onto the book case behind the conference room desk.

'Mr. Kirkland - what a guy.' John perched on the end of the table. 'Cost me fifteen bucks.'

'Fifteen bucks - what for?'

'I had to buy him lunch before he would talk.'

'How many was it for?'

'Just him.' John shook his head. He pulled out his notebook from his shirt pocket. 'OK, he quit college in '83 and enrolled into the army. Did a seven year stint before being discharged. He had a series of jobs before becoming the Pleasant View motel manager in Et Lanna.' He took his eyes from the pages and placed his foot up, resting it on the chair. 'He claims he rented out a suite to the deceased every Friday night, and Stephen always paid cash. Our Mr. Kirkland claims he was under strict instructions not to disturb the, and he quoted this,' John raised his fingers and mimed quotation brackets. '"lovers", said he saw the deceased with the same woman and identified her as Sally Martinez.'

'What about the other witness?'

'Mr. Newson hasn't arrived in town yet. I'll go back later.'

Matthew stood by the window, staring at the reporters coming out of the county jail. 'I spoke with Mrs. Moore - Sally's employer - she is available to testify. Clara is sending her a subpoena.'

'Have you thought anymore about putting our beloved client on the stand?'

Matthew pondered a moment and put his hands into his pockets. 'I don't know?'

John leaned back, folding his arms. 'So, any luck with the judge?'

Matthew noticed Deputy Patterson whispering in the governor's ear as they stood across the street. 'Yeah, he's sequestered the jury with no objections.'

'Any idea who's stirring up all this Muslim-brainwashing crap?'

Matthew ran his tongue across his teeth, making a sucking sound. 'Yeah, I have a pretty good idea.' He did not take his eyes away from Patterson.

* * *

At quarter past two, Wednesday afternoon, an officer of the court took the jury to the outskirts of Birchwood County, where they remained in a hunting lodge until the Judge summoned them to court.

They were not allowed to watch television or make any phone calls, which disgruntled them further. Some settled for a friendly card game while others shuffled through old magazines and crossword puzzles.

'They should just ask us what our verdict is now,' Juror number three, Casey Bennett, said. He placed the ace of spades on the table. 'Guilty.'

'The trial hasn't even started yet Mr...?' Juror number seven, Hannah Millstein, said. She raised her eyebrows, pursing her lips waiting for his reply.

He didn't look at her, just continued playing cards. 'Bennett and I ain't interested in no introductions.' He picked up the queens of hearts. 'I just wanna get outta here - I got a wife.'

'Listen,' Juror number two, Tatiana Grover, said, 'We all got places we wanna be but we're here. There's no need to be rude about it.' She snatched a mirror from her purse and checked her appearance. 'I say let's hear the evidence first before condemning somebody to death row.'

'I ain't interested in what you gotta say,' Casey tut-tutted. 'The bitch deserves it,' he leaned back in his chair. 'Even her husband says they should gas her.'

* * *

Anna started the engine. She waved to Linnie and the children as they stood on the porch in front of her.

She turned the radio on and drove out of Barn Mead, onto South Hall Road. She had decided to prepare a romantic meal and break the news of her pregnancy to Matthew. *Maybe the blow won't be so hard for him once he sees how much effort I put into the evening?* She thought.

Hypnotized silver eyes flew past. The headlights pierced through the darkness. A few specks of rain hit the windshield before falling suddenly from the sky like projectiles from the gods, the dry cracked road their target.

Angry spears of lightning sliced through the purple clouds creating serrated yellow edges across the sky.

She flicked the windshield wipers. They flitted frantically from one side to the other, trying desperately to clear her vision, to no avail.

She lifted her foot from the gas pedal. She was now doing thirty in a fifty zone.

Headlights approached in the rear view mirror. Pressing on the brakes lightly, she hoped the lunatic would pass her. The headlights became invisible as the Volvo was rammed. 'What the…?' A small cry escaped from her throat.

The Volvo swerved. She tried to control the spin, turning the wheel frantically left then right.

Headlights appeared then disappeared again as the Volvo was hit for the second time.

Chapter Thirty-One

Matthew had decided to have a night off. Part of him knew Anna was feeling neglected. He had not taken any notice of the work she had done on their yard. Tonight he would show her that he appreciated her efforts to make their new house a home.

Flicking his wrist, he opened the throttle. He hoped the trip to the mall had taken longer than Anna had anticipated, so he could beat her home.

In the distance, he could see flashing red and blue lights. He released his grip on the throttle; the Buell slowed to a walking pace.

Deputy Easton stood next to a road block. He stuck out his arm, instructing Matthew to stop.

'What's happened?' Matthew's voice was muffled from the confinement of his helmet. He could see an ambulance and two patrol vehicles parked opposite an oak tree.

'Hit and run,' Easton replied.

Matthew nodded and did a U-turn before flicking his wrist on the throttle.

'Wait Matt!' Easton yelled behind Matthew.

Matthew parked his motorcycle in the garage. He took off his helmet, placing it on the seat to look at his watch. 8:30pm.

The detour home had added another twenty minutes onto the journey. He narrowed his eyes at the empty driveway. An uneasy feeling twisted in his stomach.

The phone rang. Matthew stumbled up the garage steps, through the kitchen to the hall. He answered the phone just before the last ring. 'Anna?'

'Matt? It's Linnie.'

'Linnie?' He tried to hide the fact he was worried. 'What's up?'

'Oh, Matt. We're at the hospital.'

Matthew swallowed hard.

'There's been an accident.'

Chapter Thirty-Two

Matthew rose from the antiseptic plastic chair as the waiting room door opened. He hoped it was Doctor Holmes with some news on Anna's condition.

Elizabeth and Thomas entered carrying some candy from the store on the first floor.

'What's taking so long?' Matthew sighed, impatiently.

'I'm sure the doctor will see us soon,' Linnie replied, placing Thomas on her knee.

'We've been here for forty-five minutes and no one has said anything.' Matthew paced back and forth. 'I can't stand this anymore. I'm going to get some coffee - anyone want some?'

Nine Styrofoam cups sat on the small round pine table. The contents of the cups had been removed an hour ago.

Matthew stood by the window. Tiny white specks of foam lay at his feet. He did not know when he had started to dismember the cup. He put its remains on the table and rubbed the back of his head.

Doctor Holmes entered the waiting room. He was tall and slender with slick backed brown hair. A green tie showed through the opening of his white overcoat. 'Matthew?' he said.

Matthew walked toward him. 'How is she Doc? Is she going to be…?' He tried to compose himself, remembering saying those very words the last time he stood in the waiting room.

Doctor Holmes held Matthew's hand firmly. 'I'm sorry Matt...' he sighed, making eye contact. 'Anna lost her baby.'

Matthew froze. The words floated around in his head, not registering in his mind. He sank to the floor.

'She'll be all right though, Doc. Won't she?' Arthur asked, worryingly. He gripped an empty Styrofoam cup in his hand; it cracked under the pressure.

'She has a few nasty cuts and bruises and she's pretty shaken. She will have to stay in for observation until tomorrow,' Doctor Holmes replied. 'You can see her now.' He patted Matthew on the back. 'I'm truly, deeply sorry.'

Linnie wiped her tears. 'Matt, I ain't got the words.' She walked toward him, hugging him tightly.

Matthew tried to comprehend what was going on. 'Would you mind if I go in to see her first?' He whispered.

'Take all the time you need.' Linnie sniffed. 'We'll wait here, OK?'

Matthew approached a closed door at the end of the corridor. Room 23. He could see Anna through the tiny window in the door. She was lying in the hospital bed, facing the window.

He tried to control each jelly-like step as he made his way toward her. His palms were sticky with sweat.

Anna rolled over to face him. Her face was pale and drawn. The left side of her forehead was covered in band aids. Her cheeks glistened with tears. 'Oh, Matt,' she sobbed.

He rushed to her, taking her in his arms, trying to hold back the tears.

'Why is this happening to us?' She gripped her stomach. As if a simulated kick beat against her abdomen. 'I'm so sorry, Matt…. I'm so very sorry.'

Chapter Thirty-Three

Anna's grief-stricken face replayed in Matthew's mind. He would never forget the pain in her eyes. He was sure it would haunt him forever.

The house was eerily silent.

He wandered into the kitchen and sat at the breakfast bar, resting his head in his hands.

Part of him hoped the paper bag Linnie gave him had a bottle of Jack Daniels inside.

Rocky groaned loudly. He looked in the direction of the front door.

'She ain't there!' he snapped. 'Dumb dog! Why D'you have to be so stupid? I hate you.' He grabbed the paper bag from the counter and placed his hand inside, revealing a blue teddy bear. Daddy.

Rocky nudged Matthew's arm.

He pushed Rocky away. 'Leave me alone. Fuckin' dog!' Rocky cowered, his ears back and his head bowed.

Matthew stared at his faithful friend. 'Jesus. I'm sorry Rocky.' A sharp twisting pain shot through his chest. 'I should've been with her.' he said, sinking to the floor.

Rocky approached, licking Matthew's face, tasting the tears on his cheek.

All you need is a drink. A voice inside his head said. It was so comforting, he had to listen. *That will ease your pain, help you cope better.*

He stood using the kitchen stall as his prop. He pulled out a plate of leftovers from the refrigerator. 'Here. Knock yourself out,' he said, placing the plate on the floor in front of Rocky.

Just one glass. He was in a sudden state of euphoria. The voice sounded like music, warm, smooth and hypnotic.

He jumped as the phone blasted in the hall. He hesitated, waiting for his heartbeat to restore itself, and placed the phone to his ear.

'Your wife's accident was a warning,' the voice threatened. 'Drop the case or she dies.'

The dialing tone pierced Matthew's ears. With one sweeping motion, he ripped the phone from the wall.

He hunted for money, throwing cushions from the sofa, he dug deep. Nothing. 'Where would she hide it?' He scratched his head desperately. 'Upstairs.'

He found a safety deposit box in a cupboard in his room. It was locked and he could not find the key. A ferocious noise escaped from his frustrated lips. He punched the wooden closet door before flying downstairs to the garage. He snatched a tool kit from the shelf; storage boxes fell to the floor, spilling their contents. The picture of the blonde boy came to a halt at his feet.

'Bobby!' Tears streaked his face; his breath was rapid and shallow.

Sweat laced his brow and trickled down his neck. His heart slammed against his ribcage. With tremendous force, he prized open the safety deposit box and snatched the small wad of cash from inside.

Chapter Thirty-Four

Matthew sat in the Tavern bar. He held his seventh Jack Daniels. He stared at the blue bear sorrowfully and drowned the tears with one smooth flick of his wrist. He swallowed hard and ordered another.

'Don't you think you've had enough, Matt?' the barman asked.

'Just pour the drink,' Matthew replied, holding up his glass.

'Well, what do we have here?' Patterson leaned back, placing the beer bottle to his lips. 'Look at him – loser!'

The small crowd turned to face the person their friend sneered at.

'He's nothing but a lowlife drunk.' Patterson raised his voice above the jukebox. 'Lowlife drunk!'

Matthew turned to see where the jeering was coming from.

Patterson took another swig. Placing the bottle on the table in front of him he said, 'Pathetic lowlife. How can that wife of his stand it? She needs a real man.' He crossed his legs. 'I bet he can't keep her satisfied. I know what she needs,' he tugged on the crotch of his jeans, 'and I've got it right here.'

Outraged, Matthew staggered toward them.

'What are you gonna do?' Patterson laughed. 'You can't even walk straight.' He took a swing, knocking Matthew to the ground.

Matthew staggered to his feet, gesturing for Patterson to hit him again with a nod. Patterson took another swing. Matthew ducked, punching him in the stomach with tremendous force. Matthew's anger exploded through his clenched fist. It felt good.

The barman grabbed a rifle from under the bar and stormed over to the rowdy group. 'Take that outside,' he demanded.

He flashed them his .243 Winchester. The satin finish and the elegantly cut checkering reflected the lamps hanging on the wall.

The fat one helped Patterson to his feet.

'This ain't over Brennan,' Patterson threatened, trying to catch his breath. He clutched his stomach.

The barman tugged on the bolt handle and loaded the rifle.

'Take it easy, grandpa. We're leavin',' the taller one said, holding up his hands defensively.

Matthew staggered toward the men's room. The chairs, stacked on tables at the back of the bar, supported him. He fell against the back wall. Finally, he reached the men's room, ready to vomit.

He cleaned himself with a paper towel and stared at his sullen bloodshot eyes in the small mirror above the sink. His face was pale and subversive. He sighed heavily.

A maroon bruise began to appear across his right cheekbone. His lip stung with tension.

With his head hung low, he smashed his fist against the mirror. It spider webbed from the center to the end of its frame.

The cool night air brushed his cheek as he crossed the parking lot to his motorcycle.

174

'No!' He stared wide-eyed.

The floodlight reflected on the carcass from above.

His eyes filled with tears. He stood shaking in the shadows. Holding his breath unconsciously, he fell to his knees. He picked his helmet from the floor, holding it in his right hand, and stared at the blistered fragments of plastic fly screen, pieces of aluminium swing-arm and handle bar deflectors. His motorcycle lay in pieces. He threw his helmet, watching it bounce on the pavement.

Chapter Thirty-Five

Matthew opened his eyes slowly. He was fully clothed, minus his shoes and socks, lying on a brown leather sofa.

The morning sun pierced through the curtains, revealing tiny dust particles around the room. He squinted, trying to make out where the hell he was and how he had got there.

He tried to move. The room circled around him like the tail end of a twister. 'Ooh!' He lifted his hand and placed it to his forehead. He decided it was better to survey the room from a lying position.

Above him, hung on the yellow painted walls, was a twenty-two inch gold framed oil painting. It appeared to be a small town somewhere in Europe. He could not read the artist's name.

Two tall narrow windows, framed in white skirting borders, were on either side of the painting. The light came from a third window to the right of the sofa. Its beige drapes were drawn and held back with silver ties.

Almost immediately Matthew recognized the school photographs on top of an antique wooden almirah, to the right of the third window. The almirah stood elegantly against the far wall behind a small matching square coffee table.

The photographs were of three girls and a boy. The girls looked exactly like their father, toothy grins revealing perfect teeth. The boy had more of a typical seven-year-old smile, two front teeth missing awaiting the birth of his adult set.

Matthew rested back against the safety of the cushion. With every small movement he made, his stomach churned. 'Oh.' He burped. He had forgotten what it was like to have a hangover.

'How are you feeling?' John asked. He crossed the beige rug on the living room floor and handed Matthew a glass of water and a vitamin supplement.

Matthew coughed but did not reply. His mouth was dehydrated, his throat sizzled. He placed the glass to his lips. The water chilled his throat and trickled down. It joined the stomach walls in their galactic efforts to become the next human washing machine.

John sat in front of him on the edge of the coffee table. 'Last night was my fault, I'm sorry. I shouldn't have left you alone.'

'You weren't to know about Anna. I should have called you.' Matthew gripped at his hair, pulling on it out of frustration. 'I am losing myself. I can feel myself slipping away again,' tears formed in his eyes. 'I feel like I'm running; sweat is streaming down my face, my body aches but I feel like I'm accomplishing a lot so I run faster,' his voice croaked. 'Suddenly I look ahead expecting to see the finish line; instead I realize I'm on a fucking treadmill in the same dark room.' His voice faded with fatigue.

John grimaced. 'I know buddy, I know.'

*   *   *

Helen collected the software from the "computer whiz". A compilation disc of the precise locations of the patrol car, the back entrance of Ned's bar and diner, and where Sally's car was parked in relationship to them.

She proceeded to the photographic store along Hanover Street to collect the 210 x 297mm color photographs of Sally's bronco.

Chester would collect the photographs of Stephen's corpse, once they were enlarged appropriately.

Matthew had filed a motion in Limine requesting the photographs of Stephen's body be excluded; Chamberlain had denied the request.

She sat, drinking tea in Bella's Coffeeshop.

The photographs of Sally's bronco and the disc, sealed in a manila envelope, sat on the table in front of her; she placed a careful hand on the envelope.

The coffeeshop was full of reporters, locals waited outside to be seated. The sound of idle chitchat bounced off the walls relentlessly. Helen could not help but eavesdrop.

'D'you hear she does naked rituals in her cell at night?' One woman muttered in the booth behind Helen.

'I know, it's wrong,' replied another woman. 'I believe in the King James' Bible, Exodus 22:17: "you should not let a sorceress live". I say gas her before she bewitches our town!'

Helen sipped her orange juice before taking a bite of her bagel.

'What do you think Helen?' A female voice asked.

'About what, Mary-Sue?'

'About poor Anna Brennan?'

Confused, she studied Mary-Sue's chubby face. She could see anxiety flash in Mary-Sue's green eyes. 'What about Anna Brennan?' she asked.

'You haven't heard?' Mary-Sue perched herself in front of Helen. She told Helen about Anna's accident involving a hit and run driver and the loss of Anna's baby.

For a moment, she was frozen. 'I did not know Anna was pregnant,' she mumbled.

178

'Neither did Matt. Apparently he was seen staggering from the Tavern last night. You better change your number again – he'll be wanting to know where Bobby is.' Mary-Sue placed a hand on her hip. 'His grave looks wonderful-all those flowers you planted. By the way, how is the leukemia fundraiser going?'

'Good. We've raised $3,000 dollars.'

Mary-Sue nodded, standing from the booth.

Helen took her by the arm. 'Has Anna been allowed out of hospital yet?'

'Not yet, Doctor Holmes is keeping her in for observation.' Mary-Sue frowned. 'I wouldn't be surprised if her brainwashed sister had something to do with it.' She pulled a face. 'They do that, you know? Conjure up the devil they do. I think she put a curse on Anna.'

Helen nodded and began picking at her bagel with a sullen expression.

* * *

Pastor Jones handed a placard to Deputy Patterson. He took it proudly, showing off the words painted in red: To embrace Islam is to embrace Murder.

'Now, let's take our message to the people – the world will hear us!' Jones' voice echoed through the microphone over the speakers. The crowd cheered, waving their Star Spangled Banners and blowing whistles.

* * *

'I've made some breakfast,' John looked at his watch. 'Well, lunch. You have to eat buddy - keep your blood sugar levels up.'

'Thanks for last night,' Matthew croaked. 'Letting me stay here.'

179

'Hey, don't go gettin' all mushy on me. How 'bout a summer fruit smoothie?'

Matthew rubbed his head. 'I can't eat.'

'What you need is a good ole dose of vitamins to get you goin',' John replied, handing him a tall glass and a spoon.

'Oh it'll get me goin' alright,' Matthew replied, sarcastically. 'Goin' right to the bathroom. You actually eat that stuff?'

John nodded with a huge grin on his face, unfazed by Matthew's comment. 'Pete's taken care of the bike.'

Matthew nodded. He scooped deep purple mush from the glass and dared himself to eat it.

'Clara rang. The judge wants to see you at his home,' John said, sorrowfully.

Matthew sighed.

'I'm sorry buddy.' John took a seat on the arm chair to the left of Matthew. 'I interviewed the motel clerk last night, the other witness on the state's list. He saw Sally get arrested. He heard her ask Sheriff Langford where he was taking her children. The clerk seemed to think she had no idea why she was being arrested.'

Matthew half nodded. He couldn't think about the trial right now, his brain was one mass of fog. He placed the glass onto the coffee table. He could not face another mouthful. 'Can I use your shower?'

'Sure, down the hall on the right. There's a change of clothes on my bed.'

* * *

Downtown was awash with bodies dressed in blue. Sheriff Langford lit a cigar and ordered his men to stop anyone parking down West Street until the peaceful protest march had finished.

Helen nodded. 'You're doing a good job, Sheriff.'

Langford smiled. 'Glad you think so, governor,' he gasped. 'Did I say that outta turn?'

She smiled wickedly.

'I must say I'm a little disappointed governor Francis couldn't be here to enjoy the show.'

Helen swallowed hard. 'She sent me to ensure victory and expects a full report.'

He nodded, taking a large drag on his cigar.

'Shall we put the barricades up, Sir?' Officer Ward said, with a hint of nervousness in her voice.

'No leave them in the van, we won't need them,' he replied.

Reporters rushed from their mini vans armed with their cameras and microphones. Some interviewed locals standing on the sidewalk outside Betty's hair salon, complete with hair curlers and tin foil.

The Anti-Islamist Organization exited the bus and gathered on the sidewalk like a colony of ants. Pastor Jones placed the megaphone to his lips. 'Thank you for standing together in solidarity and for believing in our lord Jesus Christ, now let us pray.'

The crowd stood in silent prayer.

'We shall be heard!' he bellowed after a pause.

The crowd cheered and marched toward the courthouse wearing Star Spangled Banners and waving caricature placards of Muhammad. They chanted in unison KILL THE TRAITOR to the beat of a drum.

Sheriff Langford's radio squawked. 'The protesters are coming Sir,' the female voice said.

Helen felt uneasy, but she smiled at the Sheriff when he looked at her.

Langford pressed the button on the side and spoke into the radio. 'Thanks Mills, look sharp.' He raised his eyebrows. 'Showtime.' He blew smoke into the air.

'Yes, Showtime indeed.' Helen tried to keep the contents of her stomach from exploding from her mouth.

Patterson tapped the Sheriff on the shoulder. 'Look, Sir.' He pointed to an army of University students counter marching from the opposite direction. Black, White, and Asian Muslims walked arm-in-arm from Hanover Street toward the sea of blue uniforms. They held placards with the words RIGHTS FOR ALL written on t-shirts. They chanted RIGHTS FOR ALL in perfect unison.

'Shit,' Langford said. 'Set up barricades now!'

Patterson and several other officers rushed to the sidewalk setting up barricades across the street to divide the two tribes.

Helen's stomach flipped as she stared at the hundred people coming toward her.

Kill the traitor! Kill the traitor!

Rights for All! Rights for all!

The opposing sides moved closer.

Chapter Thirty-Six

'Good luck, buddy,' John said from the driver's seat.

They sat outside Judge Chamberlain's home, two feet from the wrought iron entrance gates.

The judge lived six miles from Billows Creek in a newly built two-storey manor.

'Do I look OK?' Matthew asked, insecurely. He pulled at the yellow Hawaiian shirt John had laid out for him to wear.

John smiled. 'It looks good on you.'

Matthew doubted that, but under the circumstances, he thought a bit of color might win over the judge? 'I can't believe you had this in your closet?'

'It's my lucky shirt. That garment is what finally ended my last marriage,' John smiled warmly, all teeth and charm.

'Divorce by Hawaiian shirt - I would have loved to have been in the court room when that was filed.'

'It was a keeper. Now get going. Call me in an hour.'

Closing the gate behind him, Matthew wandered along the immaculate paved walk, leading to the judge's front door.

Three chimneys protruded from the gray rooftops like soldiers standing to attention.

A four car garage stood to the right of the L- shaped building with en suite guest rooms above it.

He walked past the colored flower beds; rows of pink, white and yellow, contrasted against a lush green lawn.

Patterson must have told him about last night. That bastard. How else could the judge have found out so quickly? He thought. He could play it safe - grovel or even beg to stay on the case. But he could not help but think that maybe he was not fit to continue.

He approached four white pillars to the double entrance doors. He could not help but notice how clean everything looked.

The maid came to the door. Dressed in a white uniform and apron, she resembled a Victorian nanny. 'His honor is on the deck. Follow me,' she announced.

He followed the maid down the entrance foyer, past a wrought iron staircase and several double stained-glass doors, to the end of the foyer, out on to the sun deck.

A barber attended to Judge Chamberlain, combing his gray hair and snipping away with his scissors. The barber applied the last finishing touches and the maid showed him out.

The judge instructed Matthew to sit at the wrought iron table with a slight hand gesture. A long uncomfortable silence followed.

Matthew kicked himself for allowing John to talk him into wearing the loudest shirt in John's closet. *What must the judge be thinking right now?* He thought, trying to read the judge's blank expression.

The judge took a sip from his fine china cup, swallowed, and then he looked Matthew in the eye. 'You were drunk last night.' His voice was stern.

'Yes, your honor and nothing can excuse my behavior.' Matthew took a breath when he realized he was talking too fast. 'I can only say that I am truly sorry. I've let myself, my family and my client down, I know that. Today is day one.'

Silence again. Matthew looked to the floor, anticipating an ear bashing.

'I have heard about your wife. I am sorry for your loss.' Chamberlain crossed his legs, leaning back in his chair. 'Put yourself in my position Matt,' he took a breath. 'What would you do?'

Matthew paused, shielding his eyes from the sun's glare. 'I am not qualified to make a judgment, your honor. I'll leave that in your capable hands. All I can say is regardless of my relapse,' he leaned forward. 'And that's all last night was a setback, my client will receive my full and utmost attention.'

The judge looked away, directing his attention to the pool house a few yards from the patio.

Agonizing seconds past and Matthew wondered how he should react when the judge fired him.

Finally, the judge looked at him. 'Matt, you're a good young lawyer, and I have faith that what you say is true. However, I am seriously thinking of declaring a mistrial on the grounds of incompetent counsel.'

'Your honor-'

The judge raised his eyebrows and with a stern expression said, 'Don't force my hand.' Chamberlain pointed to a copy of *The Birchwood County Times*. 'Have you heard about this protest?'

'Yes, your honor.'

Chamberlain frowned. 'These are dangerous times Matthew, dangerous times in deed.'

Matthew nodded. 'Yes, your honor.'

Chamberlain sighed heavily. 'It's like Nazi Germany.'

Matthew nodded, and he stood to leave.

The judge held up his hand. 'By the way Matt.'

Matthew smiled, hoping the judge would not suddenly change his mind about not declaring a mistrial.

'I like your shirt.'

'Thank you, your honor.' Matthew replied, sheepishly.

* * *

'I can't believe he didn't declare a mistrial!' John gave a quick glance from the driver's seat as they turned left onto West Street.

'Neither can I,' Matthew confessed. He eased his elbow out of the window, enjoying the warm air as it caressed his skin. 'Why do you think he didn't?'

John shrugged. 'Maybe because he wants this trial over with quickly. Did he say who told him?'

Matthew shot John a look of disbelief. 'Are you kidding?'

'Well I can guess who it was.'

Matthew nodded. 'Me too.'

'Unbelievable!' John stamped on the brake pedal. The Chevy skidded; the brakes squealed like an animal in pain.

Matthew stared wide-eyed at the sight in front of them. He sat frozen for a moment. 'I've never seen anything like it.'

Kill the Traitor!

Kill the traitor!

Rights for all!

Rights for all!

Lines of blue held back protesters outside the courthouse; flags of Muhammad burned on sticks high above their heads like blowtorches. A woman wearing a blue dress walked past the Chevy in a daze; blood trickled from her head, staining the dress purple.

Trash littered the streets like ugly confetti; protesters picked it up and threw it in the police officer's direction.

John looked at Matthew, his jaw dropped. 'It's like something out of a movie.'

'It's that traitor's lawyer!' A male protester said, picking up a glass bottle, throwing it in the Chevy's direction. The bottle flew over them, hurling through the church window at heightening speed.

Several protesters ran toward the Chevy armed with broken bottles and bricks.

Matthew swallowed hard and turned to face John. 'Go!'

John floored the gas pedal, doing the quickest U-turn possible. Another bottle was thrown and shattered on the roof of the Chevy. 'Jesus!'

'Hurry John!'

'I'll take Hopeland, we should be able to get through to the hospital from there,' he said, speeding south away from West Street. 'Let's hope we don't end up in there ourselves!'

'I thought the protest would've been over by now?' Matthew bit his fingernail trying to calm his shaking body. 'Did you see the look on that guy's face when he saw us?' he gave a nervous laugh.

'Yeah, I thought he was gonna kill us.' John shook his head. 'Man, I wish I had my camera when that bottle went through the church window,' he chuckled breathlessly, 'his face!' He cleared his throat.

'Yours was better!' Matthew's throat tightened with dryness. 'Are you OK?'

John swallowed hard, cleared his throat again and said, 'Yeah – are you OK Buddy?'

Matthew nodded as he stared at the dashboard. 'That was close, huh?'

John shot Matthew a look.

Arriving outside the hospital, John pulled into a parking space. 'I can't wait to see Anna's face when she sees you in that shirt.'

'You should have seen the judge's face,' he chuckled.

John laughed. 'I bet the first thing *ole Chamberlain* did when you left was phone the optician's to have his eyes examined.'

Matthew stepped into the elevator. 'Probably, he should have booked you in for one too - you brought it remember?' He placed his hands into his pocket. 'John, I want to ask you something.'

'Fire away.'

'I would appreciate it if you didn't tell Anna about my relapse last night. She's got enough to deal with right now.' He shrugged. 'Although with everything going on right now it doesn't seem…'

'Yeah, I know Buddy.'

The elevator doors closed.

'You'll have to tell her about it sometime - you know that right?' John said.

Matthew nodded. 'Yeah.'

With a jolt, the elevator stopped, and the doors opened on the eleventh floor.

Anna's room had been decorated with cards and flowers since Matthew's last visit. Several vases stood around her bedside with multicolored daisies and begonias. A bouquet of lilies, their ribbon in tacked around the plastic vase, stood on the bedside table, to the right of a jug of water.

The nurse had had to move greeting cards onto the window sill and surrounding areas to stop them from falling to the floor every time the doctor came in. 'Matt,' Anna beamed. She stretched her arms out slightly, inviting him to hold her.

'How are you feeling?' he asked, kissing her forehead. He could see from her expression she had not slept since she had been in hospital.

Her reply was a slight shrug, an answer that meant she was a wreck. 'What are you wearing?' she asked, changing the subject.

He gave John a quick glance. 'It's John's.'

She looked confused. 'Why are you wearing one of John's shirts?'

'Laundry day,' he lied. 'I've taken care of it - don't worry. I just want you to concentrate on getting yourself together.'

He watched her smile at John. Her eyes were wide; trying to speak to John telepathically. In the corner of his eye, he could see John nod.

'Do you like my cards and flowers?'

'They're lovely,' John replied, placing his hand into his pocket. Trying to disguise the silent interaction.

She pointed to the lilies on the bedside table. 'These came earlier, but I don't know who they're from. There was no card.'

John frowned. 'That's strange. Perhaps it fell off in the corridor.'

* * *

'Anna seemed better today, don't you think?' Matthew spoke as if he were alone in the car, staring out to the passing fields.

'Yeah,' John replied. 'She'll be allowed home soon.' He shot Matthew a glance. 'I'll drop you home so you can collect your things.'

'My things - why where am I going?' He looked at John, waiting for his reply.

'My place. You don't want to stay home alone.'

'What about my dog?'

'He can come too. He is housetrained, right?' John replied, with a hint of conviction in his voice.

'Of course,' Matthew turned back to the fields. 'You don't have to baby-sit me. I won't drink anymore.'

They stopped at a stop sign.

189

John shot him a look from the driver's seat. 'You can stop that shit.'

'I'm sorry; I didn't mean that the way it sounded.' Matthew knew he had hurt John's feelings.

'Yes you did!' John signaled into Goodland's Avenue and continued for a few yards. The Chevy glided to a stop outside Matthew's house. 'Well, go on then.' he replied, pulling up the handbrake. He did not look in Matthew's direction. He just kept his eyes on the red pick-up truck parked curb side, ahead of them.

Matthew sat silently for a moment. He could see the vein at the side of John's neck pulsing with anger. 'John, I'm sorry. My head is…'

'I know. That's why I haven't broken your nose.'

'I wondered that.' Matthew stepped out onto the curb.

'Do you need any help?' John pressed the release button on the safety belt. The shoulder strap retracted back, dangling the silver buckle as it hit the mechanism above his left shoulder.

'Sure,' Matthew replied, in the direction of his house. 'Ritchie you're working late tonight?'

'Oh, yeah.' Ritchie sounded surprised to see Matthew standing at the end of the driveway. 'I got the fertilizer Anna ordered at the farm. Thought I'd bring it around.' He carried a bag of compost from the red pick-up truck, along the lawn. He dropped it next to the flowerbed, with a thud. He seemed to take a moment to compose himself.

Matthew figured the bag was much heavier than Ritchie had anticipated. He walked toward Ritchie with his hands in his pocket; he took out his keys.

'Heard about all the commotion today, something on the radio about a riot?' Ritchie said.

Matthew frowned. 'Yeah.'

Ritchie shook his head. 'The Sheriff called in reinforcements from several counties. Must have been hell.'

'Yeah you could say that.' Matthew rubbed his shoulder.

'Every one's talkin' about it,' he put his hands on his hips. 'I bet the hospital was full tonight?'

Matthew nodded.

'Listen Matt, I'm truly sorry for your loss, it must be hard losing a child. I hope they catch whoever did it, you know?' he said, sincerely. With tremendous thrust of his hand, he opened the bag of compost with his switch bladed knife.

Matthew nodded. 'Thanks.' He looked down at the flower garden. 'It's lookin' good. Anna will love it,' he said, changing the subject.

Ritchie placed a handful of compost along the border. 'Well, she picked the flowers I just planted them. It's comin' along, won't be long until it's all finished. How does the patio outback look?'

'Great, we haven't sat out there yet, but it looks swell.' Matthew smiled.

John joined them smiling politely not wanting to interrupt the conversation.

'Ritchie this is my partner, John Beaumont.'

The two nodded, not wanting to mix compost hands with clean ones.

'We'll let you continue,' Matthew said, turning toward the front steps. 'I think I might have made a mess of the house?' he whispered to John as he placed the front door key into the keyhole.

'You weren't joking?' John said, when they entered the hall.

Rocky emerged from a pile of cushions scattered on the floor. He pounced onto Matthew with great affection.

'Hey boy.'

John stepped over the cushions making his way into the living room. 'Wow, it looks as if the riot came through

191

here!' He placed his hands on his hips, looking at Matthew with a candid expression. 'We better clean this up before your wife sees it.'

Matthew scratched his cheek. He had never seen the aftermath of his demon before. Confronted with the damage first hand, he was not sure how to react. 'Yeah,' he replied, somewhat subdued.

'Where do these go?' John stood next to the television cabinet, holding two large Russian dolls.

It had taken them an hour to clear the objects away from the floor. The house looked as though nothing had happened; Anna would never know.

The DVD's and C-D's were now back safely in their cabinets. Luckily for Matthew, their cases were not broken. He was not so lucky with a china elephant that used to sit on top of a corner shelf, below the stereo speaker on the far wall. He would think up a good excuse to tell Anna.

'Here, put them here,' Matthew said, pointing to the empty corner shelf where the elephant used to sit. 'Good,' he gripped John's shoulder with gratitude. 'Thanks.'

Matthew collected his clothes into an overnight bag. He grabbed Rocky's leash from the downstairs closet. 'I think I've got everything?'

'OK,' John looked at his watch. 'Do you fancy Chinese? If we hurry, we might get there before Mr. Chong closes. At least we can stay away from downtown.'

Matthew's stomach had bypassed the hunger pain, but he knew if he did not eat, the cravings would surface and he would be in trouble.

For some unknown reason, Matthew remembered the last meeting he had with Doctor Adamson at the Summerdale rehabilitation center.

The athletically built man, with thick black hair and a nose as sharp as an arrow, offered Matthew a seat. He had smiled, lips closed, and had handed Matthew a survival booklet. 'Remember the word: HALT.' The deep gravel voice echoed in Matthew's ears. 'Avoid getting hungry, angry, lonely or tired. H. A. L. T.'

'HALT,' Matthew said, aloud, snapping back to reality. He stared at the curb, his hands in his pockets.

'What?' John asked, trying his best to persuade the hefty dog into the back seat. Having none of it, Rocky helped himself to the passenger seat. He stared defiantly at John, only looking away when John gave up.

'Sorry John, I forgot to tell you. Rocks hates sitting in the back.' Matthew climbed into the back pulling the lap belt across, clicking it place.

John sighed. He picked some stray fur from his seat, before climbing in. Rocky grumbled impatiently.

'He wants you to open the window.'

John tutted. 'Next you'll be telling me you prepare steak for him every night.'

Matthew laughed at his sarcasm. Matthew was sure Rocky would choose steak every night if he had a choice, which he did not.

'You didn't answer my question,' John said as he pressed the button to roll down the passenger window. 'Chinese?'

'Yeah, sounds great.' Matthew tried to sound upbeat, thoughts of the pending trial tomorrow flashed in his mind. He had no idea where the time had gone. He felt like he was back on the treadmill running to catch up with everyone else.

John flicked his eyes up to the interior mirror trying to read Matthew's expression. 'You've got that look again, Buddy.'

Matthew smiled nervously. 'Yeah.'

'Worried about the trial, huh?'

Matthew didn't answer, just raised his eyebrows and nodded. *Was it really that obvious?* He thought.

'Don't worry; you know jury trials are unpredictable. It ain't over 'til it's over.'

Matthew knew John was right, but he could not help feeling anxious. The rumors and accusations had left a bad taste in his mouth. He could see it now, the jury, poisoned by mysticism and ignoring their rational thoughts, declaring a guilty verdict, even after being sequestered. But what could he do about it? He couldn't put their opinions on trial or even his own.

Chapter Thirty-Seven

John was usually an early bird. His mother used to complain when he was a boy that he should have been born on the other side of the world. Waking up at ungodly hours when the rest of the household had just got off to sleep. It was true. He was a lark and was sure he always would be. Except today.

'Damn dog,' he mumbled. He tugged at the sheet, pulling it over his head. Kicking Rocky off the sofa, John continued to mumble to himself.

Stretching his legs to their full length, he found a comfortable position. He closed his eyes. *Just half an hour longer.* He told himself.

'Now what?'

Vibrating somewhere on the sofa, John's cellular phone indicated he had received a voicemail message.

Fumbling under the cushions, John retrieved the darn contraption. He pressed the green button and listened to the message.

'It's Sarah-Jane…I-I need to see you…I have something you need to see…You must see it, it's important…I have to go…Call me later OK?'

Sure he would call her. Later.

* * *

'How are you feeling this morning?' John asked, making his way to the driver's seat. He unwrapped a stick of nicotine gum and placed it into his mouth.

Matthew shrugged. 'Ok,' he lied.

'You didn't eat your breakfast.'

John's tone made Matthew looked at him, instantly aggravated.

'Well, if it makes you feel any better, you look real confident in that blue suit.'

Matthew smiled, climbing next to him in the passenger seat. 'Thanks, you too.'

John flashed Matthew a horrified look. 'That mutt of yours is housetrained, right?'

Matthew chuckled, shaking his head. 'Of all the things…' he cleared his throat when he realized John didn't find it amusing. 'Rocky is perfectly housetrained, I promise. Do you want me to drop him off at my place, would that make you feel more comfortable?'

John flicked his wrist, checking the time on his watch. 'No time. It's half past eight, we should get goin'.'

* * *

Matthew placed his trial notebook onto the desk and sat down with his arms crossed. Sally sat fidgeting next to him, wearing a pale yellow Hijab.

'It's OK Sal, take one deep breath and relax.' He rubbed her arm, comforting. 'Every thing's under control.' He wasn't sure if he were actually trying to reassure her or himself.

The bailiff brought the courtroom to order as the judge took his seat at the bench and instructed Helen to begin.

Sally tensed her shoulders and Matthew faked a smile in her direction, hoping she wouldn't sense how nervous he was.

'The evidence you will hear today will show on the night of June 13th, the defendant shot and killed patrolman Collins, a peace officer of the Birchwood County police department, and attempted to kill his partner, Deputy Richardson.' The jury watched Helen with distinction, devouring every word she preached.

Matthew didn't look at her. He directed his attention to the jury, studying their expressions and body movements; he was full of anxiety.

'You will hear from a witness, Shirley Baxter, who will testify she saw the defendant commit these heinous crimes.' Helen paused, to allow the words to sink in. 'We will introduce to you exhibits that prove the defendant and patrolman Collins were involved in an illicit affair and evidence that shows patrolman Collins terminated the affair days before his murder.'

Matthew rolled his eyes at Helen's repeated use of Patrolman Collins' name. It was her attempt to add more sympathy – he was a real life person and not just a victim of a crime.

She rested her hand on the jury box. 'We will show patrolman Collins threatened to tell the defendant's husband about their affair.

'We will prove beyond a reasonable doubt, the defendant drove 360 miles from her residence in Atlanta to Ned's bar and diner, here in Birchwood County.' She held the revolver in its evidence bag for the courtroom to see. 'Armed with this loaded .38 caliber revolver.

'Furthermore, we will offer testimonies from witnesses that will remove any doubt of Mrs. Martinez's state of mind, after the termination of the affair and exhibits to back up these testimonies.' She interlocked her fingers. 'Ladies and gentlemen, the facts remain. We will prove means, motive and opportunity. There will be no doubt, the verdict must be guilty. Thank you.'

The jury were wide eyed as Helen walked to the evidence cart next to the witness box. They watched her replace the revolver on top.

Matthew had chosen to give his opening statement once the state had rested its case. He felt it was important that the jury remember every detail about the trial and not become blinded by testimony from the opposition.

'Ms. Maxwell, you may call you first witness,' Chamberlain instructed.

'State calls Shirley Baxter,' Helen said. She crossed to her beautifully mounted blueprint of the diner's parking lot that rested elegantly on a tripod, next to the witness stand.

Shirley wore a short navy skirt that stopped just before her knees and a white blouse. It was buttoned halfway up her chest showing a little flesh but not too much. Her auburn hair was tied in a ponytail. She looked a little nervous, but she carried it well. She was sworn and took her seat in the witness box.

'Ms. Baxter, can you tell us in your own words what exactly you saw on the night of June 13th, outside in the parking lot of Ned's bar and diner?' Helen flashed Shirley a quick look of encouragement. She relaxed and told the court what she saw.

'She's lying,' Sally whispered.

Matthew nodded, raising a hand, a gesture for her to be quiet.

'And is that woman in the courtroom today?' Helen asked. She looked at the jury and waited for Shirley to answer.

'Yes, she's right there,' Shirley replied, pointing directly at Sally.

'Let it be noted the witness pointed directly to the defendant. You saw this woman, Sally Martinez holding a revolver at the officers?' Helen repeated.

'That's correct,' Shirley replied, looking at the jury.

198

'Ms. Baxter, is this the revolver you saw?' Helen raised the murder weapon.

'Yes that's the gun I saw,' Shirley replied, matter-of-factually. 'I saw her fire that gun at the officers, jump in her car and drive away.'

'Your honor, I would like to ask that this to be marked in as evidence number one?' Helen walked to the bench, showing the revolver to the judge.

'No objections,' Matthew replied.

The judge lifted a finger, a wave from royalty. 'So granted.'

Helen turned to her table. Chester handed photographs of Sally's Bronco to her promptly. 'And is this the car you saw drive away from the crime scene?' she asked, showing Shirley the pictures.

She studied them briefly before she said, 'Yes, that's the car I saw.'

'Your honor, can I show these pictures to the jury?' Helen said, showing them to Matthew.

Chamberlain consented with a deep throated tone and Helen proceeded to the jury box.

'Your honor, I'd like to ask that these photographs be marked in as evidence number two?'

'Any objections?'

Matthew looked up from his trial notebook. 'None your honor.'

'Thank you, Ms. Baxter. We have nothing further. Your witness.' Helen smiled, a smug look of satisfaction on her face.

'Any cross-examination?' The judge asked, leaning forward in his throne.

Matthew stood, buttoning his jacket. All eyes were on him, except Helen's. She was busy looking smug.

'Ms. Baxter, you said you were working an extra shift that night, is that correct?'

Shirley nodded.

'The witness will answer so the court reporter can hear,' Chamberlain instructed.

Shirley looked at the judge nervously and replied, 'Yes, that's correct.'

'How long had you been working when these events took place?'

'About eleven hours, but I'd had all my breaks.'

'Even so you must have been pretty tired?' Matthew said, slipping it in hoping no-one would notice that his question was leading. 'What did you use to prop open the door? Never mind, we'll come back to that later.' He walked toward the jury box and made eye contact with the front row before turning back to the witness box. 'Where were you standing at the time you saw the defendant?' He placed his hand on the jury box and leaned slightly, resting his buttocks against the wood.

'I was standing by the entrance to the kitchen as I said before,' Shirley replied, relaxing.

Matthew picked up the baton and walked toward the blueprint. 'If I may?' He pointed to the kitchen entrance. 'You were standing about here, is that correct?'

Shirley leaned forward so she could see the blueprint more clearly. 'Yes, I would say so.'

'Now, where was the defendant standing?' Matthew asked, giving her the baton.

She pointed at the diagram. 'There in the parking lot.'

Matthew nodded. 'OK. Would you say Sally Martinez was approximately ten-feet away from you?'

Shirley paused, wrinkling her nose. 'Yes, I would say approximately ten-feet.'

He placed his hand on his chin. 'I'm confused?' he replied. 'How did you see through the Dumpsters?'

She studied the diagram. 'I-I don't know what you mean?'

Clara handed Matthew photographs taken three weeks ago of the area surrounding the kitchen entrance. The photographs were timed and dated. He showed them coolly to Helen and walked back to the witness stand. 'Mondays are garbage collection day, aren't they?' He scratched his cheek. 'Doesn't Ned move the Dumpsters so the garbage men can collect the garbage without disturbing his customers?'

Shirley stared at him blankly. 'Y-yes,' she whispered.

'Your honor, I would like to ask that these photographs be marked as defense exhibit A into evidence?'

Helen nodded her approval.

The judge lifted his head from his chin. 'So granted.'

'How big would you say the Dumpsters are, Ms. Baxter?' Matthew looked at her directly waiting for her reply.

'I-I don't know.' Shirley looked as if she was about to cry. Her cheeks blushed, and her eyes were glassy.

'How about, six-feet-tall by eight-feet-wide?' Matthew said, reading off the measurements from a piece of paper. 'That's without six inches for the castors.'

Shirley stared at the floor, blinking uncontrollably. Her lips parted then closed again.

'How tall are you Ms. Baxter?'

'Five-feet-two-inches,' Shirley mumbled and raised her head, her eyes pleading. 'B-but I saw her.'

'OK Ms. Baxter.' Matthew walked back to the blueprints. He pointed to the marker positioned at the kitchen entrance. 'You said you were standing here, am I correct?'

'Y-yes,' she replied.

'And Sally Martinez was standing ten-feet away from you in the parking lot, is that also correct?'

'Y-yes.'

'And the Dumpsters were here.' Matthew slapped the photographs of the three Dumpsters onto the diagram, next to the kitchen entrance. 'How could you see above the Dumpsters?'

'The Dumpsters weren't there.' Shirley tried to compose herself. She stared at the jury members hopefully; they simply stared back.

'If the Dumpsters weren't there, what did you use to prop open the door?' Matthew asked, staring at her.

Shirley was silent. Her shoulders rounded as she sank back against the chair.

'No further questions, your honor.'

'Any redirect examination?' Chamberlain asked.

Helen did not answer. His honor repeated the question.

'No, your honor,' Helen replied, finally.

'The witness is excused.'

Shirley walked down the aisle with her head bowed. She did not look at Sheriff Langford, who sat in the front row.

Helen shuffled through papers in front of her, appearing unscathed by Shirley's testimony. She stood slowly, 'State calls Deputy Patterson.'

Matthew stared at his fingernails. He could feel Patterson's eyes burning the side of his face as the Deputy took a seat in the witness box.

'Deputy Patterson, you were the first officer on the scene is that correct?' Helen asked. She held photographs of Stephen's mutilated corpse in front of her.

Matthew noticed she tried not to look at them.

Patterson cleared his throat. 'Yes,' he replied, coolly leaning back in his seat, resting his arm on the armrest.

'And can you tell us, in your own words what you saw when you arrived?'

'There were spectators in the parking lot. I cleared them as best I could, you know to secure the area and all.' Patterson looked at the jury with 'puppy' dog eyes.

'And then what did you find?' Helen asked. She moved her weight onto her right foot.

'I saw Stephen Collins' body lying next to his marked patrol car. The bullet had penetrated his head - execution style.'

'Your honor I'd like these photographs to be marked into evidence, exhibit number three.'

Matthew was on his feet. 'Objection your honor. The evidence is unfairly prejudicial.'

Chamberlain fiddled with his glasses on his nose. 'Your objection is noted counselor, objection overruled.'

'Your honor may I show these photographs to the jury?' With a nod from the judge, Helen handed the photographs to juror number four, Wyatt Andrews.

The photographs were passed along the front row. Sudden looks of disgust and disrepute displayed openly on the jury members' faces.

Matthew watched Hannah Millstein cover her mouth with her hand and gawk in horror. She closed her eyes, passing the photographs to the juror on her left.

It was impossible to make out the exact part of Stephen's forehead. The bullet had been penetrated with precision, lots of blood and brains splattered in all directions. Matthew had a strong stomach. He had seen a lot of murder pictures over the years, but these pictures made him feel nauseated to the point where his stomach ached. They were going to be trouble for him and knew it.

The part he hated most was the enlarged image of the blood-stained protect and serve badge, pinned perfectly to Stephen's chest.

'Can you tell the court what you observed next?'

'I observed Harry, excuse me, Deputy Richardson lying four-feet from patrolman Collins' body. He was barely conscious.

'Three bullet casings were on the ground not far from the bodies and a .38 caliber revolver lay in some hedgerow.' Patterson scratched at his cheek.

Helen held up the revolver. 'Is this the .38 caliber revolver you found at the crime scene?'

Patterson examined the revolver closely. 'Yes.'

Helen's shoes clicked along the marbled floor as she crossed to the jury box. She handed the evidence bag to Wyatt Andrews. He took it daintily from her and began to study it carefully. The evidence bag crackled under the pressure of his thick fingers.

The revolver was passed down the rows to other jury members who examined it carefully.

'Can you tell us what happened next?'

'I secured the area and waited for the Sheriff to arrive.'

'Thank you Deputy. No further questions.'

'Any cross, Mr. Brennan?'

'No questions, your honor.'

Deputy Patterson was excused from the witness box and made his way toward the aisle. He grinned cockily in response to Matthew's dirty look.

'State calls Deputy Richardson to the stand.'

Matthew held his breath. The very sight of Harry in his condition was trouble for him. In the corner of his eye, he could see Sally. Her body tensed. She sat almost frail-like, hunched over clasping her hands tightly to her chest. Her eyes were transfixed on something in front of her as if too scared to move.

Matthew leaned forward. 'Every thing's going to be OK, Sal. Just relax,' he whispered, unsure what to expect from her after her actions the other day, when they were alone.

She smiled at him weakly.

He gripped her hand, trying not to let the jury in on Sally's nervousness.

The majority of the people in the courtroom had read the newspapers and had seen the reports on television. When Harry entered the courtroom, the reaction was audible. He sat in a power wheelchair, wearing blue jeans, a black polo shirt and white sneakers. He held a remote control lever on the armrest, taping it with his fingertips lightly until he reached his destination.

His knees pointed inwards supporting each other as the wheelchair made its way to the witness box slowly.

'Please state your name for the record, sir,' Helen said.

'Harry Richardson.'

'And how old are you?'

'Thirty-seven.'

'And what is your occupation?'

Harry grimaced. 'I'm a police officer.'

'And how long have you been a police officer?'

Harry swallowed hard. 'Seventeen years.'

'And where were you on June 13th at 19:45?'

'I was on duty.'

Helen stood. 'Deputy Richardson,' she said, interlocking her fingers and placing her hands in front of her. 'Thank you for comin' here today, I know this has been a difficult time for you. Please tell us in your own words, what happened that night?'

Harry began to explain why he and his partner were called to Ned's bar and diner that night.

Matthew noticed Harry didn't look in his direction.

'And how long had you and patrolman Collins worked together?'

'Six months, he transferred from Atlanta where he worked as a Deputy-' Harry stopped suddenly, clearing his throat.

'Would you like a glass of water?' Helen did a quick shuffle-step to her table.

Nice touch. Matthew thought and wondered if she had rehearsed the whole charade.

'Take your time, Deputy Richardson,' Chamberlain said, softly.

Harry took a sip from the cup. 'I approached what I thought was the abandoned vehicle, a blue Ford bronco. I noticed there were people inside. They were sleeping.'

'And what happened then?' Helen asked. She looked at the jury. Their eyes narrowed, trying to comprehend how and why this would happen.

'I knocked on the window to tell the female driver she couldn't camp there. She rolled the window down, and that's when I recognized her.'

'That's a lie!' Sally protested loud enough for the judge to hear.

Matthew grabbed her arm tightly. 'Sit down.'

Chamberlain gave Matthew an evil glare. 'You may continue, Ms Maxwell.'

'How did you recognize her?'

'She was Stephen's ex-girlfriend, Sally Martinez.'

Matthew scratched at his face. He gripped Sally's hand, a gesture to remain seated and to remain quiet.

The courtroom was animated, shuffling of feet and coughs rippled up and down the aisle.

Helen continued regardless. 'How do you know she was his *ex*?'

'I know because I was standing next to him when he phoned to dump her.' Harry replied, not taking his eyes off Sally.

'You actually heard Stephen Collins dump the defendant?'

'Yes, Ma'me.'

Matthew jumped to his feet. 'Objection your honor, calls for speculation. The witness cannot be certain the deceased actually spoke to the defendant during that phone call.'

Chamberlain was silent for a moment, adding to Matthew's anxiety. 'Sustained. The jury will disregard.'

'What happened after you recognized the defendant?'

'I askt her why she was here.'

'And what was the defendant's reply?'

'She wanted to know if Stephen were with me.'

Sally jumped to her feet in protest. She pointed her index finger at Harry. 'You'll be sorry.'

Matthew tugged on her arm. 'Sit down.'

'But this is a lie!' she whispered back.

Matthew lowered his eyebrows. 'Keep quiet.'

'What happened then, Deputy Richardson?'

Harry didn't blink. He continued to stare at Sally as if hypnotized. 'Stephen called me back to the unit, I guess to tell me that this wasn't the abandoned vehicle as it belonged to the defendant. That's when I turned around and-' He shook his head sorrowfully. 'I can still hear the gun shot.' He stared at the floor. His eyes filled with tears. He gripped his fingers into tight fists.

'And that's when you were shot, is that correct?' Helen asked, looking at the jury.

'Yes,' Harry's voice was bitter. 'Although I don't remember fully what happened. I was told I had been shot at the hospital.'

'Harry, I know this is difficult but what injuries have you sustained as a result?' Helen asked, softly.

'The bullet hit just past my lower back. I have lost the function of my legs and my hips. I have had to have surgery to stabilize my spine.'

Matthew swallowed hard as he listened to his friend. He closed his eyes hoping to be somewhere else.

'They put a metal rod in my back. They took some bone from my right leg to join the vertebrae. I am on steroids to cope with the pain, and I have counseling to help with the night terrors.' Harry's voice began to croak. 'I can't fully dress myself, and I need help when I go to the bathroom.' Tears fell from his eyes and glistened his cheekbones. He wiped them away with a flick of his finger.

Jury members shook their heads sorrowfully. The panel seemed to stare with accusing eyes in Sally's direction. The courtroom was silent.

The artist stopped sketching. She bit her lower lip.

Helen touched Harry's arm. 'Are you able to continue?'

He nodded.

'Your honor I'd like this to be marked as exhibit number four.' Helen pressed the *play* button and showed a videotape of how Harry's life had changed because of his injuries. It was filmed three days ago at the hospital. Two nurses attended to his needs, washing and dressing him and helping in and out of his wheelchair.

Matthew rubbed the bridge of his nose. He knew Harry's testimony would be difficult for his case, but he didn't expect this level of attack.

A tension headache drummed across his forehead.

As if understanding Matthew's agony, Helen stopped the video.

'As a result of your injuries, are you able to perform your duties as an officer?'

Or maybe just twisting the knife in further. He thought bitterly.

She gripped Harry's shoulder like a proud parent at an award ceremony.

'No. The Sheriff is gonna get me a desk job, but I will never be able to...' Harry's voice fell to a whisper.

'You will never be able to perform as a patrol officer again?' Helen finished.

'No.'

She tilted her head toward Harry. 'You did great Harry, well done,' she whispered. She addressed the court. 'No further questions, your honor.'

'Your witness, Mr. Brennan,' Chamberlain said, clearing his throat.

'Deputy Richardson, firstly thank you for comin' here today,' Matthew said, sincerely.

Harry stared up at him with his deep brown blood shot eyes.

'I have just a few questions.' Matthew held a green folder in his hand. The folder contained the affidavit John had asked Harry to sign. 'Mr. Richardson, do you remember my associate, John Beaumont?'

Harry looked at the defense table in John's direction. 'Yes.'

'And do you remember a conversation you had, less than two weeks ago, about your account of the night in question?'

'Yes.'

'Isn't it true you stated to my associate that you saw a black male in the defendant's passenger seat that night?'

Harry said, 'No, she was with her children.'

Matthew raised his eyebrows. 'Deputy Richardson you are under oath.' He looked to Chamberlain who slithered unexpectedly toward Harry.

'Deputy Richardson, I am reminding you of the perjury rule.' The judge appeared righteous as he retracted back.

Matthew breathed in the atmosphere. Oxygen flowed through his body like a tornado, making him feel light-headed. He walked toward Harry. Opening the folder, he said, 'Is this your signature?'

'Yes.'

'And is this a copy of the affidavit you signed in the presence of my associate?'

Harry avoided eye contact with Matthew. 'I was under a lot of medication, I don't remember signing anything.'

'Yet you can remember other details that happened weeks before that?' Matthew said, sarcastically.

'Objection.' Helen slammed her hands onto the table. 'Move to strike, your honor.'

'Sustained.' Chamberlain glared at Matthew for his outburst and instructed the jury to disregard the last comment.

'Deputy Richardson did you see who shot you?'

Harry looked to the floor. 'No.'

'So you can't identify the person who shot you?'

Harry was silent for a moment. He stared at Sally before replying, 'No.'

'No further questions, your honor.'

Helen stood, an indication she had some more questions. The judge nodded, and she proceeded. 'Deputy, so the jury is clear. Was the defendant and her children alone in the vehicle?'

'Yes. They were alone.'

'No further questions.'

'You may be excused, Deputy Richardson,' Chamberlain said, like a voice from God. He looked at his watch. 'Court is in recess until 9am tomorrow.'

*   *   *

After their day in court, Matthew and John headed downtown to Pete's garage.

Dolly Parton's 'I will always love you' bellowed from the radio. The Chevy's speakers vibrate furiously under the strain of the volume.

'I forgot to tell you yesterday your yard's looking good.'

210

'What?' Matthew shouted. He turned the volume dial down four notches.

John shot him a look of disgust and turned the dial up a notch. 'I said your yard's looking good,' he repeated. He tapped his fingers against the steering wheel to the beat of the music.

'Yeah, Ritchie's almost done.'

John turned left into Hanover Street and stopped at a red light. 'It'll be nice when Anna comes home tomorrow.'

'Yeah,' Matthew intoned. 'I wonder if Pete will say the same about my bike?' He stared out the window, praying silently the Buell would live.

Reporters lined outside Bella's Coffeeshop waiting for a seat inside. The heat was already unbearable, and the locals had taken every available seat in the air-conditioned coffeeshop, before the lunchtime rush.

The reporters talked on their cellular phones, scribbling in their notebooks ready for their next entry into newspaper slots. Much to their disappointment, the streets had been restored to their former glory.

A lady reporter stood filing her nails enthusiastically as she leaned against the decorated window, with an occasional tick-like twitch to escape the gnats.

John took a left into the parking lot of Pete's garage. Pulling up the handbrake he said, 'You know Pete - he'll sort out your bike even if it takes a hundred years.'

A short stubby black man peered around a T-bird that was sat on a jack. He was wearing blue dungarees and a Nike baseball cap. Patches of oil and grease stains were on his chest and abdomen. 'Hey, boys. How you doing today?' He stood gracefully, picking up an old rag from a worktop.

'Hey, Pete,' Matthew said as he and John entered the workshop.

211

A distinct smell of used Castrol oil and Dynatron body filler wafted from the back of the garage.

Pete wiped the grease from his hands and reached to shake hands with them. 'Heard about Anna, I'm sorry. How is she?'

Matthew shrugged.

Pete had a deep basso tone to his voice. It reminded Matthew of the actor James Earl Jones. 'She'll be out in no time, man don't worry. You've been having a rough time of it lately, huh?' He patted Matthew on the back. 'Anythang we can do, just let us know, 'Kay?'

Matthew nodded appreciatively. 'Thanks.' Changing the subject he said, 'How's my bike doing? Can you fix her?' He cringed at the thought of Pete's reply.

'Well,' Pete frowned. 'They sure did do a good job of it. You need a new fly screen. The charging system is shot. You will need a new clock, headlight and taillight, turn signals and a paint job. That Hero blue is gonna be hard to get... Two new Pirelli's... That'll cost you a few hundred, at least.' He wiped his slightly graying moustache, deep in thought.

Matthew's heart sank. He could feel his face drain of color.

'Man, don't worry. She'll be up and running in no time.' Pete smiled, convincingly, putting Matthew's mind at rest.

'What about the Volvo?' Matthew asked.

'Now, the Volvo is another story.' Pete frowned.

'Can I see it?'

'Sure you wanna see it?' Pete raised his eyebrows.

Matthew nodded.

Pete sighed. 'Alright, my man.'

They followed Pete through the workshop to a junk yard behind the garage; a hundred vehicles occupied the graveyard. Some looked as if they had been there since the beginning of time, others looked almost new.

A Mustang, which was in for an oil change, concealed the Volvo.

Matthew knelt, winded, trying to catch his breath.

The Volvo's hood had concaved, a mass of twisted metal. The windshield lay smashed, tilting inward. The roof was dented. The trunk had disappeared, and the taillights were nonexistent.

Matthew ran his hand along the spikes of metal. The jagged edges prickled his fingers, slight pressure would draw blood.

'How do you survive something like that?' John placed his hands into his pockets.

Matthew shook his head in disbelief. He thanked God for helping Anna get out of the car alive. 'What kinda person would do this?'

John shook his head. He stared at the wreckage, eyes wide. 'I don't know, buddy. There are some sick people out there.' He gripped Matthew's shoulder. 'Come on, let's go.'

'They're going to pay.' Matthew clenched his fist. Hatred and anger flooded him as he stared at the distorted grill.

John knelt next to the trunk. He ran his fingers along the crevices. 'Hey, look at this?'

They walked toward him.

Pete placed a toothpick into his mouth, rolling it along with his tongue.

'Look,' John said, 'I would say those marks are black paint?'

Pete studied the marks. 'Yep, I would say so,' he said, in a kind of question kind of answer tone.

'Pete, have you worked on any black vehicles in the past few days?' Matthew asked, still investigating the trunk.

213

'No,' Pete replied. 'I haven't, but have you checked with the other garages around here? There's one along Hopeland Street, near Ned's diner. Steve's auto's, I think it's called?' He took the toothpick from his mouth, waving in the air thoughtfully. 'The vehicle that was involved in this must have serious damage, can't have gone too far.'

Matthew stood. 'Thanks, Pete. That's a good idea.'

'You can use my phone if you like?'

Matthew flipped open the yellow pages and began searching for a garage along Hopeland Street.

John's cellular phone beeped and vibrated in his pocket. He pulled it out and glanced at the caller I.D.

'Who's that your ex?' Matthew said, placing the receiver to his ear. 'You've got that look.'

John laughed. 'No, actually it's Sarah-Jane. She keeps calling me, says she has something we need to see.'

Matthew raised his eyebrows.

'I did say *we* need to see, not *I*.'

'So call her back and arrange for us to meet her somewhere?' Matthew found a number for Steve's autos.

Matthew tilted his head, listening to the low pitched ring for what seemed like an eternity.

'No answer?' John stood with his head cocked downward, staring at his cellular phone. He fiddled with the musical buttons on the keypad.

'Nope,' Matthew scribbled the number on a scrap piece of paper. 'I'll try later. Are you gonna speak to Sarah-Jane?'

John raised his head, the cellular phone to his ear.

Matthew could hear the rumblings and murmurs of a female voice. He figured John was listening to Sarah-Jane's voice mail message. His eyes were wide. His mouth fell open in shock.

'What is it?' Matthew asked.

'We gotta go… Now.'

* * *

'Slow down, you are going to get a ticket!' Matthew exclaimed. 'I'm sure everything's fine.'

'She sounded scared; I could hear it in her voice.' John applied more pressure to the gas pedal. He continued along state highway 125, passing the regional library a block from her house.

'I think maybe you're the one who's scared.'

John turned into 26th street. He studied the door numbers. 'What's that supposed to mean?'

Matthew smirked. He lifted his sunglasses and rested them on his nose. 'I've seen the way you look at her. You've got it bad.'

John sat open-mouthed. He made a noise in the back of his throat, in protest.

'So you don't find her attractive?' Matthew replaced his sunglasses in the correct position.

'That's hardly the point.'

'Maybe, maybe not?'

John parked in the street, in front of Sarah-Jane's carport; a white Honda and a bicycle occupied it. The bicycle was propped against the side of the house.

'Did the garage tell you anything?' he said, changing the subject.

'No, nothing. They haven't had any damaged vehicles in the past seventy-two hours.' Matthew scratched his cheek. 'We'll have to keep trying.'

'Sarah-Jane said she saw someone in a black Jeep at the diner acting suspiciously.'

Matthew stared at the side of John's head. 'So?'

John gave Matthew a quick sideways glance. 'Is it possible the splinters we found on the Volvo came from the same black Jeep she saw?'

215

Matthew was not sure how to answer that question. He was not convinced the two were related. There was no hard evidence to suggest the splinters even came from a vehicle, let alone a black Jeep.

Still, it would not hurt to ask Sarah-Jane if she remembered any other details of what the car looked like.

The pressing question was, what was so important they needed to see?

They exited the Chevy and walked along the bricked walk towards Sarah-Jane's house. It was a two bed-roomed one floor ranch-style house. It was painted in two-tone colors of red, the only one in the entire neighborhood.

Suddenly the earth shook beneath their feet. They were thrown backward.

Debris and glass flew in all directions, bouncing off vehicles, onto the sidewalk.

They lay stunned on the ground.

Matthew rolled onto all fours. Blood dripped from his ears and trickled down his cheek. The sound of drums echoed noisily in his head. A nauseated feeling washed over him as the world spun around him like the tail end of a twister.

'Are you all right?' A male neighbor yelled from across the street. 'The police are on their way.' He ran toward them.

John crawled toward Matthew. 'Are you OK, buddy?' He coughed deeply, blowing thick brown dust from his face.

Matthew gave a weak smile before passing out.

Chapter Thirty-Eight

A female voice could be heard in the darkness. Matthew tried to make out what it was saying.

'Can you hear me, sweetie?'

Matthew groaned. 'A-Anna?' His face stung as he moved his jaw from side- to-side.

'Yes, Matt it's me,' her voice was soothing. 'You're in the hospital. You're gonna be OK. Doctor Holmes said you've slight concussion.' She stroked Matthew's forehead. 'He said you may suffer from dizziness and nausea for a while. How do you feel?'

He opened his eyes slowly. He blinked trying to clear his distorted and blurry vision. 'Like my body has been smashed to pieces.' He wiped dried blood from his chin. He tried to remember what happened frantically. His mind was a maze of images, but nothing registered. 'What happened? John, is he…?' His tongue rebelled furiously, stinging and throbbing as he spoke.

'John's fine. He said he needed to find out what happened, he's there now.' She gripped his hand. Her eyes filled with tears. 'I thought I'd lost you too,' she sobbed.

* * *

John had never seen so many people. Blue uniforms, khaki uniforms, in a sea of black uniforms.

Seven marked police units parked strategically in the street next to three blue trucks, the words *bomb squad* painted in white on the side.

Sheriff Langford leaned against his patrol car. He folded his arms across his beer gut uncomfortably. He was in deep conversation with Deputy Patterson.

Intrigued, John walked toward them. 'Hi Sheriff. What's happenin'?' He turned and faced the wreckage.

'One female body, Mid-to-late twenties, killed instantly. A Sarah-Jane Meadows owns the property. A witness said Sarah-Jane entered minutes before it went up.' Sheriff Langford pointed to a tall woman in a gray suit. 'That's Kate. She's a bomb expert from Atlanta. Says fragments of an explosive device were found, could have been remote controlled.' He placed his hand to his mouth as if he were about to retch.

'Any leads?' John scratched his head sorrowfully.

'I am guessin' somebody who didn't like the property owner,' Patterson sneered.

Asshole. John thought, narrowing his eyes. 'D'you mind if I look around?' He glared at Patterson and watched him walk away.

The Sheriff shrugged, wiping the sweat from his forehead with the back of his arm.

'See if you can find her other leg?' Patterson said over his shoulder.

John clenched his fists but did not give Patterson the satisfaction of a reply. He walked around the rubble and charcoal that used to be a house. He shook his head sorrowfully. It was hard to comprehend why someone would want to do such a thing. Sure, he had defended some pretty awful characters over the years and had seen some gruesome sights, but he had always been detached from it. It had never happened to someone he knew. Someone he liked.

John stepped over fragments as if he were walking over a gravesite. He kicked smoldering pieces of wood gently with his shoe.

The putrid smell of burnt flesh made him want to vomit. He covered his mouth with a handkerchief.

Deputy Easton stood interviewing a woman in her late sixties. She was tall of slender build, wearing a pair of gold-rimmed eyeglasses.

John crossed the lawn so he could eavesdrop on their conversation.

'...I saw a red pickup parked over there,' the woman said. She gestured with a speckled hand in the mailbox's direction across the street. Wisps of her graying curly hair blew gently into her face as she turned toward the mailbox. 'It was there for 'bout an hour. A man got out and went to the house. He disappeared around the back and then went back to his car. I thought he was a gentleman caller if you know what I mean?' She raised her dark brown penciled eyebrows. 'They have been having a lot of those lately. Lord knows what those two get up to.' She shook her head distastefully. 'Anyhow, I thought he would drive away, but he didn't. He just sat there lookin' kinda funny, weird like.'

John raised his head and looked at the woman.

'Would you repeat this information to the Sheriff, Ma'me?'

The woman nodded.

Deputy Easton crossed the lawn toward the Sheriff.

John saw his chance. 'Mornin' Ma'am, you say you saw a man parked over there, near the mailbox?' He pointed in its direction.

'Yes, that's right. He was parked right there,' the lady repeated. She nodded her rounded head with certainty.

'What did the man look like?' John smiled invitingly, making the woman feel at ease.

219

'Well, I…' The woman scratched her wrinkled face. She smacked her lips together. 'He wore a black shirt and gray pants. Tall I guess, but ever'one's taller than me.' She chuckled to herself. 'Oh, he had a baseball cap on and somethin' around his neck. I can't remember anythang else.'

'Something around his neck?' John repeated. 'Like a scarf or a…huh? Bandana?'

'Yeah, somethang like that.'

'How old was the man, you saw?'

'Oh? I don't know. Young, yeah, he was young. I'd say about fifty, could have been fifty-five but no older.' The lady scratched her face, unsure of her estimate of the man's age. 'But I'm not really sure.'

'OK, I appreciate your time,' John replied. 'And you're sure the man was driving a red pickup truck?'

The woman nodded. 'You think I'll be on T.V?' she asked excitedly as a television van bounced around the corner.

John was sure the vultures would want to include everyone in their next big feast. 'Maybe, if you're lucky,' he intoned.

* * *

Matthew placed an apple to his swollen lips. He spoke into the loud speaker resting on the arm of the sofa. 'Professional job, you say?'

'That's what the bomb expert said when I caught up with her,' John replied. 'She sounded as if she had an idea who could have been responsible. She wouldn't comment any further, but the device was handmade.'

Matthew frowned. 'So whoever it was had some kind of expert training.'

'I would say so,' John sighed heavily. His breath vibrated across the line making it crackle.

'I'm sorry John, she was a nice girl.' Matthew placed a cold flannel against his forehead, trying to numb the throbbing behind his eyes.

'I knew she was in trouble, and I did nothing.'

'You weren't to know what kind of trouble she was in. It could have been an ex-boyfriend or something. You said she had a period of low cashflow - loan sharks know people in high places.'

'Yeah, I just wish I'd listened to my instinct that's all.'

Matthew leaned forward. He placed the phone to his ear, turning the loud speaker off. 'Did you ever find out what she wanted to show us?'

'No,' John sniffed, making it sound as if he was crying. 'Get some rest buddy, I'll be home later.'

For the first time, Matthew was lost for words. For months he had been the one in need of consoling and John had sat on the phone for hours trying to comfort him. He felt nervous being on the other side of the fence. 'Listen John…' He stared at the photographs of John's children on the almirah and swallowed hard.

As if those words were their secret code, John replied, 'Thanks buddy.' He exhaled, and it vibrated across the line. 'Don't wait up, you need to rest. I'll be home soon.'

Chapter Thirty-Nine

Matthew thought the Judge looked particularly pensive this morning and wondered what was wrong.

'I regret to inform you that another member of the jury has been taken to hospital this morning,' the judge's face was stern. 'She shall be replaced by an alternate.'

Gasps echoed around the courtroom.

Chamberlain waved his hand toward the jury box. 'Please step up and take your seat.'

The female alternate stood slowly and did as she was instructed.

Chamberlain cleared his throat, 'Please continue Ms. Maxwell.'

'State calls Sheriff Langford.'

Matthew wondered what had happened to jury number one and three and hoped it had nothing to do with the riots in town.

The Sheriff stood boldly. He straightened his sleeves walking robustly to the witness stand. He carried an air of authority with him as he was sworn and seated.

Helen smiled. 'Sheriff Langford, you were the arresting officer is that correct?'

'That's correct.' He looked directly at the jury.

'Where's John?' Sally whispered.

Matthew shrugged. 'He was gone when I woke up. He left a note – something about going outta town.'

'Would you tell us in your own words what happened that evening?' Helen glanced at the jury members. Their oval shaped faces reflected intense concentration as they listened intently to the Sheriff.

'After some preliminary investigations we discovered the defendant was staying at the Northgate circle motel in room number 307. We arrived at precisely 2300 hours and proceeded to the room. I identified myself and the suspect exited the motel room with two children.'

'And did you obtain any identification from the suspect?'

'Yes. She told us her driving license was in the glove box of her car. A blue Ford bronco, parked directly outside her room. It identified the suspect as Sally Lynn Martinez, the same name on the warrant.'

'And is that woman in the court room today?' Helen asked, folding her arms matter-of-factually.

'Yes, she's right there.' He nodded and pointed directly at Sally.

'Your honor, we would like the record to show the witness has identified the defendant, Sally Martinez.'

'So granted.'

'And did you take the suspect into custody?'

'Yes.' The Sheriff could not hide the pride in his voice. 'I read her the Miranda warnings and handcuffed her.'

'What happened then?' Helen asked. She placed her fingers interlocked in front of her. She turned on her heels, looking at the Sheriff.

'From our investigations we discovered the defendant had booked the motel room three days in advance, and she had contacted the victim several times, via text message, to tell him she was in Birchwood County and wanted to meet him.'

'Thank you Sheriff, no further questions.'

'Any cross examination, Mr. Brennan?' Chamberlain asked.

Matthew stood sharply. 'Yes your honor.' He gripped Sally's shoulder.

Sheriff Langford rolled his eyes. He looked down at his newly polished shoes.

'Sheriff Langford, did Sally say where she wanted to meet the victim in the text messages?'

Sheriff Langford rolled his tongue across his mouth. 'No.'

'The witness will speak up so the court reporter can hear,' Chamberlain bellowed, his voice thick with authority.

'Did Sally tell the victim she was at Ned's bar and diner?' Matthew continued as he crossed toward the jury box.

Sheriff Langford sighed heavily. 'No.'

'Did Sally tell the victim where she was staying in any of the text messages?' Matthew raised his eyebrows.

The Sheriff scratched at a bead of sweat rolling down his neck. 'No.'

Matthew leaned on one foot. 'While you were reading the defendant her rights and cuffing her, did she say anything to you? Make any statement?'

'Yes. She wanted to know why she was being arrested.' The Sheriff chuckled under his breath.

'She wanted to know why she was being arrested.' Matthew repeated. He made eye contact with Sally.

'Yes.'

'But didn't you say you read Sally Martinez her rights and informed her of the charges?' He placed his hands into his pockets.

'That is correct. I did read her rights.' The Sheriff's tone lowered an octave. He shifted in his chair.

'Did the defendant say anything else to you, while she was lying face down in the dirt?'

'Objection your honor.' Helen stood abruptly, shouting at the bench. 'Move to strike.'

Chamberlain peered over his glasses at the jury. 'The last comment will be stricken from the record. The jurors will disregard that last comment. Counselors approach the bench.'

Chamberlain covered the microphone. He leaned forward toward the counselors. 'Tread very carefully Mr. Brennan, another outburst like that and I'll hold you in contempt of court. Do I make myself clear?' His gray eyes glared.

'Yes your honor,' Matthew said.

'Proceed Mr. Brennan.' The Judge re-positioned his glasses onto the end of his nose. He poured himself another glass of water from the jug in front of him.

'Sheriff Langford,' Matthew began. 'Did the defendant say anything to you while she was being arrested?' he repeated.

The Sheriff rolled his eyes toward Matthew. 'Yes, she asked where her children were being taken.'

'Have you made arrests before this afternoon?' Matthew turned and looked at the jury from his position in front of the defense table.

The Sheriff leaned forward in his chair, offended by Matthew's question. He contracted and lowered his eyebrows. 'I have been the Sheriff in this county for thirteen years, Mr. Brennan and I have made numerous arrests throughout my career to protect the people of this community. It is my duty as Sheriff to provide a safe secure environment.'

Matthew looked toward the bench. 'I object your honor, move to strike.'

'Objection sustained.' Chamberlain leaned toward the witness stand. 'The witness is instructed to answer yes or no to the questions being asked.'

The Sheriff snorted under his breath in protest.

'Have you ever, in your distinguished career, arrested a criminal whose one concern was the safety of her children?' Matthew asked.

The Sheriff mumbled something unintelligible under his breath.

'The witness will speak up,' Chamberlain instructed.

The Sheriff replied, 'No.'

'And have you ever arrested a suspect who,' Matthew held a copy of the arrest warrant and read from it. 'Is "considered armed and dangerous", who brings their children along for the ride?' Matthew shrugged, turning back toward his seat.

'Maybe she wanted to teach them how to use a loaded firearm.' The Sheriff smirked.

Matthew spun on his heels, facing the bench. 'Objection your honor, move to strike.'

'Sustained. The jury will disregard that last comment.' The judge glared at the Sheriff like a sharpshooter at a gunfight.

Matthew did not need a direct answer. The seed was already planted in the jury's mind. 'No further questions, your honor.'

'State calls Professor Cathy Woodall.' Helen rose from her chair.

Professor Woodall was sworn. She took her seat in the witness box. She had a well-educated and well financed air about her as she crossed her legs. She interlocked her long fingers, gripping her knee.

'Professor Woodall, you are an expert in finger print analyses, is that correct?' Helen asked, looking at the jury.

'That's correct,' she replied, with a deep husky voice.

'And where did you graduate from?'

Professor Woodall flashed the court room her colorful credentials and her impressive and highly expensive education. She smiled as she reeled off her Curriculum Vitae. Degrees and diplomas from three universities, training at the academy and her current twelve year career working with the FBI, and a string of professional societies to which she either co-founded or was chair.

Simultaneously the jury members raised their eyebrows at the extent of the professor's knowledge and highly tutored career.

'Your honor I request Professor Woodall be accepted as an expert witness?'

'Defense counsel, do you have any foundational questions you would like to ask the witness?'

Matthew shook his head. 'None, your honor.'

'Very well, I rule the witness is qualified to give expert testimony, proceed Ms. Maxwell.'

'When you examined the finger prints on the revolver did the prints match those of Sally Martinez?' Helen asked. She placed her hand on the wooden jury box and studied their expressions.

'Yes,' the professor replied. She cleared her throat matter-of-factually.

'Thank you professor. No further questions.' Helen said, walking back to her seat.

Matthew scrolled down his trial notebook, reminding himself of the questions he wanted to ask the witness.

'Your witness, Mr. Brennan,' Chamberlain said.

'Professor Woodall, when you completed your analysis did you find any other prints on the murder weapon?'

The professor smiled. 'No.'

'Were there any fingerprints on the bullet casings themselves?'

The professor tilted her head downwards. 'No.'

227

'So what are you suggesting the defendant put gloves on to load the weapon and took them off to fire it?' Matthew said, sarcastically.

A nervous smile. 'Maybe the gun was already loaded. It's registered to her husband, maybe he loaded it?'

'You just told the court there were no finger prints on the bullet casings?'

'No there were not, I was hypothesizing.'

The courtroom came alive with voices. They were audible enough for the judge to look up from whatever he was engaged in reading. The voices ceased.

Matthew paused for effect, glancing at the jury. 'No further questions.'

Helen called the forensic expert, Nelson Boone, to the stand.

Matthew leaned toward Clara. 'Any word from Judy?'

Clara shook her head.

As Matthew expected, Nelson Boone testified Sally's clothes were covered in gun powder residue, indicating she had fired the weapon.

'Any cross-examination?'

Matthew rose from his chair. 'Mr. Boone, did you examine my client's hands for gun powder residue?'

The over confident man stopped smiling at the jury. 'Of course.'

'And what were your findings?'

Nelson Boone cleared his throat. He re-checked his red tie was still neatly behind his jacket. 'You have to understand certain chemicals can...'

Matthew held up his hand, cutting off the witness. 'Answer the question, Mr. Boone.'

Boone looked at Helen for moral support.

'Did you find any traces of gun powder residue on my client's hands?' Matthew repeated.

'No.'

228

'Thank you. No further questions.'

'State calls, Mr. Kirkland.'

The witness entered the courtroom through the double entrance doors. He was a short burly man, wearing a brown suit. He was bald with dark bushy eyebrows. He walked with a slight limp.

'What's he doing here?' Sally placed a hand to her face as if she was hoping the witness would not recognize her.

'Why do you think?' Matthew whispered. He flicked through his trial notebook, reminding himself of any questions he wanted to ask on cross-examination. The page under Mr. Kirkland's name was empty.

'Mr. Kirkland, you are the manager of a motel in Atlanta, is that correct?' Helen smiled warmly at the witness.

He appeared to Matthew to resemble a person waiting to see a dentist. He could not see Mr. Kirkland's palms, but he was sure they were sticky with sweat.

The witness cleared his throat. 'Yes.'

'Can you tell us what you witnessed at your motel on the afternoon of 27th February?'

'Patrolman Collins and a woman checked into one of my vacant rooms. They seemed like they were in love. They were holding hands.'

'What made you remember this woman?' Helen asked.

'It was the way she kept looking over her shoulder. Something in her voice. Then I noticed her ring - he wasn't wearing one - that's when I knew he was banging a married woman.' His grin faded as he realized no one else found the scenario amusing.

'Objection, your honor. Calls for speculation,' Matthew said from his seat.

'Sustained, jury will disregard.'

'And can you see the woman that was at your motel on that afternoon in the courtroom?'

'Sure, she's right there.' The witness pointed at Sally.

Helen looked at the jury. 'Mr. Kirkland, what precisely gave you the impression the deceased and the defendant were using the room for sex?'

Matthew jumped up. 'Objection your honor, calls for speculation.'

Judge Chamberlain raised a finger. 'Overruled, the witness will answer the question.'

With a wry smile, the witness answered. 'Because he asked for some change for the condom machine.'

'Thank you Mr. Kirkland. No further questions.'

'Any cross?'

'No questions your honor.' Matthew scribbled in his trial notebook. He needed to research Mr. Kirkland's testimony further and see if he could find a witness to contradict the testimony. He hoped, by the look of this sleaze-ball, Kirkland had skeletons in *his* closet.

* * *

Billy-Ray Collins sat broken and pale on the stand. The blue thread on his suit appeared to be the only thing holding him together.

'Mr. Collins, during the early hours of June 14th were you asked to identify your son at the county morgue?'

'Yes,' his voice was raspy. He sat hunched over, a lost gray look deep in his eyes.

Helen approached the witness stand. She asked softly, 'and did you in fact identify your son's remains?'

'Yes.'

Sally placed her hand onto Matthew's arm. She gripped it, unable to take her eyes away from her lover's father.

Matthew wondered what she was thinking and if she could really have pulled the trigger.

Helen lifted a small tape machine from her desk. She asked the judge for permission and on his approval, she pressed the play button.

Sally turned away, as if the movement would somehow block the hatred in Stephen's voice.

The jury box became like a silent movie, simultaneous body movements, without the informative captions.

Helen stopped the tape. 'Can you tell the court whose voice is on this tape?' She scratched her nose.

Billy-Ray Collins nodded, staring blankly at the only audible object left of his son. 'Yes, that's my son,' he croaked.

'Your honor, I would like this to be marked as exhibit number five.'

'Any objections?'

'None your honor.'

Helen walked to her seat. 'No further questions, your witness.'

Matthew had no questions for Mr. Collins. Nothing could be gained from cross-examination. Yes, Stephen Collins was dead, and yes his father had identified his voice on the tape.

'State calls, Mr. Newson.'

Mr. Newson was tall with thick blonde hair and a bushy moustache. He was dressed in a gray suit, minus a tie. A tacky gold chain hung from his neck.

'You live in the Atlanta district, is that correct?'

'Yes.'

'And how long have you been a resident at your home in Hawthorne River?'

The witness pondered a moment, trying to figure out the exact number of years. 'Nine years.'

Matthew looked to Sally with a perplexed expression. She shrugged, avoiding eye contact and continued to fiddle

231

with her fingers. He was not sure how to take her response; he had a strange feeling in the pit of his stomach.

'Do you know the defendant and her family?'

'Yes, they live right across the street.'

Matthew glanced behind to the courtroom doors. There was still no sign of John.

'Can you describe, in your own words, what you saw on the night of June 10th?'

Matthew placed his index finger to his lips, biting a hangnail. John was supposed to go back to the motel and find out what Sally's neighbor was testifying to. Matthew kicked himself, *why didn't I follow up?* He thought angrily. He felt nauseous suddenly, anticipating the witness's answer.

'I was walking back from the store at around eight. As I approached Mrs. Martinez's home, I heard shouting. It was clear there were two voices, a male and a female.' Mr. Newson rubbed the arch of his nose. 'I continued past when Mrs. Martinez's front door opened. A man walked down the driveway.'

'Did you recognize the man on the defendant's driveway?'

'Yes. It was patrol sergeant Collins.'

'Then what happened, Mr. Newson?'

'Just as I was about to cross the street toward my home, I saw the defendant run after him. She was carrying a gun. She fired two shots in the sergeant's direction.'

Matthew chocked back bile. He wiped his watery eyes and sat up in his chair.

'Thank you Mr. Newson. Prosecution rests your honor,' Helen said, hovering in a half standing half sitting position.

'Court is in recess until Monday. Defense will begin at 9am.' Judge Chamberlain slammed his gavel. 'Court is adjourned.'

Matthew sat bewildered, unable to move for a moment.

*   *   *

Something continued to irritate John. It was like a wedge in the pit of his stomach. This morning he had decided to embrace whatever it was that would not be laid to rest. He had a feeling it was the phantom black Jeep.

In his mind, it was all connected somehow. The murder. The diner. Anna's accident and he was still convinced the hit on Sarah-Jane was related. Somehow.

Unable to sleep during the early hours, he had spent the time trolling through pages of internet advertising, in search of as many local garages and auto repair shops he could find.

Armed with a list of seventy-five addresses and a double espresso, he was determined to find the black Jeep.

Arriving outside Birchwood County autos, he pulled alongside a silver pickup parked in front of a paint and body shop.

John knocked on the office window.

No answer.

To the left of the paint and body shop was another building. The shutters where half way down, revealing what looked like a Toyota sitting on a jack.

The sound of country and western music echoed around the work shop.

John crossed the lot. 'Hello?'

A young girl, dressed in a blue boiler suit sang to the music, oblivious to John's presence. She was tall and slim with auburn hair, tied in a ponytail at the back of her head. She rolled a tire along the floor towards the Toyota.

John crossed the work shop, trying to catch the girl's attention. 'Excuse me?'

Startled, the girl sprang from her seat, holding her preferred weapon, a custom made pink single action pistol.

'No, no…it's OK.' Slowly, he placed his hand into his pocket and pulled out his wallet. 'I'm a lawyer. My name is John Beaumont.' Tossing his wallet toward her, he held up his hands in defense.

The girl knelt, careful not to be distracted. She picked up the wallet from the ground. For a split second, her eyes focused on John's ID. 'What do you want?'

'I'm looking for a black vehicle with serious damage to the front end. It was involved in a hit and run.' He raised his eyebrows. 'Can I put my hands down now?'

The girl relaxed. 'Sure,' she lowered her weapon. 'Shouldn't the cops be handling that?' She pulled a yellow cloth from the loop in her overalls and wiped her hands.

John ignored the girl's comment. He flipped his wallet, taking out a small photograph of Anna's car. 'Have you seen any vehicles like that in the last week?'

The girl looked at the photograph in horror. 'Lord…' she gasped. 'Man that's some accident.' She paused briefly, trying to recall what the original question was. 'In the last week you say?'

He nodded and replaced the photograph into his wallet.

'Nope, I can't say I have. Why don't you check out Trusty's body shop up the road?' She nodded her head in the direction of Trusty's. 'It's 'bout a mile that way.'

He figured he was going to need another double espresso. 'Thanks for your time, Miss.' Maybe two?

Chapter Forty

'We lost,' Matthew said, somberly.

'We have the weekend,' John replied, 'that's forty-eight hours - we can find a witness. It's not over, 'til it's over.' He placed two sandwiches, wrapped neatly in cellophane, onto the pine table in front of him. He took his cellular phone from his back pocket. 'I missed another call,' he intoned, placing the phone on the table, before sitting opposite Matthew.

'Who was it from?' Matthew asked.

John took a closer look at the caller's details. 'I dunno. Probably a wrong number.'

'Where were you?' Matthew realized he sounded a lot like Anna.

John took a bite of his sandwich. 'I was on a wild goose chase trying to find the black Jeep.'

Matthew sighed. 'It's long gone if it were even involved in the first place.' He sipped his coffee. 'Did you hear about Clare Anderson, otherwise known as jury number one?'

John shook his head.

Matthew put down his Styrofoam cup. 'Someone broke into her apartment last night and attacked her.'

John raised his eyebrows. 'Gees, is she all right?'

'Head injuries, but stable.'

A female guard accompanied Sally as she entered the interview room. The guard removed the handcuffs and waited outside in the corridor.

'I believed in you!' Matthew exploded. 'I put my life on the line for you!'

John raised his hand - referee. 'OK let's just take a breath.' He pointed at Sally. 'You - have a seat.'

She did as instructed.

'Now, tell us what happened on the night this neighbor testified to? Was it Miguel's gun?' John took a bite of his ham and salad sandwich.

'Yes,' she replied, shaking her head. 'I didn't even want the damn thing.' She slumped back against the chair, staring at the corner of the table. 'Just before Miguel left for work, he took it out to show me. He must have forgotten to put it away again. It was on the counter when Stephen came over.'

'What's-his-name, your neighbor?' John ran his fingers along the table trying to jog his memory. 'Newson, he said he heard arguing coming from your home?'

She nodded. 'Stephen and I got into a fight.'

'Physical?'

'No. No. Stephen would never have hit me.' She looked at Matthew. He did not make eye contact, just sat with his arms folded across his chest, breathing heavily through his nostrils.

'But you hit him?' John said, bitterly.

'I threw stuff at him, yeah.'

'What was the argument about?' John looked to Matthew for some input.

Matthew rolled his eyes. He did not know why John was bothering to discuss it. She was guilty and had played them both from the beginning.

'I don't know why I picked it up,' she said, avoiding the question. 'I haven't the first damn clue how to use it.'

'What was the argument about?' John repeated. His voice rose a little in frustration.

She looked to Matthew with weeping eyes. He knew she wanted some kind of response, some warm gesture that he understood why she lied and made them look like idiots. He raised his eyebrows, a gesture for her answer the question; he was losing his patience.

'That was the night Stephen said he wanted to cool it for a while.'

'Why didn't you tell us all this before?' John said, irritably. He raised his arm and then he lowered it onto the table.

'I thought if I told you before, you would think I was guilty and not defend me. I was angry that night, that's all.'

John shook his head in Matthew's direction. 'Some people would say angry enough to kill him?' He said jumping in.

'Were you?' Matthew's eyes widened. He glared, awaiting her answer.

'What?' she asked, confusion evident on her face.

Matthew tutted. 'Angry enough to kill him?'

'No. No. I just wanted to him realize how much he meant to me. I would never have hurt him. I loved him.'

'And the fact he was planning to tell Miguel had nothing to do with it?' Matthew snapped. He leaned forward like a wild animal, his jaws locked and his teeth exposed.

'No. No. I didn't kill Stephen, I didn't,' she sobbed. 'You have to believe me.'

Matthew flung his arms. He crossed to the window behind her chair. He stood sucking in the air through his teeth, trying to calm himself. 'You expect us to believe Miguel left a loaded gun out with the kids walking around?' He shook his head. 'This is bullshit, and I'm tired of it.'

'Wait a minute. I thought you said the gun went missing?' John remembered.

Sally wiped her eyes. 'Yes, yes it did. Right after that night.'

'Bullshit!' Matthew spun on his heels and slammed his fist onto the table. 'Tell us the truth!' Where had this anger come from? He did not care. It was too late. He had lost it and could see from the tears streaming down her face he had lost it big, she cowered, covering her face with her hands.

Moments past. For Matthew, it felt like an eternity. Finally, his voice cut through the silence with a haunting whisper. 'I'm sorry.' He wiped his face with his hand. The continued silence surprised him. He looked up from the floor. 'Truly,' he said. 'I'm truly sorry.'

John gave a brittle smile.

'I'm the one who should be apologizing.' She wiped her tear stained cheek with the back of her sleeve. She looked at the ceiling, swallowing hard. 'I should have told you the truth from the beginning. I was afraid.'

John rested his hands onto the desk, rolling his tongue to remove some food between his teeth. 'So tell us now?'

'The real reason I came down here on the night Stephen was killed, was to apologize for firing the gun at him. I would never have actually shot him. I couldn't...I loved him,' she pleaded. She wiped another tear from her blood shot eyes. 'He wouldn't take my phone calls or reply to any messages I left. I had to do something. I thought if he saw me face-to-face we could work things out.' Her lips closed, and then parted again. 'Do you think he forgives me?'

Matthew did not know how to reply. He was not sure what she meant by Stephen forgiving her. *Did she mean for the incident with the gun or the fact she actually killed him?* He sighed and rubbed his face wearily.

Matthew could see John at the bottom of the jail steps with his cellular phone to his ear. He contemplated dodging John's watchful eyes and heading straight for the Tavern bar. But the episode with Sally had fatigued him. The Tavern bar was too far to walk; he needed somewhere closer.

Damn. He thought bitterly as he realized John was making his way over to him.

'That was a garage in Spring Hill. They have a black Jeep in their repair shop.' John placed his cellular phone into his back pocket. 'It came in right around the time Anna got hit.'

Matthew frowned. 'Spring Hill? You certainly wore out those shoes of yours.'

John laughed. 'I'm good but I'm not that good. The owner of the last garage I went to - his cousin owns the one in Spring Hill - he gave him my card.' He gestured with his hand toward the parking lot. 'I'm heading over there now before they close. I'll drop you home, I'm sure Anna has missed you since she got outta hospital.'

Matthew walked toward the passenger side and opened the door. 'Well, let's go to Spring Hill.'

'Are you sure I can't drop you home?'

'Naw.' Matthew could not face Anna right now. He was sure she would smell the desire on his breath. No. He could not listen to her lecture him all night. 'Besides, Linnie's there with the kids.' And he definitely couldn't deal with that right now.

John started the engine and manoeuvred around the parking lot until they were out in the street. 'It was a tough day today, huh?' he said, trying to soften the atmosphere.

'Still, we've got the weekend to sort it out. I bet you're glad *ole chamberlain* allowed a continuance?'

Saturday trials were rare in south-west Georgia, but they were not uncommon. Some judges preferred to use the extra day to cut down the workload, others preferred to use the time to brush up on their golf handicap.

'No shit!' Matthew snapped. Suddenly he retracted. 'I'm sorry. I don't know what's wrong with me?' He sat back and stared at the dashboard.

John looked at Matthew's trembling hands. 'Maybe I should drop you home? You can call Doctor Adamson. I can go to the garage, and I'll call you when I'm done?' he suggested.

'Please, just drive ok?' Matthew folded his arms, tucking his hands under his armpits self-consciously.

Most of the journey to Spring Hill was made in silence. Matthew was deep in thought. He had two days to figure out what the hell he was going to do about the trial. But he could not think about that now. His brain hurt too much. Jack. Jack. Jack. He could not stop the voices in his head yearning for its smooth bitter taste.

He had hardly noticed the countryside along highway 82 as it past the window. Nor had he noticed John pull off the highway, into the garage.

John took the key from the ignition and turned to face him. He knew what was coming.

'Why don't you wait here? I'll be back in a moment.'

Matthew felt like a two-year-old. *Maybe I should start sucking my thumb?* He thought sarcastically.

Without saying a word, Matthew exited the car and wandered around the lot.

For a garage, it was quiet. No sound of a radio playing. No droning of tools or echoing of metal against metal. Nothing. Matthew felt almost alien standing in the stillness of his surroundings.

The only sound came from the traffic cruising along the highway half a mile away.

The garage was centered neatly in between a junk yard and a small shack. Matthew guessed the shack was the owner's home or maybe a storage shed of some kind. Either way he felt the place needed a paint job.

To the right of the shack, was a neon sign that said *open*.

'Matt.' John waved him over. 'The owner's back here.'

Matthew followed him behind a white door, which had *private* painted in black lettering, at the far end of the building.

Papers and books stacked high occupied shelving units. Boxes of nuts and bolts, batteries and cans of oil were stashed under a small steel table. The whole place made Matthew feel claustrophobic.

'Good to meet you.' A tall lanky man in his mid fifties held out his hand to Matthew. The man seemed like a giant in the tiny space. 'My name is Harley, Todd Harley.'

Matthew returned the gesture.

'Now you boys wanna know about a 1998 black Grand Cherokee, huh?'

'That's right,' John replied.

'Insurance job huh? Well follow me.'

Neither of them corrected the man.

Out in the workshop, stored on an overhead jack, was the Jeep. The grill, light and bumper on the right side were distorted. Grey splinters of metal splashed across the hood like a severed vein.

'So what insurance company you guys with?' Harley asked.

John nodded to Matthew, a signal, before turning back to the garage owner. 'Where's your bathroom?'

'The door on the left.' Harley pointed in the direction of another inner door just behind John.

'You finish up here, I'm gonna take a whiz.'

Matthew took out his legal pad, flipping it over to a clean page. He looked around the Jeep making little doodles in his notebook, continuing with the pretense he was investigating for an insurance company.

Moments later John returned. He gestured that they should leave.

'Well, thanks for your time.' John shook the garage owner's hand firmly. 'We'll be in touch.'

'So what did you find?' Matthew slid across the truck stop's booth.

They had pulled over in the nearest rest stop along highway 82.

'The owner is a guy called Roy Elderberry.' John nodded to the waitress, a burly woman in her late fifties. She took a small pencil from behind her ear and stood expectantly next to their table. 'Two specials please Ma'me.'

'Coffee?' Her voice was surprisingly deep, almost unnatural for a woman.

Matthew did not dare take a closer look to see if she were in fact, a *he.*

'Two waters, thanks.'

The waitress nodded in Matthew's direction. 'Don't he talk?'

John grinned, before rolling his eyes and turning to face Matthew. 'You gonna get our order?' He avoided eye contact with the waitress deliberately.

She mumbled something under her breath as she walked away.

'Roy Elderberry?' Matthew scratched his cheek. 'Never heard of him. What has he got to do with this?'

John placed his knife and folk in front of him. 'What would you say if I were to tell you Roy Elderberry is…is,' he sighed heavily. He looked as if he were trying to say something he would regret.

'Who?' Matthew glanced at his cellular phone. It vibrated persistently in his hands, Anna's name flashed on the caller ID. He replaced it in his pocket, he couldn't deal with her right now.

The waitress placed their waters on the table in front of them and disappeared behind a green door.

'You know him, he's a regular in town,' John struggled.

Matthew rolled his eyes. 'Just tell me, who?'

'Roy the reta-' John winced.

Matthew's mouth fell open. 'Roy the retard! You're telling me Roy the retard ran my wife off the road?'

'Shh! I'm saying it's his car.'

'Why, what reason would he have against Anna?'

The waitress placed two plates of hot off the grill beef burgers, loaded with trimmings in front of them.

John covered the inside with hot sauce immediately. He took a huge bite, spilling hot sauce down his chin. He wiped it with a napkin. 'He wouldn't have any reason, he wouldn't hurt a fly.' He swallowed the remnants of his burger.

'So, someone put him up to it.' Matthew picked at the lettuce protruding from the sesame seed bun on his plate.

'Yeah and I can guess who.' John relaxed back, his arms resting on the table. 'Governor Francis.' He sat with a smug expression, his palms up toward the ceiling.

Matthew sighed. 'Why would he do what she told him?'

'He's her cousin. You know she's power hungry. I bet she set this whole thing up to get Sally convicted and maybe he got carried away. Maybe he wasn't meant to run Anna off the road, just scare her.'

Matthew sat back. He dropped his hands by his side. It all made sense. Why hadn't he figured it out before? 'The phone calls, the vandals, the junk about Sally being an Islam extremist,' he shook his head. 'That reporter said she had a reliable source – doesn't come more reliable than the bloody governor.'

John nodded.

'Jesus,' Matthew mumbled. 'Ok, here's what we're gonna do,' he sat upright. 'We're gonna concentrate on this Bernie guy and the gang, create some reasonable doubt.'

Nodding, John took another bite of his burger. 'I'll drop you home. I can be in Et Lanna by…' He looked at his watch, calculating the time it would take him if he drove. 'Ten o'clock the latest. I'll go to Williams' address first thing in the morning.'

'And the state's witnesses, Mr. Kirkland and Mr. Newson, we have to find something on them too.'

'No problem, I'm in Et Lanna. I'll swing by and find some dirt on them too.'

Matthew was silent for a moment, deep in thought. 'No, it's too much ground for you to cover alone. We only have forty-eight hours left to prepare. Drop me home I'll pack some stuff and come with you.'

John shrugged. 'Fine, I'll pick you up in an hour.'

* * *

Anna had calculated she had called Matthew at least forty times in the past two hours. There had been no answer.

She knew Fridays were early clock off day; court was adjourned at four o'clock. She checked the digits on the VCR again. 8pm.

She prayed he was off somewhere researching the case, hoping John was keeping an eye on him.

She shivered. She could not help but feel nervous about being home alone.

She paced the hall. 'Where is he? Why hasn't he answered his cell?'

Suddenly someone approached the front porch. She could hear the shuffling of shoes against the wood and the jingle of keys. Rocky charged, barking at the front door excitedly.

'Where have you been?' She tried not to sound panicked but it was too late.

Matthew glared, his eyes narrowed. 'Out.'

'Out? I've been worried sick. Why didn't you answer your cell?'

They stood like tribal leaders ready to attack. The foyer closed in around them, one move could cause injury.

He took his cellular phone from his pocket and placed it next to his keys on the sill. 'I was busy.' He opened the downstairs closet and pulled out an overnight bag. 'I'm going to Atlanta to interview some witnesses.'

'What?' She threw her arms in the air. 'No Matt, no. You're not leaving me here alone. No.' Her voice raised an octave, she spat and hissed. 'Some sicko has tried to kill me – we're still gettin' phone calls and someone vandalized my parent's home this afternoon! Don't you walk away from me you son of a bitch!'

He spun on his heels, his eyes red with rage.

She cowered backward. She could not help but hold her breath.

He recoiled, staring at her for a moment before storming upstairs and slamming the bedroom door.

She tried to regain control of her breathing. The sudden surge of adrenaline made her head spin.

* * *

'For a second there, I thought you were that guy again.' Anna stood by the living room window with her arms folded.

Matthew had stayed upstairs for as long as he could. He did not dare to look her in the eyes after his performance. He just could not control himself. The anger. He had no idea who he was angry at. Anna? Sally? Or himself? He did not know. But he knew he had to find out before he did something he would regret.

He slouched on the sofa, the overnight bag, now full, by his leg. 'I'm fine now,' he said. He contemplated telling her about his relapse that all he could think about was running to the bar. But he feared she wouldn't understand. 'I'm sorry about earlier for my behavior.' He shook his head, kicking himself for not telling her the truth. 'I had no idea about the vandalism on your parent's home; I'll tell John I can't go with him to Atlanta.' He took out his cell phone and tapped on the screen sending John a text message.

She turned toward him. Her lips closed, her eyes wandered but did not look at him. 'Maybe if you answered your cell you'd know... Look I'm sorry. I'm just on edge right now.' She sat down next to him, tucking her legs under her.

He wanted to explain about his day in court and why he too was on edge. But even though she was right next to him, she seemed so far away.

He wanted to talk desperately about the accident and about the... baby. The thought cut into his chest. No. It was too painful to think about. He had to bury the thought, pretend like it never happened.

'So who're these witnesses?' she said, changing the subject.

'They live near Sally.'

She nodded, taking his hand. 'Thanks for staying with me, did John mind?' she said, changing the subject.

He sat upright. 'Anna, if I had to go to Atlanta, you'd come with me if you could, right?'

246

She turned to face him, a confused expression on her face. 'Yeah,' she said, slowly. 'Why? You're not thinking what I think you're thinking, are you?'

His body exploded with excitement. 'Listen, hear me out. The witnesses live in Atlanta and had to travel down here. They're staying in a luxury motel – they're not gonna come here and leave their husbands and wives home alone, right?' His face light up. 'I wouldn't, would you?'

She smiled awkwardly. 'No, I guess not.' Her expression changed as she figured out what he was saying. 'So the witnesses you want to talk to might already be here, in Billows Creek.'

He nodded. 'Exactly. I'll call the motel.' He leapt from the sofa and grabbed the phone from the coffee table. 'Hey Jill, it's Matt Brennan.'

'Matt, how are you darlin'. Long time no see!' Her voice was bright and bubbly. 'What can I do for you?'

He smiled. 'You have a Mr. Newson from Atlanta saying there, don't you?'

'A-ha.'

'Did anyone else check in with him?'

'A-ha, his wife.'

He nodded. 'Thanks Jill, that's all I wanted to know.' He hoped Newson was preoccupied the night he saw Sally fire a gun at Stephen, maybe then Newson had not seen what he thought he had?

* * *

It had taken John three and a half hours to drive the 212 miles to Hawthorne River, Atlanta. He had enjoyed his adventure, cruising north up I-75, something he had not experienced since the good ole days, upon leaving university.

247

He had pre-booked a room at the Holiday Inn, just three blocks from where Mr. Newson lived on Grace Street SW.

A pit-faced kid sat behind the counter. His short blonde hair was greased back and a faint shadow of stubble lined his nineteen-year-old chin.

'Evening?' the motel clerk said as John entered the lobby. The clerk's blue eyes were blood-shot and tired.

'Hi, I booked a room for the night,' John replied, looking around the lobby.

Pot plants, which were placed in a somewhat strategic order, surrounded the lobby. A brown leather sofa stood against the front wall. A rocking chair sat in the corner.

John guessed the rocking chair was for the boy's grandmother, when she was over for a vacation. He could picture her rocking away, knitting jumpers for the grandchildren.

He looked back to the clerk. Black rings lined the bottom of his eyes. His small black pupils were lost somewhere in the sea of purple, red and gray. A tell-tale sign of a good night's partying drinking vodka and smoking stuff that sends you to Pluto.

'Name?' the clerk mumbled. He did not take his eyes off the television, sat on a stand in the corner, behind the desk.

'John Beaumont.'

The kid continued to stare at the television. His mouth was open like a catfish. 'Eighty bucks.'

'Eighty?' John repeated. He took out his wallet and grabbed a wad of cash from inside the sleeve.

The clerk's head spun around as if a force field from the cash had pulled at his eyes. 'Plus, fifty dollars security deposit. Non refundable,' he said, licking his lips. He stood up and grabbed the eighty dollars off the counter. He placed it into the register before John had a chance to say otherwise.

'Fifty dollars security deposit, huh?' John replied. He stared at the clerk with narrowed eyes. Nobody conned John Beaumont.

'Yeah, non refundable.' The clerk ran his fingers along the counter expectantly.

John licked the end of his finger and placed the cash onto the counter. The clerk pounced on it eagerly. John slammed his fist on the clerk's fingers.

'Jeez.' He pulled his fingers away sticking them into his mouth to stop the sting. 'Man, what did you do that for?' he groaned.

'That was the tip,' John smirked.

The clerk snatched a key from the wall behind him and handed it to John.

'Number 7,' he mumbled.

'My lucky number,' John said as he left the kid sucking his fingers.

Chapter Forty-One

John rolled onto his stomach. He threw his pillow at the air conditioning unit fixed on the wall nearest the door. Its relentless droning had kept him awake all night.

He would not have minded so much if the temperature had cooled enough to turn the damn thing off.

He stared at the LED clock at the side of his bed. 5:45am.

Throwing the sheet back, he debated whether to get up or stay in the comfort of the human-sized marshmallow that was his bed.

The thick curtains blocked any light from the window, making it hard to tell if it really were morning.

In the blackness of the room, he made his way to the light switch. His fingers fumbled along the wall before finding what they were hunting for. The switch.

After showering, John headed for the breakfast bar across the parking lot.

The buffet table was arranged with baskets of pastries and small plastic bowls of fruit.

A microwave oven and a hotplate were on another counter to the right of the buffet table. A tray of bacon and sausages sizzled under the hotplate.

Eight tables with wipe clean table cloths, all with the same floral design, stood in front of the counter.

A girl in her early twenties entered the dining area, from a room leading off at the far end, near the breakfast bar. She was carrying a tray filled with freshly baked bread rolls.

He approached the girl, smiling warmly. 'Morning, do I just help myself?'

She looked at him as if his presence had startled her. 'Oh, morning sir.' Her face softened. 'Sure, help yourself,' she gestured toward the tray. 'I've got some muffins on the go, if you would like to wait a minute?'

'Thanks, but I have my eye on those.' He pointed to a plate of pancakes.

She smiled, placing the warm bread into a large basket next to the plate of pancakes. 'I'll get outta your way then. Enjoy your breakfast,' she said, making her way toward the door she had just come through.

'Don't leave on my account. Actually I was wondering if you could help me?'

She turned resting the empty tray onto the counter. 'Sure, how can I help?'

He filled his plate with fresh fruit and pancakes. 'Do you mind if I sit - I'm so hungry.' He pulled a chair and began to pour syrup onto the golden mountain. 'My name is John Beaumont; I'm a lawyer down in Birchwood County. I'm looking for an old friend.'

She smirked. 'An old friend, huh?' Her facial expression told him she did not believe him; she looked as if she had heard that one before.

'Yeah, Bernie's his name. He lives in on Cypress Street, in Eastville. I was wondering if you knew how to get there?' He used the side of his folk to cut a piece of pancake. The syrup dripped as he placed it into his mouth. 'Mmm, excuse me.' He wiped the sticky goo from his lips. 'It's good.' He noticed the girl relax.

Her dark eyes smiled, as she stood leaning on her right foot, her elbow resting on the tray. She was pretty but not beautiful. Her white sneakers had seen better days. He figured she wore them to work, saving her best shoes for when she clocked off at the end of the day.

'Eastville… was it?' She tilted her head toward him. 'Cypress Street.'

'Yeah.' He tried not to talk with his mouthful.

She frowned. 'Sorry I can't help you, I'm useless when it comes to directions.'

He nodded. 'Thanks anyway.'

'Wait, why don't you ask Miss Morgan over at the beauty salon. She'll know.'

'Thanks I will,' he replied. 'D'you mind if I have some more pancakes?' He smiled, cheekily.

* * *

Matthew stood in the motel's foyer. He watched a Cab pull up in front of the entrance and a woman carrying a shopping bag climb out.

The foyer was elegantly designed with cream furnishings and a log fireplace. A chandelier hung from the ceiling above a hand crafted coffee table.

The woman entered the motel through the rotating doors.

'Mrs. Newson?'

She didn't smile at him, just raised her eyebrows suspiciously.

'Morning Ma'me, my name is Matthew Brennan, I'm a lawyer.' He handed the stick thin woman his card.

'I know who you are, seen you on T.V.' She placed a cigarette to her mouth and gestured for him to follow her back outside. She took a long drag, before blowing out the smoke. 'What do you want with me?'

252

He smiled, trying to put her at ease. 'Mrs. Newson, may I ask you some questions about what your husband testified?'

'Huh,' she took another drag on her cigarette, flicking ash into an ashtray hung on the wall. 'What do you wanna know?'

'On the night of June 10th your husband said he saw your neighbor Sally Martinez fire a gun at patrolman Collins?'

She stamped out her cigarette into the ash tray and gave a little laugh.

He was confused at her response. 'Is that correct?'

'Mr. Brennan is it?'

He nodded.

'My husband ain't a big drinker - neither of us is.'

He wondered where this was going.

'He just got promoted, first one in five years,' she continued. She pulled her cardigan across her small chest, tugging at the belt to make it tighter. 'Tyson Reed, my husband's colleague, suggested they all go out an' celebrate. They left us women at home, mind you.' She raised her eyebrows, and then shook her head. 'Anyhow, he was gone most of the evening. Drank himself into a coma.'

Matthew took out his notepad and began to scribble some notes.

'You wanna ask me what my husband said he saw was true right, Mr. Brennan?'

He put down his pencil and looked her in the eye. 'A woman's life depends on it.'

She nodded thoughtfully. 'My husband is a loving caring man, I couldn't be without him. Lord knows you know what kind there are out there - you defend them.'

He could not help but wince. He was just about to point out not all his clients were guilty when she said, 'My husband was drunk that night, passed out on the sofa; he had a hangover for three days. Now…' she moved closer. 'I ain't calling my husband a liar, you understand. If says he saw her then he saw her.'

Matthew nodded. 'Did you see her that night too.'

'Yes I saw her and I could hear her screaming and yelling too.'

'What about the gun?'

She shook her head. 'No Sir, I didn't see a gun or hear one fired neither.'

'Thank you Mrs. Newson. I know it's difficult but would you be willing to testify to that in court?'

'My husband won't get in trouble?'

'Oh no.' He shook his head.

'Alright then.'

'Do you happen to have Mr. Reed's address?'

She shrugged. 'Sure,' she said, pulling an address book from her purse. She licked her finger and flicked through the pages until she found Reed's address.

* * *

Matthew placed a bottle of water, fresh from the fridge, to his aching forehead. He sat in his office with the phone to his ear. 'Reed lives three doors down from Sally, number 878.'

'I'll swing by and give him the subpoena,' John said.

Matthew nodded. 'Thanks,' he sighed, heavily. 'Listen, I did some more research into Roy-the-retard's whereabouts. It turns out he works for the Birchwood County Times!'

'So, what are you thinking?'

Matthew frowned. 'I dunno. Maybe he stirred up all this Muslim crap?'

'Roy?' John chuckled. 'Remind me never to leave you alone anymore.'

'Well someone blasted it all over the papers.'

254

John sighed. 'It's not important who it was, let's concentrate on winning.'

Matthew nodded. 'Any luck with Bernie Williams?' he said, changing the subject. He heard rustling in the background. It sounded as if a chip packet was being opened.

'Nope, not yet,' John replied, with his mouthful. 'I have found a witness though who will testify that her son was murdered after receiving death threats from the Comancheros gang...'

Matthew could hear more rustling in the background and then shuffling of papers.

'A Mrs. Chuang, also from Hawthorne River, will be arriving tomorrow at 2pm. I told her you'd set up a meetin' with her once she's settled in her motel suite.'

'Where is she staying?' Matthew reached into his jacket pocket and pulled out his notepad and biro.

'North circle – sorry it was the only one available.'

'Shit,' Matthew sighed.

Chapter Forty-Two

The weekend had past Matthew in a haze. He sat alone in the living room, agonizing over his opening statement. *Why did I leave it until the last minute?* He thought.

In less than four hours, he would have to address the entire courtroom and do his best to prove Sally did not commit the crimes.

He sighed and stared at a mark on the wall in front of him. Thoughts and scenarios played around in his fatigued head.

He remembered what it tasted like, the sweet bitter taste that cut at his throat and fired in his stomach. All he needed was one glass. All he desired.

Hazy sunshine began to seep from the horizon. It spilled into the living room from a small gap in the curtains, creating walking shadows along the carpeted floor.

The door creaked open, snapping Matthew back to reality. Anna entered wearing the white silk nightdress he had brought for their anniversary last April.

'Sorry, did I wake you?' he asked, solemnly. He did not have the energy to move. It was too much effort. Even breathing made his body ache.

She crossed to the table lamp, flicking the switch. 'No. I couldn't sleep either.' She sat next to him, curling her legs up on the sofa.

He tapped her leg, squeezing it lightly, thankful she was next to him.

'What are you thinking about...Sorry stupid question,' she said, rolling her eyes.

He stared at the same mark on the wall and as if talking to it replied, 'I'm thinking maybe your sister was wrong.'

'About what?'

'About hirin' me. I thought I could do this. I thought I was ready.' He shook his head.

'Matt, don't do this OK? This isn't about you anymore. This is about Sally and my parents, it's about those children and me.' She placed her feet to the floor and turned to face him. 'We're your family Matt. We're the people who love you. I know you're scared. We're all scared, but you know what? You have to fight it and never give up.' She placed her fingers on his chin, turning his head to face her.

He had never known her to be so forthright with him. She seemed reinforced with determination and confidence. Everything about her body language reflected the words coming out her mouth. 'Listen to me, you're a great lawyer. Sally didn't do this, and the jury will see that with your help. You've got to get rid of the ghosts Matt or they'll haunt you forever.'

He could not help but feel turned on by her sudden vote of confidence. Closing his eyes he said, 'she's lied so many times. I'm not sure...'

'You think she's guilty, don't you?' she asked, jumping in.

He shrugged.

'Are you going to put her on the stand?'

'Do you honestly believe her?' he asked.

She paused, pulling at her nightshirt to cover her knees. 'Whatever I think of Sally, I know in my heart and soul she would never endanger her children. If she planned to kill Stephen, which I doubt, she's a lot of things but a murderer?' She shook her head. 'I know she would have made certain her children were someplace safe, not sitting in view of it all.'

He raised his eyebrows. If he were honest, with everything else that had happened, he had over looked that. 'Yeah, you're right.'

'I know now that's why you decided to defend Sally - because of Lizzie and Tom,' she told him.

He nodded. 'I can't bear the thought of them being without their mom.' He tapped her hand. 'I have to make the jury feel the same way. Sally has to testify,' he said. 'The jury has to see her as a loving caring mother, not some adulterous murderer. If I could just get her story straight?'

She squeezed his forearm encouragingly.

'You wanna help me with my opening statement?'

She nodded and leaned in, kissing him passionately.

Part of him wanted to pull away from her and finish his opening statement, but the other more dominant part of him surrendered to her caress. He kissed her back, slipping the straps off her shoulders.

* * *

At 7:30am, Matthew arrived at his office wearing his best suit. He grabbed the last minute files from Clara and headed for the courthouse.

Three boxes of case files would be couriered over later; it was too much to carry alone.

Five reporters flew at him with unintelligible questions. He pushed them away with his arm. 'No comment,' he repeated to no avail. He placed his briefcase on the small pine table in the interview room and waited for Sally to enter.

He watched her cross from the door to the pine table like a zombie.

'I'm putting you on the stand,' he blurted.

'You're what?' Her mouth fell open, her eyes darting back and forth trying to work out if what he had said was a joke.

'You heard me.' His tone was intense. 'Before I rest the case, you're going to testify.'

'I can't,' she leapt from the chair, pacing up and down the small room. 'No, fuck you I won't do it!'

He slammed his notepad onto the desk, it echoed off the walls. 'Oh yes you will and we're going to work on your story right now.'

Her lip trembled. 'I can't do this Matt,' she looked away. 'I'm scared.'

'I'm done playing games with you, Sal.' With one sweeping motion, he pulled the chair from under the table, placed it in the center of the room and gestured for Sally to sit.

* * *

Hawthorne River had forty-five educational facilities in its district. Each of them boasted about their high standards.

Sally lived in the college community of Grace Street, six miles from the William B Hartsfield Atlanta international airport.

John turned left onto Peachtree Avenue, passing the airport runway on his left. He continued under the railroad tracks until he came to a stop sign.

It was a far cry from the huge skyscrapers and the hustle and bustle of downtown Atlanta.

The roads were sweeping, almost like Billows Creek, but not nearly as picturesque as far as John was concerned.

He was thankful the traffic today was exactly like home.

He turned right onto Grace Street, slowing down to check house numbers.

Finally, the Chevy rolled to a stop outside a small detached bungalow, Sally's home, number 881.

He placed his hands onto his hips and studied the street.

The Newson's lived at number 884, right across the street from Sally's front lawn.

Lifting the first page on his clip board, John re-read Mr. Newson's statement. He wanted to be in the exact position Newson had said he was when he saw Sally fire the revolver.

Could Mr. Newson really have seen Sally's driveway from where he said he walked that night? Sure it was a well lit open street; he would have had a clear view.

He sighed, heading further down the street until he came to the Reed's residence. Tyson Reed lived a couple of blocks from the Newson's, in a rented condo.

He was a fat bald man, with freckles on his nose. He wore sunglasses on his head, like some macho heavyweight.

'You were drinking with Mr. Newson on the night of June 10th, is that correct?'

'Yeah.'

John tried not to become irritated by the arrogant prick standing in front of him, mouth open, chewing a stick of gum. 'Would you be willing to testify to that in court, I could get a subpoena?'

Reed held up his hands defensively. 'No black man's gonna threaten a Reed.'

John glared.

'But I ain't in a fightin' mood. I'll testify he had four Martini's coz I bought them.'

'Fine.' He handed Reed an envelope. 'Be there at that time.'

*   *   *

Matthew checked his watch. 8:30am. He had time. He stood in the courthouse men's room. He vomited and splashed his face with cold water, patting around his eyes with a paper towel. *You can do this.* He thought as he stared at his reflection in the mirror. He took a deep breath. This was it.

Three men entered the room, carrying briefcases and wearing shiny new suits.

Matthew pretended he was washing his hands. *Fresh meat.* He thought. He remembered when he had graduated from law school. How daunted he felt when he entered the courthouse.   The courthouse personnel seemed to look through him like he was transparent in the maze of bodies, rushing to this department and that department.

He smiled at the memory as he threw the crumpled paper towel into the Trash Can. He straightened his tie and with one last deep motivational breath, left the men's room.

The courtroom was bursting with police officers and members of their families. There seemed to be even more today than at the start of the trial. Matthew could feel them glaring at him; it sent a shiver up his spine.

Reporters lined the front balcony, note pads and pens at the ready.

Chamberlain had denied the use of television cameras. It was well documented he found electronic equipment to be obtrusive during criminal trials. Of course that did not stop local television companies, from filing request forms, in the hope the old codger would change his mind.

Matthew relaxed when he had discovered the judge had denied the requests. He was sure he would not have coped if he had a camera in his face the entire time.

With surprising confidence, he took his seat, placed his files and trial notebook in front of him and interlocked his fingers on the table.

He sat going over his power-thinking mantra in his head, waiting for Sally to enter the courtroom. *This is my place; this is where I work my magic. This is what I was born to do. I will make the jury see Sally could not have committed these crimes.*

Linnie and Arthur entered the courtroom. Elizabeth and Thomas, dressed in their Sunday best, followed their grandparents shyly. They all took their seats just behind the defense table.

'How's it goin'?' Arthur whispered to Matthew.

He turned around. 'OK, Art. OK.' He smiled weakly at Linnie and she returned the favor. 'Didn't Anna come with you?'

'No. She had some errands to run, said she's on her way,' Arthur replied.

The sketch artist began to work a couple of lines as Sally entered the court room. She walked toward the defense table, her eyes transfixed on her children. 'My babies!' she whispered, trying to hold in her emotions. She held them over the wooden partition, kissing their foreheads. 'I'll do everything you say Matt,' she whispered.

He nodded. He hoped the jury was studying Sally's performance. He knew it was genuine, but what was a little exaggeration? If he could get her to act like that on the stand, perhaps they had a chance?

'Gas her!' a male voice yelled.

Matthew led Sally by the arm to her seat as the bailiff brought the courtroom to order. He could see she was upset by the abuse. She bowed her head and picked at her thumb nail.

'All rise.'

'Where's Anna?' Sally whispered. 'And John?'

'John's on his way back from Atlanta, I hope. I don't know where Anna is.' He looked over his shoulder and made eyes at Linnie and Arthur, 'Where is she?' They shrugged and looked past the second row of spectators, to the courtroom doors, to see if she were with the late arrivals. There was no sign of her.

Chamberlain made himself comfortable in his seat. 'You may proceed Mr. Brennan.'

Matthew stood tall. He glided to center stage, toward his audience. The spotlight was on him. He took a breath, absorbing the anticipated silence, adrenalin pumping wildly through his veins.

His opening statement started with sincerity. He said the murder of patrolman Collins and the assault on Deputy Richardson were heinous crimes. He was not here to prove otherwise. To do so would be an even bigger crime against two peace officers of the community. He was not here to tarnish the memory of patrolman Collins or to make light of the injuries Deputy Richardson sustained.

But with this crime came pressure: pressure on the county Sheriff's department to find the killer. The community pleaded with the Sheriff's department. The governor pleaded with the Sheriff's department. 'Arrest somebody. Arrest anybody.'

The point of an opening statement was to give an overview, a sort of road map, for the jury to follow during the presentation of evidence. It was not for arguing defects with the other side's version of events. That would come later in closing.

Matthew was sure Helen was about to object to his statement, but he was done arguing. For now.

He walked along the jury box. He wanted his ending to stick in their minds. 'Helen Maxwell and the prosecution team have to prove beyond a reasonable doubt that Sally Martinez committed these crimes, and we, the defense, will produce evidence that brings reasonable doubt to their case. Yes, Sally Martinez was at the diner that night, but she didn't kill anyone. Therefore, you must acquit her of all charges.' He crossed to the defense table, a signal to the judge that he was finished.

'Call your first witness.'

'Your honor, defense calls Mrs. Moore.'

Matthew's first impression of Sally's manager was of a short petite lady, almost fragile-looking, someone that made you feel as if you needed to protect her from life.

When Mrs. Moore had come to Matthew's office for a run through of the questions he would ask during the trial, he was shocked at how tall she actually was. She was almost six two.

'Mrs. Moore please tell the court how long Sally Martinez has worked for you at your store?'

'Six years.' She tucked her black maxi dress under her thighs to stop it dragging on the ground under her seat.

'And what kind of responsibilities did Sally have while she worked at your store?'

She smiled warmly in Sally's direction. 'Sally served customers, dealt with cash and credit card slips. Occasionally she would answer inquires on the phone. She locked up three times a week.'

'And what does that include, when she locks up the store?'

She scratched at her nose. 'Well, there's a whole list of duties. You have to count the cash and credit card slips, clean the floor and the shelves.' Mrs. Moore looked to the jury box. 'Once the store is closed and the money is collected, it all has to go over to the bank. The stock has to be checked and documented for the next order of supplies.'

'That sounds like a lot of responsibility? Was Sally reliable?'

'Oh Yes.' She smiled at Sally.

'And had Mrs. Martinez ever been late?'

'No never. She always called first if there were a problem, like if one of her kids got sick or something.'

'And how did you feel when you heard the news of her arrest?'

Matthew was trying to establish Sally's character. If they saw her as a hard working mother, maybe they would not be so quick to send her to the gas chamber?

Mrs. Moore looked wide-eyed. 'I was shocked. Sally would never hurt anyone. But when I heard on the radio her children were with her, I knew then there was no way she did what they said. She loves her children so very much. She would never endanger them in anyway. She is a good mother.' She looked at the jury. 'She always puts those children first.'

'Thank you Mrs. Moore. No further questions,' Matthew said.

Helen stood and approached the witness box. She did not bother to wait for the judge to ask if she wanted to cross-examine. 'Mrs. Moore on the Monday prior to June 13th, did you and the defendant have a conversation about vacations?'

'Yes.'

'Can you tell us about that conversation please?'

'Sally was overdue a vacation and she asked me if she could have the following week off. She was taking the children away for a few days.'

'Thank you, Mrs. Moore. No further questions.'

Chamberlain jumped in, 'Any re-direct?'

Helen was trying to imply Sally planned the murder because she had pre-booked a week off work in order to drive down from Atlanta.

Matthew stood abruptly. 'Mrs. Moore, did you think the request was particularly short notice?'

'Not at all. Her husband works long distance, and she often gives me a weeks notice.'

'So you didn't think the request was particularly unusual?'

'No.'

'No further questions, your honor.' Matthew flipped over his trial notebook to remind himself of the questions he wanted to ask his next witness. 'Defense calls Sheriff Drano.' Matthew had recognized the Sheriff as soon as he walked into Matthew's office. The image Matthew had of the man was exact, except Matthew was certain Drano didn't weigh three hundred pounds – maybe two.

Dressed in his brown uniform, minus his hat, Drano resembled a bear. He walked with surprising grace, in his heavy industrial-style boots, down the aisle to his seat in the witness box.

'Sheriff Drano, how long have you been the Sheriff in Atlanta?'

'Six years.'

'And how long have you had experience in law enforcement?'

Drano smiled. 'Twenty years, give or take a coupla months.'

Matthew nodded, lifting some papers from his desk. 'And what was your relationship to the deceased, Stephen Collins?'

Drano lifted his baseball glove hands into his lap. 'He was my patrol sergeant for a coupla years.'

'Would you say Mr. Collins was good at his job?'

Drano nodded. 'One of the best. He won policeman of the year three years running. He had an arrest rate longer than my,' Drano paused, remembering he was in a courtroom, and re-thought his answer. 'Longer than anyone I know.'

Matthew smirked, cleared his throat and said, 'Can you tell us in your own words what happened on the night of December 17th 2005?'

'Stephen had been working a case involving the Comancheros, a notorious gang in our neighborhood, that night he brought in the leader, Jay Keller, for dealing.'

'What happened when the leader, A.K.A Killer J, was brought into the holding cell?'

Helen did not bother to stand. 'Objection your honor, relevance?'

'Your honor, I ask the court for a little latitude, all will become clear.'

The judge interlocked his fingers. He looked at Helen as if he needed her permission to proceed. 'Make your point Mr. Brennan. The witness will answer the question.'

Drano nodded at the judge. 'He somehow managed to take a swing at patrolman Collins - gave Collins a black eye and threatened to have him removed from the planet.'

'He threatened patrolman Collins' life?'

'Yeah a coupla times.'

'Did you think these threats were real?'

Drano nodded, looking at the jury. 'Sure, J has connections you know,' he rubbed his nose. 'Hit men, other gangs in Florida - you name it - if he wanted Stephen dead he was gonna be, in my opinion.'

'Other gangs in Florida?'

'Yeah. J was arrested last fall down in Florida for armed robbery. He was working alongside the Mexican gang there. He did time in jail too.'

'In Florida?'

'Yes, sir. He's no stranger down there.'

Matthew looked at the papers he was holding. Reading from them he said, 'Can you tell us what happened on May 26th?'

'Yeah, Stephen put in a request to be transferred here, to Birchwood County.'

'And on the Saturday before his transfer, did the officers hold a farewell party in a nightclub, in the center of town?'

Drano rested his arms onto the armrest. 'Yes.'

'Can you tell us who was at the party?'

Helen rose from her seat. 'Objection your honor, relevance?'

Judge Chamberlain took a sip of water from his cup. 'Over-ruled.'

Matthew nodded and gestured with a hand for Drano to answer the question.

'Stephen's friends and family were there. We also invited a local reporter to do a piece on Stephen.'

Matthew looked up to the bench. 'Your honor, may I approach the witness?'

Chamberlain nodded.

'Can you identify this newspaper column?'

Drano studied it. He smiled, remembering that night. 'Yeah, this is the column Jackie Milson wrote on Stephen.'

Matthew rested his arm on the jury box. 'Can you read the highlighted section please?'

Drano cleared his throat, flipping the newspaper to the highlighted section. '"Patrolman Collins leaves for Birchwood County, southwest Georgia, where he will continue his role as a peace officer."'

Matthew took the newspaper from Sheriff Drano. 'Your honor I would like to ask that this be marked in as defense exhibit B.'

'So granted.'

'No further questions your honor.'

Chamberlain scratched his chin. 'Any cross?'

Helen shook her head. 'No questions, your honor.'

'Defense calls Ms. Chuang to the stand.'

Ms. Chuang was younger than Matthew had imagined. She had had her son at seventeen and raised him with the help of her mother, her only living relative. The years of struggling had taken its toll on her once beautiful appearance. Her hair was thinning, lifeless and dull, and she looked washed out and tired.

'Please state your name for the record, Ma'me' Matthew said.

'Valerie Chuang.' Her voice was soft, almost inaudible, with a strong Chinese accent.

'And how old are you?'

'Thirty-five.'

'And what is your occupation?'

'I'm a maid.'

'And how long have you been a maid?'

'Seventeen years.'

'Do you have any children, Ms. Chuang?'

She swallowed hard, looked at the floor and replied, 'I have an eighteen-year-old son.'

Matthew interlocked his fingers, he took a slow breath. He had not thought that asking questions about a woman's son would be so difficult. 'Ms. Chuang, can you tell us what happened on Tuesday May 15th?'

'Y-yes, my son was at a party with some friends, and I guess a fight broke out. My son was threatened by Jay Keller the leader of a gang in our neighborhood.'

'How did he threaten your son, Ms. Chuang?'

She bit her lip. 'He punch him and tell him he was going to kill him. Then later that night someone threw a brick through my window. It had paper wrapped around it, it say: "You going to die".'

'Did you think this threat was real?'

Ms. Chuang nodded.

'The witness will answer the question so the courtroom can hear.' Chamberlain said, softly.

'Y-yes I was afraid for my son.'

'Ms. Chuang, can you tell us what happened on the night of May 17th, two nights after this threat?'

She cleared her throat. 'My son was shot and killed while walking home from his girlfriend's.'

Matthew nodded. 'Thank you Ms. Chuang. No further questions your honor.'

'Defense calls Alan Morris.'

Alan Morris proceeded down the aisle toward the witness box. He was dressed in a cream patterned shirt, black pants and a matching tie. His clear rimmed glasses magnified his huge hazel eyes.

'Mr. Morris, can you tell the court what your occupation is?'

He licked his pencil thin lips. 'I am the editor of *Your Town* newspaper in Atlanta.'

Matthew interlocked his fingers in front of him. 'And what is *Your Town* newspaper?'

'It is a monthly newspaper that is dedicated to publishing news and stories covering people, culture and business that will help to bring members of our community together in Atlanta.'

Matthew smiled. 'And can you tell us how many publications you have produced within the Atlanta community?'

'We publish over 43,000 copies each month.'

'And where do you distribute these publications?'

Morris cleared his throat and looked at the jury. 'We distribute to over twelve neighborhoods within the Atlanta district including Ansley Park, Sandy Springs and Hawthorne River. We also mail 23,000 papers, using the U.S Postal service, to other neighborhoods within the Atlanta district.' He looked back at Matthew. 'The other 10,000 papers are distributed to local restaurants, small businesses and community centers inside Atlanta.'

Matthew nodded. 'Can you tell the court who Jackie Milson is?'

He nodded and smiled. 'Jackie is one of our most highly sought after journalists.'

Matthew approached the evidence cart and picked up the newspaper he had asked Sheriff Drano to read from. 'Can you identify this newspaper?' He handed Alan the newspaper with its highlighted section.

He did not study it for long. 'Yes, this is a copy of my newspaper, Your Town.'

'Thank you Mr. Morris. No further questions.'

'Any cross?'

Helen sighed heavily. 'No your honor.'

'Defense calls Mr. Ned Holland.'

Ned walked casually down the aisle and took his seat in the box. 'Mr. Holland, can you tell us what you do for a living?' Matthew smiled at how awkward he felt calling Ned "Mr. Holland".

'I own Ned's bar and diner, here in Birchwood County.'

Matthew turned to face the jury. 'So the jury is clear, is that the same establishment where the crimes took place?'

Ned nodded sorrowfully. 'Yes, that's correct.'

'And can you tell us where your establishment is situated?'

'Just off Interstate 75.'

Matthew turned back to face Ned. 'And can you tell us how many customers you had on June 13th?'

Ned raised his eyebrows. 'I can't really say. It was real busy because I was auditioning a band that night. We had college kids coming and going and,' he scratched his nose, 'it's the holidays too, so people come from all over.'

'Would it be fair to say there were more customers than usual?'

Ned nodded. 'Definitely.'

'Thank you, no further questions, your honor.'

Matthew was trying to establish that if Jay Keller wanted Stephen dead, like Ms. Chuang's son, all he had to do was read a copy of *Your Town* magazine to find out where Stephen was transferring to.

It would have been easy to follow Stephen to Birchwood County, using I-75, hang out at Ned's diner until Stephen arrived, remove him from the planet and then get back to Atlanta.

Chapter Forty-Three

Anna was dressed in a blue suit with matching pencil skirt. She pulled the pillows back and hunted for her safety deposit box. 'Where is it?' She had spent twenty minutes looking for the box and was becoming increasingly aggravated by her lack of memory. She looked at her watch. 10am. 'Crap.' She had told Matthew she would be at the courthouse by eight-thirty.

She remembered she had it the day she packed some boxes, before putting them in the garage.

The wooden railing creaked with the pressure of her hand as she jogged downstairs, making her way to the garage.

On the floor, she noticed the safety deposit box, lying next to a crowbar; the latch was broken. Without even counting the money inside, she knew 100 dollars were missing.

'Oh Matt.'

She slouched on the stairs in the hall. She held a Kleenex in her left hand, the phone, rested against her ear, in the other. She called Matthew's doctor to ask his advice. It was obvious Matthew had relapsed, and she needed to know how to handle the situation.

'Sorry Doctor Adamson, there's someone at the door. Can I call you back?' She was surprised to see Ritchie on her porch. 'Oh hi Ritchie, I was just on my way to the trial. I haven't forgot your payment – would you like it now?'

'Yes, if it's no trouble – I'm in a hurry myself.'

Rocky growled at Ritchie, teeth snarling, saliva spitting from his jaws.

'Oh, let me just put Rocky away,' she said, sheepishly. She took Rocky by the collar, ushering him into the kitchen, out into the garage and closed the inner door.

Rocky continued to bark in the background as she made her way back down the hall to where Ritchie was standing.

'Quit scratching the floor Rocky!' She smiled. 'Sorry Ritchie, I'm a mess this morning. Make yourself at home.'

He laid his jacket over the arm of the sofa and followed her toward the kitchen.

'I'm trying to find my check book – it's around here somewhere.' She rifled through some drawers. 'A-ha here it is!' She placed the checkbook on the counter before realizing she didn't have a pen.

'The yard's lookin' good – those seeds are doing well – mind if I take a peek?'

'Sure help yourself,' she said, hurrying to the next drawer to search for a pen.

She entered the living room, hoping Matthew had left a pen by the telephone. He hadn't, but she noticed Ritchie's jacket on the arm of the sofa and figured he wouldn't mind if she borrowed a pen.

She pulled a gold fountain-pen from the inside sleeve. Receipts fell from the pocket landing at her feet. She sighed heavily, shaking her head, and picked them up.

She froze, staring at the Ned's bar and diner logo printed in bold.

'June 13th.' Her words came out slowly, cutting through the silence at a deafening pitch. '19:40,' she gasped.

Suddenly, she was aware of someone standing behind her.

'Yes, June 13th.' His voice was cold and threatening. '19:40'

Chapter Forty-Four

Wendy Morgan had been a huge help. John was convinced she was a human road atlas, giving him exact landmarks and exit numbers to Eastville. It was only thirty miles from Hawthorne River, along the spaghetti-like interstate that was the 285. He was surprised the traffic was lighter than he had expected.

He smiled to himself. He listened to the radio, the wind blowing through the open window. While he was traveling at such speed, there was no need to turn on the air conditioning.

He parked in front of number eight.

The front yard had a child's bicycle on the front lawn and some plastic toys. A small inflated PVC pool lay next to shrubberies, to the right of the house. He knocked on the screen door.

'They won't be back for hours, honey,' said an elderly voice. 'Can I help you?'

He looked over his shoulder. A woman, in her late seventies, supported her weight on a white side gate.

'Mornin' ma'am,' he said, politely. 'I'm lookin' for Mr. Williams. Does he live here?'

'Erm, Bernie Williams?' The woman played with her thick plaited ponytail.

'Yeah, that's him.'

'Are you here to collect his stuff?' Her face softened.

'His stuff?' he said, curiously.

She smiled embarrassingly. 'I'm sorry, I thought you were here to collect Bernie's things. He moved, you see and left some boxes here until he had settled. I kept them for him. It's been a few months now, and I was hoping you were here to collect them.'

John smiled. 'Yes that's right. I'm a buddy of his,' he lied.

The lady narrowed her eyes suspiciously. 'Really? Did y'all work together at the academy?'

The academy? He nodded.

'Well, why don't you come on in and have some tea? I've just made some and we can get out of this heat.' She led John into her back yard and into her house via a patio door.

'Here have a seat,' she said as they entered the air-conditioned dining room. She gestured for John to sit down and poured a glass of tea from an elegantly designed carafe. 'Oh, where are my manners? My name is Lucille, Lucille Beckwith.'

'Charmed, J...' John corrected himself. 'James Cromwell.' He hoped she was not a huge movie fan and did not recognize the actor's name. 'My, what wonderful decorations.'

The dining room walls were covered with oriental wall fans. Each one had a symbolic meaning.

A Japanese silk painting hung to the right of a blue dining table set, encased in a wooden cabinet along the back wall.

A Buddha and some jade elephants sat neatly along the front of the cabinet with two pot plants either side of them.

'My son. He travels with his job. He buys all these things for me.' She smiled.

He returned the smile. 'They are truly remarkable.'

277

'So how long have you known Bernie?' she asked, changing the subject.

'Oh, seems like a lifetime,' he lied. 'What a guy.'

Her smiled faded. 'Yeah, he deserves a medal for what he's been through the past six months.'

He nodded, remembering what Matthew had told him about the death of Bernie Williams' wife. 'He sure does.'

She shook her head. 'It ripped him apart. His wife was a wonderful woman.' She smacked her lips together. 'He was heart broken after the hearing - accidental my foot! Poor man ended up in a psychiatric hospital for a coupla months.'

His eyes widened. 'That's terrible.' He took a sip from the glass in front of him. His taste buds danced in protest; the bitter taste stung his throat as it traveled down to his stomach. He blinked trying to clear his watery vision. 'I didn't know he had to go into a hospital. Which one?'

She placed a light hand on her cheek. 'Oh, I can't remember. I'm sure there is some correspondence among Bernie's things. He won't mind if we look.' She stood from her chair, supporting her weight with the dining room table and gestured for John to follow her.

'This can't be Bernie?' he said, unable to hide the surprise in his voice. He stared at the photograph for a long moment.

'It is, why do you say that?' She narrowed her eyes suspiciously.

He chuckled, trying to lighten the atmosphere. 'He just looks so young, that's all. Listen, I must be going. Thanks for your time.' His words came out rushed and anxious as he hurried down the hall, toward the front door.

* * *

Fumbling with her checkbook Anna said, 'H-here, I borrowed your pen. That's all I owe you, right?' She handed Ritchie the check, trying to remain calm.

'Yes, that's right.' He didn't look at the check and studied her expression.

'Well, I have to get to court.' She headed toward the front door.

He blocked her way. 'I was there that night, but you know that, don't you?'

She stared at him, biting her lower lip. 'I-I have to get to court.'

He paused for a moment, studying her expression. 'The murder happened at 19:45, didn't it?'

She smiled nervously for a moment, not knowing how to respond. 'D-did it? I don't know.'

'Don't lie to me,' he threw her against the wooden railing. 'You're not going anywhere.' He pulled some handcuffs from his pant pocket and handcuffed her to the railing.

'Please let me go. Why are you doing this?'

He slapped her hard across the cheek. The pain shot up the side of her face, igniting her skin. Her eyes blurred, water streamed over her lids.

He wiped the sweat from his forehead with a black patterned bandana, before tying it around his neck.

'Please Ritchie?' Her words floated past him as if he were immune to her voice.

'You had to snoop, didn't you? You couldn't just give me my money and let me go home!' He curled his fingers into fists. 'Stupid bitch!'

Chapter Forty-Five

Matthew had spent, what seemed like an eternity, going over Tyson Reed's statement with him in the conference room during recess. It was not that the guy's statement was complicated or that Matthew was not prepared. He already had enough to impeach Newson's statement from his wife alone, but Reed would nail it for them.

'I tell you what, how about if I say it like this?' Reed scratched at his unshaven face. 'No, I'll pause - you know for effect? - Then I'll flash the ladies a little smile?'

Matthew rubbed his temples. He was losing his patience. 'Look I'll ask you how many Martini's you brought and you just say four, OK.' He stood from the courthouse conference chair. 'Just say it normally and naturally OK?'

Reed relaxed in his chair, stretching out his leg. 'Well, I think it would be good if I said it the way I want.'

Matthew crossed to the exit. 'Whatever.' He mumbled under his breath.

He could feel the tension building in his muscles as the courtroom was called to order.

'You may call your next witness, Mr. Brennan.'

'Defense calls Mrs. Newson.' He did not move from his standing position at the defense table. He would ask his questions from there.

The witness was sworn and seated. She tucked her floral print dress under her legs, before making herself comfortable.

Her hair was styled neatly with two small pins either side of her head, keeping her short layers away from her face.

'Mrs. Newson you are married to the state witness, Mr. Newson, is that correct?'

She smiled. 'Yes. We've been married for twenty-three years.'

He returned the smile. 'Please tell us in your own words what happened on the night of June 10th?'

She told the court that her husband was intoxicated that night.

'Thank you Mrs. Newson. No further questions.'

With no cross examination, the witness was excused from the stand. Matthew proceeded with Mr. Reed. He tried not to show his animosity toward the arrogant prick as the witness took the stand.

He was thankful that Mr. Reed had changed into a more appropriate courtroom attire. A black suit and tie, no doubt his work clothes.

The witness answered Matthew's questions as he had been instructed. He was convinced Reed had practiced his answers as discussed hundreds of times, so he used the correct facial expressions.

Helen had no questions for Reed, and he was excused.

Matthew gripped Sally's hand. With a few whispered words of encouragement, he turned to the judge. 'Defense calls Sally Martinez to the stand.'

*   *   *

John snatched his driving license and registration from the officer's hand. 'Thank- you officer, as usual you've done an excellent job,' he replied, sarcastically.

'Do you realize you were doing sixty in a forty zone?'

John gripped the steering wheel in frustration. 'As I've told you officer, it is a matter of life and death that I get back to Birchwood County. People are in danger!'

'A-ha. Whatever you say.'

*   *   *

Sally stared at her children from the witness box. Matthew had warned Helen would have some questions and told her to prepare herself for the worst.

Helen, a ball point pen in her left hand, walked toward Sally. 'How would you describe your relationship with the deceased, Stephen Collins?'

Matthew did not take his eyes from Sally.

She answered with confidence. 'We were lovers for little over a year.'

'And who ended that relationship?'

'He did.' She looked at Matthew for some reassurance. He did not respond.

'He ended your fourteen month relationship?' Helen confirmed.

'Yes.' She looked Helen straight in the eye.

'How did that make you feel?'

She shrugged. 'Naturally I was upset.'

'Upset?'

'Yes.' She licked her dry mouth. 'I loved him.'

'How upset were you, Mrs. Martinez? Did you harass Stephen, with text messages and phone calls?'

She closed her eyes. 'I think harass is a little strong. I phoned him - yes.'

282

Helen cocked her head. 'Isn't it true, you harassed him so many times he threatened to tell your husband about your affair if you didn't leave him alone?'

She swallowed hard, turning to face Matthew. 'I don't remember him threatening me.'

'Would you like to hear the tape again, Mrs. Martinez? No?'

Sally did not respond.

'You have stated you were at Ned's bar and diner that night. Did you phone Stephen Collins to tell him you were driving here to see him?'

'Yes.'

'Isn't it true, Mrs. Martinez you were so upset about Stephen threatening to tell your husband of your affair, you drove here, where Stephen Collins resided, begged him to meet you at the parking lot of Ned's bar and diner and shot him?'

Sally did not blink. She took a deep breath. 'No, that's not true,' her voice quivered. 'I loved him.'

'You expect us to believe that, Mrs. Martinez?' Helen said, returning to her seat.

'Objection, move to strike.' Matthew slammed his hand on the desk.

'Jury will disregard,' Chamberlain said.

'No more questions, your honor.'

Matthew followed Helen with his eyes back to her seat. He was drawn to a young woman who entered the courtroom. *It can't be.* He thought.

The bailiff walked toward Matthew and handed him a note. He looked back at the woman, and she gestured she needed to speak to him. 'Your honor defense requests a short recess?'

Chamberlain flicked his wrist, checking the time on his two hundred dollar watch. 'Very well. Court is in recess until 2pm.'

283

Chapter Forty-Six

'Sarah-Jane?' Matthew said, surprised. 'We thought you were dead?'

She stood in the conference room, leaning on one foot. She was dressed in the only pair of clothes she owned. A pink cotton dress and a white shrug tied across her chest. Her white sandals were scuffed and graying. She had attempted to make her hair presentable, tying it back with a graying scrunchie.

'It was Amanda they found. I had asked to her stay home to wait in for the mailman...' her voice faded. She rested her backside on the corner of the table. 'I was expecting a delivery.'

He could see she was shaking as she gripped her hands tightly. 'Let me get you some coffee,' he said, softly.

'No, please I'm fine.' She faked a smile. 'Pastor Dean is taking care of me.' She took a deep breath, pushing a stray hair away from her eyes. 'I tried calling John on his cell, but I never got a reply.'

'Oh that was you? John thought it was a wrong number.'

She wiped her nose with the back of her hand. 'The disc was destroyed.'

'What disc?'

'The security disc from the diner. I had it.'

He raised a hand. 'Wait a minute. You took the disc?'

'Yeah, I saw what happened.' She shook her head. 'He caught me watching.' She placed her hands around her throat, mimicking what had happened. 'He squeezed so tightly I thought he was gonna kill me. He told me to give him the disc, but I wouldn't.' She gasped. Her eyes filled with tears as her hands fell to her side. 'Amanda's dead because of me.'

'No, listen to me it's not your fault. You may have saved a woman's life by coming here today.'

* * *

'Please let me go?' Anna tried not to sound afraid through her tears.

Ritchie towered above her. His face was full of pity, such sadness. 'We were going sailing around the world together just Monette and me. She had already packed for our journey.' He smiled. 'She was so excited.' The smile faded.

She had never seen that look in the kind man's eyes before. It shot chills up her spine.

'That son of a bitch murdered her,' he mimed the actions, his thumb and forefinger becoming a gun. He pointed at her, pressing his finger against her temple. 'Right here BANG.'

She jumped, closing her eyes.

'Oh he made it look like an accident, but I know he murdered her. I saw the look in his eyes at the inquiry, he smirked. That son of a bitch smirked. I told him he would pay for what he'd done. I told him I'd catch him.'

'Please Ritchie, don't do this?'

He gave an evil laugh that she was sure began to freeze the blood in her veins. 'That's the clever part.' He crouched in front of her, making himself comfortable. 'See, I'd been following Stephen Collins for months. I knew every part of his sad, pathetic life. I saw him with your sister,' his eyes widened at her apparent shock. 'What? You're wondering how I knew she was your sister?' A smirk touched the corner of his mouth.

She wanted to scream, but no sound would come out. Her eyes scanned the room for something. Anything to prize herself away from the railing. Nothing.

Rocky continued to bark from the garage. She could tell by his sudden high-pitched tone that he was getting anxious.

'I had a lot of time in the hospital to think thangs through. They said they were committing me to help me and it did.' He nodded. 'You see that bastard would have recognized the Williams name, so I had to change it so I could kill him.

'I had read a lot of newspapers in hospital - came across a kid who was murdered in a gangland shootin'- I took his name.'

She narrowed her eyes, staring point blank at him. 'Ritchie Tate?'

He chuckled. 'No, he came later. Joseph Mullen. All I had to do was get close to your sister and what-do-you-know? She had advertised for a handyman. Perfect.' The smile returned. 'It was going to be easy; her husband even had his own gun that he kept in a shoebox at the back of his closet. I would make it look like Sally's husband murdered Stephen - he would have the perfect motive.' He gritted his teeth. 'But then Stephen got transferred here, to Birchwood County.' He thumped a fist into a cupped hand.

She kicked out her legs hoping desperately to reach the sack of shit in front of her.

'Now that just won't do.' He slapped at her legs. 'Stop it Anna, you won't get your surprise?' With one quick motion, he grabbed her throat. She stared at him with

286

anxious eyes. She gasped. Gripping. Slapping. Trying to free herself.

*   *   *

'Call your next witness, Mr. Brennan.' Chamberlain took a sip of water and replaced the cup in front of him.

Matthew stood from his chair. He leaned forward slightly, his hands resting on the table in front of him. 'Defense calls, Sarah-Jane Meadows.'

Helen was quick to stand and make her objections. She hissed and spat like a cornered cat. 'This witness was not on the list. What happened to the discovery rule?' She turned toward the courtroom, almost looking to them for support.

Matthew straightened his back, his palms facing the ceiling. 'This witness has vital evidence that could exonerate my client. She is on trial for her life, your honor.'

The judge interlocked his fingers. 'Counselors approach the bench.'

They approached swiftly.

Chamberlain covered the microphone in front of him. 'I don't know what kind of charade you're playing at Mr. Brennan, but you will not make a mockery of this court.'

'Your honor, this witness has vital evidence that could exonerate my client. A woman's life is at stake here. I am trying to establish the facts…'

Chamberlain held up a hand cutting Matthew off. 'All right, I've heard enough,' he paused. 'I'll allow the witness but tread carefully Mr. Brennan.'

Helen mumbled something under her breath, before taking her seat. Matthew looked at the judge expecting some form of repercussion for her little grumble, but the judge had not heard from way up in the heavens.

The witness took her seat in the box. She appeared confident, her shoulders relaxed as she flicked her fringe out of her eyes.

'Miss Meadows, can you tell the court what you do for a living.'

'I am a waitress and I work at Ned's bar and diner.'

'And were you working on the night in question?'

'Yes.'

'And did you serve the defendant that night?'

'Yes.'

'What happened then?'

She looked at the nearest jury member, Tatiana Grover. 'I gave the defendant her check and went out back to the management office so I could sneak outside for a cigarette.' She smiled at Tatiana, with a shameful shrug. 'We're not supposed to smoke on the grounds – Ned forbids it - but no one can see you from the parking lot if you stand outside the office window.'

'And what happened then?' He walked toward the jury box, his hands placed in his pockets as if he were thinking her testimony through.

'As I walked into the office to go outside, I caught a glimpse of the CCTV security monitor from the camera above the parking lot. I saw a man and the woman I served...the defendant, standing near a police car.'

'What happened then?'

She turned to Matthew. 'I saw Deputy Richardson walk away, I saw the man pull something from inside his pocket. He pointed it at the back of the Deputy's head; I saw it was a gun.'

Matthew walked to the evidence cart. He lifted the revolver in its bag. 'Is this the gun you saw?'

She nodded. 'Yes.'

He replaced the revolver onto the cart. 'Please tell the court what happened next?'

Panic shot across her face as if she were witnessing the scene all over again. 'The man fired. Deputy Richardson fell to the ground, the other officer shot back, but the man seemed to be invincible,' she gave a nervous laugh at the thought. 'The bullets just kept missing. The man stood firm. He walked closer to the officer and placed the gun to his head...' She placed her hands over her ears. Tears fell from her eyes. 'There was a flash – like lightening...And the officer was... dead.' Her body shook. She folded her arms across her chest. 'There was so much blood.'

The courtroom was silent. Matthew turned to check he was not the only person in the room. 'Why didn't you come forward before this afternoon?' He put his hands into his pockets, tilted his head toward the witness box.

'Because of the phone calls. He threatened to kill me if I spoke to the police.'

She stared at the floor. 'He killed my best friend.' Her lip quivered. 'And destroyed my home.'

'At any time did you see the defendant with the weapon?' he asked, softly.

She shook her head. 'No.'

Matthew did not mention the loss of the CCTV disc. It was of no help to his case, and there was no physical evidence to prove what the disc showed or even that it existed in the first place.

The jury would draw its own conclusions.

'Any redirect?'

Helen didn't bother to stand. 'No your honor, the state rests.'

'Very well,' Chamberlain took a sip of water. 'We'll take a ten minute recess and begin closing arguments at 3pm.'

Chapter Forty-Seven

Ritchie's fingers released. 'Now be a good girl,' he said, patting Anna on her head.

She coughed deep and hard. A sharp pain shot up her neck; a bone clicked into place.

He flicked his wrist, looking at his watch. 'I had been in Stephen's apartment when Sally phoned to say she was on her way down to see him. That incident with the gun had finally severed any chance of them ever seeing each other again. She scared him good, nearly blew his head off before I could.

'I took the gun away from her - couldn't have her taking away my responsibility now, could I?

'That afternoon, I called to report an abandoned vehicle on the pay phone outside the diner to get Stephen right where I wanted him. Your sister was the perfect candidate to take the fall.' He closed his eyes. 'I saw her, my Monette, she smiled at me as his body hit the floor. I know now she's at peace.'

'What does this have to do with me? I won't tell anyone.' Her voice was coarse. 'Please let me go?' tears seeped over her eyelids and trickled down her cheeks.

He stared at her for a moment.

'Please...' she hoped her plea would encourage him to let her go.

'It'll all be over soon, Anna,' he said.

She stiffened at the word *over*. 'You're going to kill me, aren't you?' her words came out in one fast tempo.

He turned away from her and fiddled with something. 'Yes.'

Chapter Forty-Eight

Matthew addressed the jury. They stared up at him with poker faces. He tried to exaggerate his movements, like a stage actor, control his powerful voice and relax as much as possible.

He started his closing argument with Shirley's testimony. 'How could she be sure she actually saw Sally fire the weapon – her view was blocked by the Dumpsters? Does she have X-Ray vision?' He chuckled. 'Now, the prosecution want you to think Sally fired the weapon because her finger prints were found on it yet no finger prints were found on the bullet casings themselves. If Sally wore gloves to load it as the prosecution want you to think, why would she take them off to fire it – if the act were premeditated?'

He paused in all the right places keeping the audience in suspense. He sipped from a cup of water as if running through his own thoughts aloud in the comfort of his office. He made eye contact with the jury only, including them in his educated ramblings.

'And officer Richardson, he signed an affidavit stating he saw two adults in the vehicle, and he didn't see who shot him. Now the prosecution want you to believe he was under medication at the time and couldn't remember signing anything. However, he could remember minute details about that day and even after his operation!' He rested his buttocks against his desk and stared at the jury.

'Now we have Patrolman Collins, a decorated officer, one of the best – policeman of the year three years running – arrests a notorious drug dealer in his home town, who threatens to kill him. It's documented within the Atlanta PD that Jay Keller carries out his threats, and it was reported in local newspapers of where Stephen was being transferred to.' He paused long enough for the doubts to sink into the jury's mind.

'The verdict, ladies and gentlemen, has to be not guilty – Sally is innocent – send her home to her children.'

At four, Chamberlain gave the jury some final instructions, and they filed out of the courtroom.

Matthew watched until the last juror was out of sight. He hoped he had done enough to save Sally. He hoped he had done enough to save himself.

* * *

'Surprise!' Ritchie showed Anna a homemade explosive device - it ticked away as his thumb flipped the red button down.

'Ritchie please, don't do this?'

He placed the device above the living room door, in front of her so she could watch the digits count down.

'Please!'

He kissed her on the cheek. 'I'm sorry – you know too much.' He stood, straightened his back and headed for the door. 'Goodbye Anna,' he said, stepping out onto the porch. 'Can't stand around talkin' all day - I've got work to do.'

* * *

Sally gripped Matthew's hand and bit her lip.

'All rise.'

The jury filed into the courtroom. Each member stood in front of their seats. Matthew thought for a brief moment that they appeared to be as nervous as he and Sally were.

'Have the jury reached a verdict?' Chamberlain asked.

The head spokesman juror, stood tall with his chest puffed out, replied, 'Yes, your honor.'

The judge instructed David Featherly to read out the verdict. He cleared his throat and stood tall. 'We the jury find the defendant, Sally Martinez, not guilty.'

Matthew took a breath finally. He had not realized he had been holding it for so long.

Sally hugged him tightly. 'Thank you, thank you.' She wiped tears from her cheek.

Arthur and Linnie reached over from the partition. They pulled Matthew and Sally close, kissing and crying as the courtroom descended through the doors.

'I can't thank you enough, Matt!' Sally held her children tightly. She kissed Elizabeth's forehead.

'Just doing my job,' he replied, bashfully.

'I understand why Anna didn't come. I have really hurt her in the past. Maybe our relationship is truly over?'

He shook his head as he collected the papers and files from the defense table in front of him. 'No, I'm sure it isn't over Sal. Anna loves you, you're her sister. I have no idea why she isn't here - there must be a legitimate reason.' He stood wide-eyed as the image of the safety deposit box flashed in his mind.

Hastily, he made his way outside. He pushed through the reporters, huddled in the corridor, he could not stay for questions. He had to get home and speak to Anna...to explain.

'Miguel?' he was sure Miguel sat across the street from the courthouse in his black pick-up truck, but he didn't have time to get a better look.

What if she's left me for good? He thought. He placed his cellular phone to his ear. If she would just pick up the phone, he could explain everything to her?

I've blown it now! She's left me. 'Please Anna pick up the phone?' he pleaded. 'Shit.' He ran now down West Street toward Goodland's Avenue.

*   *   *

Anna tried to free herself from the handcuffs. They pinched at her skin as she tried desperately to squeeze her wrists from their grasp. 'Help!' She heard the garage door release. Rocky barked at the front door. 'Run Rocky! Run!'

Chapter Forty-Nine

John arrived in Billows Creek and drove straight to the courthouse.

He pushed through the crowd until he found a familiar face. 'Sally, have you seen Matt?'

'No, he left about five minutes ago. What's wrong?' she called after him.

He did not reply. He jumped back into his car and sped off down the street. He searched West Street for Matthew. Suddenly, he spotted Matthew jogging down South Hall Road.

'Matt!' John yelled. 'Jump in.'

Panting, Matthew replied, 'I'm glad to see you.' He placed his seat belt across his chest. His shirt clung to his body soaked in sweat. 'I have to get home. I think Anna knows about my relapse, that's why she didn't come to court today.'

'I've got some more good news for you buddy.' John signaled into Goodland's Avenue. 'I found out about Bernie Williams. The guy's a nut. He blamed Stephen Collins for murdering his wife.'

Matthew stared at John.

'Get this, he's been posing as your gardener, and he's ex-bomb squad.'

'R.i.t.chie?' Matthew's mind went blank. He couldn't comprehend what John had just told him.

* * *

'Anna!' Matthew kicked at the front door. It was
jammed. He cupped his hands against the window. 'I can
see her, she's in the hall.'

'Matt! Don't come in - there's a bomb!'

'John keep trying the front, I'm going around back.' He
jumped over the hedgerows at the side of their neighbor's
house and made his way to his back door. It was locked. 'I
need something to prize it open with,' he said, aloud. 'The
crowbar!'

He picked up the crowbar from the garage floor. Taking
a firm grip, he smashed at the panels of the inner door,
spikes of wood flew in all directions.

* * *

Anna watched the timer. Two minutes flashed on the
display. She prayed. Tears streamed down her face as she
tried again to free herself from the handcuffs. They rattled
against the wood.

'Anna!' Matthew wiped the sweat from his forehead. He
stared at the device on the wall.

'Matt! Leave! Get out there's not enough time!'

One minute 50 seconds flashed on the timer.

Matthew tried to prize away the wooden railing. It
buckled but did not break.

'Matt! Please just get out of here.'

30 seconds flashed on the timer.

'I'm not losing you Anna, I can't!'

'There's not enough time, please?'

He stared at his wife. 'I'm not losing you.' Shaking, he
pulled the bomb from the wall and ran toward the
backdoor.

297

Chapter Fifty

Anna pulled against the buckled railing. It creaked under the pressure. Sweat-laced her brow as she pushed and pulled, trying to free the handcuffs. 'Come on, please!'

Her ears had become immune to the sound of banging; John kicked at the front door. Suddenly the hinges ripped from the door frame. The door crashed to the floor.

'Help me, John!'

Sucking in as much air as he could, he took a grip on the railing and with one sharp push, the railing snapped in two.

'Where's Matt? Have you seen him?' She turned toward the kitchen.

John grabbed her arm. 'Come on Anna let's go!'

* * *

Helen pulled up outside the Brennan home. Rocky poked his head from the passenger window, tongue hanging from his jaw.

'What the...?'

The ground shook.

For a brief moment, she could not move. She had never heard such a terrifying sound. Fumbling she reached for her cellular phone, staring blind-eyed as Anna and John fell onto the front lawn.

She watched them huddle together; Anna looked over her shoulder desperately.

One word came to Helen's lips. 'Matt?

Chapter Fifty-One

Matthew stumbled from behind the house and fell into Anna's arms.

'Oh Matt, I thought you were...' her voice broke away. She kissed him hard on the lips. 'Don't you ever do that to me again!' She kissed him again and he sank into her body, caressing her neck with his thumb.

She pulled away from him, staring at the blood on her hands. 'Your forehead's bleeding. You're hurt!'

'I threw the device over the fence,' he puffed. 'The windows shattered, there's glass everywhere.' He wiped the blood with the back of his hand. 'It's just a scratch, I'm OK.'

'The ambulance is on its way.' Porter called from his patrol car. 'Come on let's go across the street. What the hell happened?'

Sitting sideways on the backseat, John filled Porter in on Bernie Williams. 'He's alias was a gardener called Ritchie Tate.'

Matthew held Anna; her body trembled.

'Did he say anything to you about where he was going?' Porter unlocked the handcuffs and Anna rubbed her wrists.

'He said he was going to work,' she replied, her teeth chattering from shock.

'The Sheriff's here,' John said, standing up. The sound of sirens echoed around the cul-de-sac as the ambulance, and several other police units entered the street.

Porter explained the situation to the Sheriff; the bomb squad entered the Brennan home.

Anna slouched on the ambulance bed; she had her head in her hands. The paramedic draped a blanket across her shoulders.

'Anna,' the Sheriff nodded at Matthew. 'Are you sure he said he was going to work?'

'Yes, Sheriff,' her voice was coarse.

The second paramedic attended to Matthew's wounds. 'Rocky!' His hand didn't leave Rocky's head. 'Where have you been?' He scratched behind Rocky's ears.

Rocky licked his fingers.

'He must have followed your scent to the courthouse,' Helen said, shrugging. 'Is everyone all right?' She approached slowly.

Matthew nodded. 'Thanks for bringing back my dog,' he winced as the antiseptic lotion was applied to his forehead.

'You're welcome.'

The Sheriff scratched his chin, before lighting a cigar. 'The guy had several occupations; I wonder which one he meant?'

John placed the blanket, draped over his shoulders, on the end of the ambulance bed. 'He could be half way back to Atlanta by now.'

The stench of burning wood and smoldering plastic filled the air. Heat wafted from the debris. Matthew choked on the fumes as they scratched his throat. He noticed Arthur's truck pull up at the curb. He tapped Anna's hand and pointed in the Owens' direction.

'Momma?' Anna stood from the bed.

'Oh my…' Linnie gasped as she caught sight of the parade of police vehicles. She waddled as quickly as she could in four inch stilettos, toward her daughter.

'Anna!' Linnie scooped Anna in her arms like she had done when Anna was a small child. She shook her head. 'What happened?'

Anna did not reply.

Matthew swallowed hard as he watched the reunion. He couldn't help but think of what would've happened if he and John hadn't got to the house in time.

Arthur made his way over to his wife, scratching his head before playing with his moustache nervously.

Anna looked at her mother. 'Where are Sally and the kids?' Her eyebrows pulled together as she anticipated the reply.

'They're at home, she didn't want to…impose, everything's gonna be OK.' Linnie replied softly, stroking Anna's hair. 'I wish you two would make up now all this is behind us.'

'Momma?' Anna pulled away. 'Is Ritchie supposed to work on your yard today?'

'Why yes, the lawn needs to be mowed,' Linnie replied, confused.

Anna threw the blanket off her shoulders and turned to face Matthew. 'He's got Sally.'

Chapter Fifty-Two

Matthew ran to the Owens' front porch. 'Sally! Sally open the door!' He banged on the wood until it burned his knuckles.

'Matt? What is it?' Sally asked, standing in the doorway. 'What on earth happened to you?'

'Where are the kids?' He stumbled into the hall.

She looked at him confused. 'I-I don't know, playing?' she stared wide-eyed at him. 'What happened, Matt?'

'You're in danger,' he panted, wiping the sweat from his forehead with the back of his hand.

She swallowed hard, pulling her eyebrows together. 'Kids?' her voice was high-pitched and shaky. 'Where are you?' she yelled, running into her mother's kitchen. He followed, grabbing a knife from the counter. They stepped out onto the back porch.

'Lizzie? Tom?' She stopped in her tracks.

Ritchie kneeled in front of her, his hands covering her children's mouths. 'Glad you could make the party,' he said. 'And the lawyer too.'

'Let them go. Please don't hurt them!' she pleaded.

'Let them go,' Matthew said, stepping forward. He gripped the kitchen knife.

'Don't come any closer.' He tugged at the children's faces.

303

Elizabeth groaned as her earring dug into the side of her neck.

Thomas's tears seeped into the crevices of Ritchie's dark skin.

Sally held up her hands. 'OK, Joe OK. I'll do what ever you want. Just let them go.'

Matthew's jaw fell. He stared back at Sally. 'J.o.e Mullen?'

Police sirens could be heard coming from a distance. They grew nearer and nearer, then stopped suddenly. Slamming of car doors echoed around the Owens' home and were followed by the sound of shuffling feet.

'Joe, huh?' he scoffed, releasing Thomas.

Thomas ran to Sally; she held him tightly in her arms.

'OK,' Matthew stepped forward slowly, 'Let Elizabeth go,' he said softly.

Ritchie tugged on Elizabeth's face, she stiffened, groaning in fear.

'I won't come any closer,' Matthew said. 'Just let her go, OK?'

Sally knelt. Tears streamed down her face. 'Please, please let her go.' She kissed Thomas' head, trying to comfort him.

Ritchie opened his jacket.

Sally gasped in horror.

Matthew stared at the brightly colored device strapped to Ritchie's body, a mass of red and blue wires protruding from a flat white plastic block.

Ritchie pulled the white L-shaped trigger out from his pocket. He clutched Elizabeth tightly to his chest; her nose was inches away from the device.

Chapter Fifty-Three

'You don't have to do this,' Matthew said. He knelt slowly, putting the knife on the lawn. 'She's just a little girl,' he swallowed hard as he looked at the fear in her eyes. 'What would Monette say if she were here right now?'

Ritchie fiddled with the trigger.

'No! Please…' Sally sobbed.

Matthew stepped forward, he was two feet away. 'She wouldn't want you to do this.' He held up his hands, defensively.

Ritchie stared at Elizabeth's covered head. He looked back up at Matthew and then at the trigger, contemplating. Calculating.

'Just take it easy.' Matthew kept his voice low. He could see the Sheriff at the side gate, just over Ritchie's shoulder, gun poised ready to fire. Matthew signaled with a flick of his finger not to approach. The Sheriff spoke into his radio quietly.

Matthew prayed they were good shots.

Ritchie lowered his trigger arm.

'That's good.' Matthew tilted his head to one side, pleading. 'Now let her go.'

With one quick movement, Ritchie pushed Elizabeth away and raised his trigger arm again. Matthew stumbled. He punched Ritchie on the nose and tried desperately to free the trigger from Ritchie's iron grip. Ritchie kicked Matthew in the stomach; a cry escaped his lips as the wind was sucked out of him.

Matthew fell and rolled onto his back, kicking Ritchie to the ground. He slapped at Ritchie's arm, hoping to reach the trigger.

Ritchie lashed out his fist into Matthew's nose, blood spattered onto the ground.

'Matt!' Sally screamed.

Matthew slammed his elbow into Ritchie's face; the struggling ceased. He prized Ritchie's fingers open and held the trigger between his finger and thumb as if it were made from tissue paper.

Ritchie did not struggle. He was read his Miranda's and carted away in handcuffs. The device was disposed of.

'He'll probably get off on insanity, huh Matt?' Porter asked, standing next to his patrol vehicle.

Matthew did not answer. He watched the police unit disappear around the corner. *Maybe it's time to stop pretending?* He thought. He wiped the blood from his nose with a kitchen cloth.

* * *

'Matt, you joining the party?' John called from the Owens' front porch. He clutched a glass of homemade lemonade in his hand, a paper party hat protruding from his crown.

The smell of Arthur's barbecue wafted from the Owens' back yard. The faint sound of music on the radio could be heard from the open front door.

Matthew shook his head. 'I'll be right back, there's something I have to do.'

* * *

The sun shone around the headstone like a halo. An array of summer flowers surrounded the grave. Matthew noticed their sweet fragrance immediately.

Taking a deep breath, he continued toward the headstone until he was standing within four inches of it.

Our beloved son,
Sweetly sleeping, until we meet again.

A pain so sharp stabbed in his chest, he fell to his knees. He could not fight the tears back any longer.

He cried so hard, he could feel his body begin to numb with every gasp of air that filled his lungs.

Chapter Fifty-Four

It had been a long arduous day for Helen. Shortly after returning Rocky, she was called in for another meeting with the mayor and the governor. It seemed a position on the career ladder was unavailable, at least for this term. She had figured as much.

She had not bothered with the left over paperwork. She chose, instead to pay a visit to the florists on her way home picking the brightest colored lilies she could find.

She had not visited her son's grave for three weeks. She needed to unload the burden of her day onto him.

She crossed the grass verge and followed the bricked walk around the churchyard.

The rambling sound of a goldfinch could be heard coming from a small tree to the left of the walk.

She caught a glimpse of Matthew kneeling, his arms resting on their son's headstone. His face was covered, but she knew he was crying.

She stopped, and for a moment watched from a distance. She could not help but feel relieved. Finally, he was letting go of his guilt.

She turned on her heels; she did not want to disturb him.

* * *

Matthew could see someone in the corner of his eye. 'Helen?' he sniffed, wiping his nose with a handkerchief.

'Hey,' she said, biting her lower lip.

He stood and wiped his face, before placing his hands in his pockets. 'I just came to say…'

'Please, don't explain… You don't have to.'

They exchanged glances for a moment.

She walked toward him and arranged the lilies around the headstone. 'Omar told me they arrested a man in connection with the Collins murder.'

'Yeah,' he tried to clear his sore throat.

'He confessed, you know?' she said, concentrating on the lilies.

He did not reply. *Just say you're sorry. Tell her how you feel.* 'I want to… I,' he stuttered. 'I mean thank you for the lilies, for Anna. I know it was you who sent them when she was in the hospital.'

She was silent for a moment. 'That's OK. I'm glad she is well again.'

He was thankful she did not mention the baby. 'I'm sorry about before I didn't mean what I said about you being up the governor's…well I was out of line.'

She swallowed hard. 'No you were right. I wasn't thinking clearly about…Oh Matt, I've done something terrible-'

He cut her off. 'Hey now, it's OK.' He rubbed her shoulder, trying to comfort her. 'Whatever it is I'm sure it can be sorted out.'

She pulled away from him. 'Not this…I'm sorry,' she sobbed. 'It was me, the whole time. I'm the one who should be locked up – me and the governor!'

He raised his arm. 'Wait, what are you talking about?'

'The rumors, the riot, all the media attention. I did it. The governor said it…Oh, what have I done?'

'I don't understand.' He shook his head. 'Why?'

She didn't turn to face him. 'I wanted recognition. I wanted something to show for all the work I've put into this town the past three years. I've worked so hard and I have nothing to show for it,' she sobbed. 'People with less experience and less passion come along and get everything they want – career, family, money – I deserve it! The governor's job was mine!

'It was never meant to go this far.' She turned to face him. 'Please believe I had nothing to do with Anna's accident.'

'That was part of the plan? That was part of this scheme to manipulate voters?' He grabbed her. 'What's wrong with you? Are you crazy?'

'It was the governor and her cousin, please stop you're hurting me!'

He released her. 'I don't know who you are anymore,' he said, shaking his head.

Chapter Fifty-Five

The windows in the Brennan home were finished finally. The window fitters were packing up ready to leave.

Matthew had not told Anna where he had been, and she had not asked. He felt guilty as if he had done something wrong going to Bobby's grave, but something told him those feelings were unnecessary.

'The Sheriff's got his hands full tonight,' John said, his voice vibrating across the phone line.

Matthew smirked. 'Makes a change,' he said, sarcastically. He leaned back against the sofa cushions and rubbed his aching neck.

'Roy was arrested in connection with Anna's accident.'

Matthew nodded. 'Good.'

'Of course there wouldn't be an arrest at all if it hadn't been for Helen's confession this afternoon. She's made a deal and is gonna testify.'

Matthew raised his eyebrows. 'She confessed?'

'Yeah, walked right up to the Sheriff and spilled her guts. They arrested the governor an hour ago.'

Matthew smiled.

'See you bright an' early.'

Matthew shook his head, closing his eyes. 'No, I'm taking a vacation.'

John laughed. 'See you next week.'

He hung up the phone.

'Matt, can you come here?' Anna called from somewhere at the far end of the house. The tone of her voice made him think something was going on. He proceeded to the kitchen, where she stood holding a blindfold.

'What's going on?' he asked, trying not to smile.

She gestured for him to come closer and placed the blindfold across his eyes.

'What's this all about?'

She fastened the black fabric.

'Ouch!' he said as the fabric caught his wound.

'I'm sorry, are you OK?' She placed her fingers to her mouth.

He smiled at her guilt. 'It's OK – just sensitive that's all. Why do I need a blindfold?'

She laughed. 'So many questions. Just relax OK.' She took his hands in hers. 'Now walk forward and follow my voice.'

He relied on his other senses. The acoustics in the room changed as their footsteps echoed. He could feel a slight breeze across his face. 'Now there's a step here,' she said.

He recognized the stench of paint and knew they were now in the garage.

'OK, I'm gonna take this off now,' she said.

He tried to adjust his eyes to the sudden brightness coming from the open garage door. Suddenly, there it was standing like a wild beast in front of him.

'My bike! It looks as good as new!' He grabbed her, embracing her passionately. 'Let's take it for a spin,' he beamed.

Author Biography

N.J. Warner was told as a child she had a highly active imagination. Her passion for acting became apparent at an early age and when she wasn't acting in school plays, her love of writing took over, writing her first novella aged 7.

At 12, she fell ill and was diagnosed with M.E/CFS forcing her to put her writing and acting dreams and indeed her life on hold. Her debut novel, Nowhere to Run, was written while bedridden with the condition in her early twenties.

She has since been featured in The Times newspaper and Interaction magazine for the Action for M.E charity bringing hope to thousands of sufferers across the UK.

For more information visit: njwarner.net

Lightning Source UK Ltd.
Milton Keynes UK
UKOW04f1543190913

217524UK00001B/4/P